BY

DARYL BANNER

Books By Daryl Banner

The **Beautiful Dead** Trilogies:

A post-apocalyptic fantasy series starring Winter, an undead teenage girl. Each trilogy can be read independently, but it's best to read them in order.

The Original Trilogy

#1 - The Beautiful Dead
#2 - Dead Of Winter
#3 - Almost Alive

The Sunless Reach Trilogy

#4 - The Whispers
#5 - The Winters *(coming soon)*
#6 - The Wakings *(coming soon)*

The OUTLIER Series:

An epic dystopian saga with a strong ensemble of unique & unlikely heroes who incite a rebellion. Join them on their journey for truth, love, and justice.

The Series

#1 - Outlier: Rebellion
#2 - Outlier: Legacy
#3 - Outlier: Reign Of Madness *(coming soon)*
#4 - Outlier: Beyond Oblivion *(coming soon)*
#5 - Outlier: Five Kings *(coming soon)*

Kings & Queens: A collection of companion novellas

The Slum Queen
The Twice King *(coming soon)*
The Queen Of Wrath *(coming soon)*

The Brazen Boys:

A series of steamy standalone M/M romance novellas.

Dorm Game / On The Edge / Owned By The Freshman
Dog Tags / All Yours Tonight / Straight Up / Houseboy Rules
Slippery When Wet / Commando (Dog Tags 2)

The College Obsession Series

A series of full-length standalone romances linked together by a group of college friends. Though characters are shared between the books, each one can be read on its own.

#1 - Read My Lips
#2 - Beneath The Skin

Other Books by Daryl Banner:

super psycho future killers
Psychology Of Want
Love And Other Bad Ideas
(a collection of seven short plays)

Read My Lips
A College Obsession Romance
#1

Published by Frozenfyre Publishing

Cover Artist : Kari Ayasha at Cover To Cover Designs
Interior Design : Daryl Banner

List of Chapters

First and foremost, thank you, the reader, for picking up this book and giving it a try. I hope you enjoy getting to know Dessie & Clayton.

I'm a proud alumni of the University of Houston with a degree in Theatre and Psychology, and I want to dedicate this book to all the other actors, techies, designers, and dreamers who created art with me and shared in some cool-ass experiences during my time there.

While writing the second half of this novel, I experienced the very sudden loss of a friend who was also a fellow Theatre U of H alumni. His name was Timmy Wood. He was a hilarious and caring comedic actor whom everyone knew and loved—and I do mean *everyone*. Timmy was involved in freakin' everything. He was always in a play or working on some new project. Simply put, he was a creative machine who just couldn't be stopped. Every memory I had with him rushed forth as I finished this book. So I dedicate this to you, Timmy. Tell Doc, Lanford, and Jenny hi for me, and I hope you're all partying hard up there!

And to my witty, proudly deaf professor with whom I took four eye-opening semesters of American Sign Language, and to the friends—both hearing and not—who I met along the way, this is for you too.

With so much love & Happy Reading,
Daryl

READ MY
lips
A COLLEGE OBSESSION ROMANCE

Prologue

DESSIE

I went to college to find myself. I didn't expect to find *him*.

My whole life was a delicate, artful plan set in place by my delicate, artful family. From my mother, the famous actor of stage and film, to my world-renowned lighting designer father and insufferably perfect sister, I was doomed to a life in the Theatre spotlight.

And the Lebeau family name was forever tainted with average, unremarkable, untalented me.

After graduating high school, I enjoyed a few years of disappointing my parents. Thirty-three bad auditions and two private academies later found me begging them for one last favor: a normal college experience.

And it was at that totally normal small-town Texas college that I met *him*, the muscular, tatted bad-boy who would soon become my obsession.

His eyes smoldered me with just one look. His touch awakened the woman inside me. His breath drew out the inspiration deep in my soul that I did not know was there.

And through his lips, his perfect, plush, kissable lips, I would find my voice at last ... the voice that would someday fill a New York City stage, the voice that would set me apart from my tragically perfect family, the voice that would finally break me free ...

If only he could hear a word of it.

DESSIE

"I can't hear you!"

The noise that fills the courtyard of the Quad is deafening. Families bustle about carrying belongings to the dorms. A group of frat boys play Frisbee, their shirtless torsos sweaty and lean. A guy shouts orders from a window up above to his parents below, who can't make out what he's saying. A circle of girls chant some sorority thing over and over nearby. Two dudes who look like they haven't bathed since Daylight Savings began stand on the rim of a fountain with guitars as they serenade the masses, their lyrics lost in the cacophony of shouting and laughter.

And standing before all that mess is little excited me, a heavy bag hanging at my side, a massive case of luggage-on-wheels by my feet, and a phone pressed to my fast-reddening ear.

"What? I can't hear you!" I shout again. "Mother?"

The call cuts off. I stow my phone away in a pocket. Besides, the whole reason I'm here is to get *away* from my nauseatingly arty, weird, fame-whoring family. *"Please,"* I begged my mother two months ago when she was between photo shoots. *"All I want is a* normal *college experience. I don't want the expensive schools and the private lessons and the pretentious crap."* To that, she hiccupped, raised her martini glass, and sweetly replied, *"Doll, the Theatre world* is *pretention."* It was my father who caved and said he knew a person down in Texas who could pull a string or two to get me into a school this late in the summer.

And here I am—and excitedly so. *This is it!* I only have a battlefield of frat boys and Frisbees to wade through before I'm safe in the comfortable confines of my very own dorm room.

"What do you mean I don't get my very own dorm room?" I ask half an hour later when I've finally made it to the front of the line at the reception desk.

The woman stares at me over the thick rims of her glasses. She's clearly had a day.

"I'm supposed to have my own place," I explain, all too aware of the line of anxiously waiting people behind me. "A condo, some upperclassmen suite, or ... or my own dorm room at the very least. I spoke with a Betsy ... or Bettie? Bridget? And she said I would get my own room. I'm sure it's just a mistake."

"Priority living arrangements are reserved for upperclassmen. Not for incoming freshmen."

"But I'm *not* an incoming freshman, Donna," I explain, trying my best to lean over the counter so that I don't have to shout. These people should have offices; the whole line can hear every word of our little chat, I'm sure. "I'm a transferring sophomore."

"It's Diana. Are you new to Klangburg University? Then you're a freshman in our eyes. Current students get priority. If you wanted solitude, you should have rented an apartment on Periwinkle Avenue."

"In *this* neighborhood??" I hiss back. My bag has become so heavy, I let it drop to the germ-infested floor. "Listen, I ... I really don't mean to cause a big scene, but—"

"Of course you do. You're an actress." She slides a key and a slip of paper across the counter. "Theatre major, right? I could smell the drama a mile away. You're in West Hall, room 202. Your roommate's a Music major. Name, Samantha Hart. Go make yourself a best friend."

A Music major? Great. I'll have to contend with a roommate who gives blowjobs to an oboe all day long. *Is the AC in here broken?* I pull my hair over a shoulder and off of my neck as beads of sweat populate my forehead. First lesson: Texas weather is Hell's weather. "She sounds lovely. Listen, Diana, I—"

"Oh! 'Listen,' you say. What a novel concept." Diana the Desk Demon snorts. "You keep telling me to listen, but it's *you* who doesn't hear a damn thing I say. The rooms were assigned months ago. You even got your room assignment in the mail."

"I didn't. I haven't gotten any..." But even as I say the words, I picture my controlling mother pulling the mail from the box and not giving a care in the world about anything addressed to me. I bet it's even my mom's email that's in the school database, not mine, because she controls everything about my life. *"I understand your desire to run away to a faraway 'normal' college,"* mother told me this morning over cups of peppermint tea, just before I left for the airport. *"You're scared of New York, doll. You're a guppy in a world full of sharks. Your sister—now* she's *a shark."*

If there's anything worse than being called a *guppy*, it's being compared to my insufferably perfect sister Celia—or Cece, as she insists on being called. She gets cast in leading roles. She's as beautiful as a princess and annoyingly well-read. She always has handsome, adorable, sexy boyfriends at her side. It's not that I'm jealous; I love my sister. But sometimes I wish *I* was the one who scored a leading role now and then. I wish *I* was the one with a hot guy hooked to my arm at some gala my parents drag me to.

I'm not the one guys stare at. It's always her.

Surprisingly, my sister has nothing to do with my current predicament. Maybe my roommate will turn out to be cool, or have parents who bring us home-cooked delicacies, sparing us the frights from the campus kitchens. What do normal college kids eat? Maybe we'll have lots of Easy Mac and Ramen. On second thought, that sounds like a carb nightmare.

"Thank you," I murmur to my new best friend, Diana the Desk Demon, and take the key.

"It's been a pleasure," she mutters back, sounding like it's been anything but. "There's a freshman mixer in the courtyard at seven. Good day."

I'm not a freshman! But I keep the words to myself and lift my bag once again, heading for the door. The second I'm outside, three shirtless boys nearly topple me over in their effort to claim a rogue Frisbee, which I end up catching midair to prevent it from giving me an unintended nose job. I hand the disc to the nearest one, trying not to stare at his lean, sweaty torso. Pulling my luggage along, I cut through the noise to the West Hall, a slate-grey building in the shape of an L that forms one of the four corners of the Quad and seems to be the liveliest of them all. Its heavy door bursts open the moment I approach, releasing four loud freshmen and a worried set of parents. I wonder if they're taking bets on which of their children will contract dorm room herpes first.

I step inside only to mourn an onslaught of stairs before me. Enlisting the strength and dexterity from my basic combat training in New York (or rather, *stage* combat training), I choreograph and execute a one-woman routine of dragging my suitcase up five steps, sliding it across the narrow landing, then up eleven more. Arriving at the second floor, I squeeze past a crowd of guys guffawing at a spilled box of soda cans two paces from my room, 202. They're daring each other to open a can when I make it to my door, ready to reveal my college dorm room to my eager eyes.

The door swings open, revealing two beds, two dressers, and two desks. The smell is hundred-year-old musk and even older mildew. The bare walls, pocked with scratches and holes, are the color of a rash my sister got once that she made me swear never to tell anyone about. How adorable. The bathroom appears to be a small chamber of doom that connects to the neighboring dorm, suite-style.

I smile. No one in the world would recognize it as one, but it's there. My college experience is going to have to include sharing a bathroom with three other girls I've never met. In a bleak room that's just short of padded walls.

I fight a rare urge to call my mother and demand that she give me a bigger allowance and allow me the mercy of getting an apartment like any other twenty-two year old *adult.* Then, I gently remind myself that this is what I wanted. No privilege. No personal chefs. No driver who takes me around town. No ritz and glitz. No fancy cocktails. Just a fixed allowance and meal plan like every other student.

For once, a normal life among normal people doing normal, college-y things.

I have a sudden craving for this gourmet lobster bisque that only my mother's chef Julian makes.

Focus, Dessie! Piece by piece, I unpack my suitcase and hang each article of clothing in the tiny closet, which is a quarter the size of mine at home, leaving one half of it empty for my mystery roommate. Then, I sit on the bed I've made up with my new sheets and feather pillow I brought from home. It creaks happily under my weight. I listen to the noise in the hallway of families moving their kids into their dorms, the sound of laughter and banter and shuffling furniture and boxes reaching my ears and vibrating the walls.

My parents told me to call them when I was all moved in. I prefer that they presume I'm lost or dead. So caught up in mother's performance in London next month, I doubt they'll even give me a thought until well into my father's fourth glass of chardonnay when he finally looks up from his lighting design charts to ask, "Did we hear from Dessie yet?"

It's already almost seven, so I push myself off the bed, freshen up in the bathroom mirror, and spritz myself with a light scent. I pray there's more than just freshmen at this courtyard mixer. When I open my door, I'm greeted with the sight of the room across the hall, its door propped open. Scarves of varying shades of purple adorn the ceiling in bilious clouds of silk, giving the room the look of a 16th century gypsy's tent. A lamp burns orange on the desk within my view, which is littered in glass trinkets that pick up the light. It is night and day from the starkness of my room to the glamour of hers. Beads line the closet door, and they rattle when the room's occupant moves through them carrying a thin book pinched open in one hand and a bottle of lemon vitamin water in the other.

She turns, spotting me. "Hi," all eighty-nothing pounds of her says lamely, her tight braids dancing with her every step as her needle eyes focus on me. She stands at her doorway. "You're living in 202?"

"It seems to be my tragic situation," I admit. *She's reading a play,* I realize with a closer look. *She's a Theatre major, too. Befriend her, damn it!* I give a subtle nod to her décor. "I like what you've done with your—"

"I have a lot of reading to do, if you don't mind." She gives me a curt nod, then taps the rim of her playbook with the closed end of her vitamin water.

"*As Bees In Honey Drown?*" I note, catching the title off of the cover. "I played Alexa in Brendan Iron's production in New York last spring."

"New York, you say?" A light flashes in her eyes. "You don't look like a freshman. Are you a transfer? New York? Where in New York?"

Now I'm suddenly worth her time. It's amazing, the power of a simple name-drop. I discreetly leave out the fact that it was less of a production in New York and more of a botched audition. "I'm a transfer from Rigby & Claudio's Acting, Dan—"

"Acting, Dancing, and Musical Academy," she finishes for me. The whites of her eyes are ablaze, deepening the rich color of her smooth, mahogany skin. "And ... you transferred here? What brought you from there to ... to here?"

A fierce vision comes forth of my former director, Claudio Vergas himself, as he hollers at my indignant face, flecks of his morning coffee dusting the stage floor between us. It was the first time he'd ever lost his temper enough to throw his favorite mug. I can still hear the porcelain as it shattered against the lip of the stage. I didn't even flinch. I lifted my chin and called him a stiff-necked, pretentious, know-it-all panty-wad. It was not my best moment.

"Artistic differences," I answer vaguely.

"New York," she moans, all her childhood dreams of being in the limelight painted across her glassy eyes. "I'm Victoria," my new best friend says, shoving the script under an arm and extending her hand. "Victoria Li. Third year Theatre major. Don't call me Vicki. I have violent reactions to being called Vicki. I'll cut a bitch. But not you. Unless you call me Vicki."

My phone in one hand, I accept her handshake with my free one. It's cold as ice. "I'm Dessie."

"Great name. I *love* Desiree Peters. Her portrayal of Elphaba on the last national tour of *Wicked* had me in tears. I have her autograph on my CD soundtrack *and* the playbill which I, of course, framed. I had to stand by the stage door afterwards for forty-eight minutes in ten degree weather. Worth it."

"It's not short for Desiree," I clarify. "It's short for ... for Desdemona."

Victoria stares at me. "As in *Othello*'s Desdemona?"

Hurray for having Theatre parents. "That would be the one. Anyway, it's almost seven already, so I was going to head to the mixer. Are you going?"

"It's not until eight," she tells me, leaning on her doorframe and taking a sip of her lemon water. She's suddenly so much friendlier than she was a second ago. "How'd you hear about it?"

"I was told it's at seven. Well, according to Diane the Desk Demon," I add with a roll of my eyes.

"No, no. Eight o'clock at the theater."

I lift a brow. "There's a Theatre one?"

"You thought I meant the fishbowl? No, honey. You're coming with me," she states. "You're new here, and you don't want to get lost on this big ol' campus after dark, end up somewhere on fraternity row, and get robbed ... or worse. Can't trust a frat boy for anything. It would not be a lovely way to spend your first evening here."

"It's really that bad here?"

"This campus is the pillow on the bed between two bitchy ex-lovers: the rich neighborhood full of snobs to the north, and the have-nots and gunshots to the south. Campus security is a joke, but it does exist. Remember, safety in numbers! So, we'll leave in thirty. Hey, where's your roomie?" she asks suddenly, craning her neck to get a look.

"Not here yet, I guess." What the hell kind of crime-ridden so-called normal college did my father send me to down here in Texas? "School starts the day after tomorrow, so she might come in tonight, or—"

"Or not at all," she points out. "Sometimes, there's a last minute transfer or change of plans. My friend Lena had a room all to herself last semester."

"Don't get my hopes up."

My phone buzzes. I look down to see my mother's headshot staring up at me, all glamorous and ready to blink at the flashing cameras. I slap the screen to my chest, unwilling to chance whether or not Victoria knows who she is. I'm not ready for a firestorm to be caused by anyone figuring out whose daughter I am.

"Mommy and Daddy?"

"Something like that," I admit, still chokeholding my phone into submission.

"You were spared the company of my parents by about five minutes. No one wants to see a black woman and a tiny Chinese man arguing."

"Oh, you're half-Chinese?"

The phone keeps vibrating against my chest. I continue to politely suffocate it.

"He's my stepdad, but I call him Dad since they married when I was two. My bio dad took off." The phone stops buzzing. She notices and offers me a wistful smile. "Looks like you're safe for now. See you in thirty, Des."

She disappears into her room. A green voicemail notification pops up on the screen of my phone. I swipe it out of existence and, inspired suddenly, I text Randy, my one and only friend that I kept in touch with from that creatively stifling elitist academy. He's a deliriously gay playwright my age, who I desperately wish I could've brought to Texas with me. He might be the only regret I have about leaving that cruel, snobby school. I text him, asking how he's doing and why I haven't heard from him. Then, I stare at the screen and excitedly wait for him to answer.

I'm still waiting half an hour later when Victoria knocks on my door to go.

The walk is far less scary than she made it out to be. From the dorms, the School of Theatre is just a stroll past a large courtyard and fountain, through a tunnel over which the Art building squats, beside the University Center itself, and around the tall, glass-windowed School of Music where I imagine the corpse of my mystery roommate to be buried.

The School of Theatre is a giant red block of a building with a three-story tower jutting out from its rear like the tail of a threatened scorpion. The front is a row of glass teeth, punctuated at either end by double doors that read: *Theatre, Dancing, Excellence.*

As we approach the doors, for some reason I can hear the bottles of my parents' champagne popping off at some ritzy cast party in my mind, mocking me. I hear mother's cold words to me all over again, the ones she said when I first came home after quitting Rigby & Claudio's: *"You're simply not ready for the stage, doll. You'll find your spotlight someday."* I hear my father's: *"A good actor listens before she speaks. A better actor only listens."* Whatever the hell that means.

When Victoria doesn't lead us through the front glass doors, I make an observation. "The lights are all out. Do we have to wait for a member of faculty?"

"Oh. No, honey. This isn't a faculty-organized thing. The seniors do it at the start of every year. There will be booze. I'm fairly sure that some faculty know about it, but they pretend not to. Only certain underclassmen are allowed to attend."

"Which underclassmen?"

She gives me a knowing smirk. "The ones that matter."

The side door is propped open, a pool of light touching it from the parking lot. There's a guy leaning against the wall amidst a cloud of smoke generated from that cancer stick in his fingers. Shaggy haired, skeletal, and looking like he lives under a sheet of cardboard on Bleecker street, he regards me with heavy-lidded eyes and a nod. I'm about to greet him when Victoria steers me into the side door and whispers, "That's Arnie. He's a prop rat, hates life, and I'm pretty sure he's stoned out of his mind twenty-five hours a day."

The side door empties into a small lounging area, which is entirely unoccupied. We continue to follow the light down a hallway and into what I take to be a rehearsal space, which looks like half a basketball court minus the baskets. Across the room, a pair of double doors empty into the wings of the stage.

"Wow, this is new," she murmurs, our footsteps slapping against the hard floor as we go. "Party must be in the main auditorium."

"Are we going to get in trouble for this?"

She answers my question with a shrug, then bursts with energy at the sight of a girlfriend, cutting across the stage to greet her and leaving me entirely on my own. The darkened wings of the stage, framed by long red curtains that hang down from the heavens, are littered with racks of unhung lights, coiled cable, and a big machine on wheels that looks like some sound system from the 90's. Onstage, there are clusters of students chatting and laughing, only a spray of bleak white light coloring them. In the audience seating, there's a row or two with a handful of other people kicking back and chatting. Somewhere in the aisle–though it's hard to see with the bright light in my face–there appears to be a shirtless guy dancing, egged on by whooping friends nearby. Victoria claimed this little theatrical shindig started at eight, but from the looks of it, it started much sooner.

"You're a new one."

I turn toward the loose, gruff voice. Standing next to me is a short bald man with a beard and sparkling eyes. His body is stout and muscular with a belly that pulls at his green, plaid shirt. His beard, red and trimmed, sits like a rug against his pale, freckled skin.

"Hi," I return with a smile.

"Have a beer." He offers a second cup to me I didn't realize he was holding. I accept it, but don't dare take a sip. "You look too old to be a freshman."

Quite the charmer. "Thanks."

"Freddie," he says, extending his free hand. I shake it and regret it immediately, his hand being wet as frog skin. "You're an actress, obviously."

He didn't even ask for my name. "Obviously," I agree, looking around for someone to rescue me.

"I'm directing a play in the black box. Goes up in November. You should totally audition for it."

"Should I?" Where the hell did Victoria run off to?

"You'd be perfect for, like, all the parts. Every one. Even the dudes. You're amazing."

I step back and realize I'm a step from falling off the stage. Close call. That would be a lovely way to meet everyone: with broken limbs and a concussion.

"How old are you? Twenty-two? Twenty-three?" he asks, his words slurring.

"I'm an actress," I answer. "I'm all the ages."

Freddie laughs a little too hard at that. "Holy fuck, you're funny, too!"

Out of the shadows, Victoria appears at my side, her eyes flashing brightly. "Dessie!"

Saved. "Hey there, Victoria! You, um ... wanted to show me something?" I urge her, hoping she picks up what I'm putting down.

She's smart as a whip and does. "Totally. Excuse us, Freddie." She pulls me to the steps leading down to the seats while Freddie gives a sad, wordless moan of a goodbye.

"*You ditched me*," I hiss at her.

"Sorry, hadn't seen Marcella all summer. The bitch thinks she can take the role of Emily. She *should* go for the stage manager. We're sorta stage sisters," she explains, "doomed to audition for all the same parts."

"Stage manager? That's a tech position."

"No, no. The acting part. The 'Stage Manager' role in the play *Our Town*. That's the first fall production. Catch up, Dessie!" She stretches out her arms. "Erik! Other Eric! Ellis! Stanley!" She embraces each of her friends one by one, who stand in a cluster at the end of the fifth row. "This is my hall mate Dessie," she says for a modest introduction, then adds, "*She's from New York*," in a cocky aside.

"Hi," I murmur, then lift the cup that Freddie had given me. "Anyone like some roofied beer?"

"Have you tried it?" Victoria asks excitedly.

"I'd rather not. As I implied, it's probably roofied, and it smells like cat pee."

The one she just called "Other Eric", slender and olive-skinned, gently takes the cup from my hand. "It's homebrewed cat pee." With a shy smile, he adds, "It's *my* homebrewed cat pee."

"Oh." My face flushes at once. "I'm s-sorry, Other Eric. I just panicked. That bushy orange-bearded guy gave me a drink and started the whole director's couch thing on me and I just—"

"Freddie." Other Eric shrugs. "He's not a bad guy. He's just Irish."

"I bet this auditorium is, like, nothing compared to what you're used to in New York," says a girl from the floor, her jet black hair choppy and erratic, and her eyes bleeding dark eyeliner like tears.

"Actually, the theaters in New York are pretty small," I admit. This one's surprisingly big and almost two-tiered, an aisle dividing the back six rows of the house from the front. I guess everything *is* bigger in Texas; they have more space to play with than cramped-up, built-on-top-of-itself New York City.

"Smaller ones are easier to fill," notes Other Eric. "We never sell out the house."

Victoria grips my arm suddenly. "She studied at Rigby & Claudio's. This chick's *been places!*"

"So, you're here for the grad program?" asks the girl from the floor.

"No. I'm a sophomore. I left that school after one year. It ... It wasn't a right fit for me." Inspired by all the attention, I let my mouth run off. "An arts school in New York really ... isn't all that. I learned nothing I didn't already know. All the students think they know everything." *I can't shut up.* "The professors are failed actors, bitter and blaming their failures on you. Half the time, it was *me* schooling *them*." The resentment pours out of me like soured wine. "Claudio Vergas ... is a *prick*." I feel shivers up my arms, just saying that one harsh word.

"And Rigby? You'd be lucky to even see him once a semester. Don't get me started on the fools who run the dance department."

"Please," Victoria urges me, "get started on the fools who run the dance department." That inspires a laugh from the others.

"It's all so pretentious!" I go on. I've craved this release. My parents wouldn't listen. I need to get this out so badly. "They make you pay so much money just to fund their own shoddy off-off-off Broadway productions–and they're never hits. They had a whole play once where the entire set was constructed from just ... *chairs*. Chairs stacked together to form a bed, to form a wall, to form ... *a bigger chair*."

"That sounds kinda cool," murmurs goth girl from the floor.

"It wasn't," I assure her. "Then, during a grueling five-hour rehearsal of this weird, modernized, full-of-itself, leather-daddy rendition of *Romeo & Juliet* last spring, I found myself realizing–"

Then, my words catch in my throat at the sight in front of me.

From backstage emerges a man whose face catches the stage light so potently, his creamy skin glows.

I hear my own breathing in my ears, nothing else.

My heart stutters.

His killer face is carved from stone, sharp and dusted with a hint of five o'clock shadow. Even from the seats, his fuck-me eyes glisten like chips of glass.

I swallow hard.

I want to tangle my fingers in his messy brown hair, which casts a shadow down his forehead.

Then, there's his body. *Damn*. His magnificent, big body. I have seen countless stunning male actors, but instantly forget all of them in the presence of *him*.

And I'm still trying to finish my damn sentence. "And ... And I found myself realizing ..."

He wears his heather-grey tee like it was hand-stitched to fit his every delicious contour, from his strong broad shoulders to his thick biceps—I can already picture him lifting me with just one arm.

"And ..." I'm still trying to make words. "And I found myself ..."

His jeans, light blue and torn at the knees, hang low on his hips, the sight of which guts me and sends me down a path of naughty thoughts.

"And ..."

"Go on," Victoria encourages me.

He's standing now at the table with the beer, and the firmness of his ass is a one-man show all on its own. I want to grab it or tear his pants into shreds. He's turning me into a damn animal.

I am never like this. I'm so ashamed of myself.

"And I found myself," I finish. Maybe that was the sentence I was looking for all along. "You know what? I think I *will* try that beer."

"Drank it," says Eric apologetically, wiggling the empty cup.

"I planned to get one that wasn't roofied," I joke distractedly. "I'll ... I'll be right back."

I turn and walk up the steps to the stage. With each footstep, my nerves grow tighter and tighter. *I don't think I can do this.* Seeing him at the table with his beer, I strongly consider changing my mind. This is so insanely out of character for me, I feel like a different person with each of my slow and slower footsteps, dragging my feet through a swamp of molasses. My thighs threaten to drop me to the stage floor in an embarrassing heap of limbs.

My sister does this so easily. She approaches the hottest guys like they should be lucky to share oxygen in her vicinity.

But this is my turn. She's not here. I am.

One step at a time.

One breath at a time.

You're just walking into an audition, except it's ten billion times worse, and the casting director is the hottest guy you have ever seen. Suddenly, all I can hear are my own breaths, in and out. Then come my footsteps as I cross the stage, each slap of shoe against wood rattling my brain.

I draw so close, I bump into the table. He doesn't seem to notice, turned away slightly and seeming to be trapped in a web of dark, bothersome thoughts. *A tortured artist*, I decide with a smirk. *He's a man of many mysteries.* That's okay. I'm mysterious, too.

Then I inhale, and that might be the greatest mistake of all. *He smells amazing.* The hint of some unnamed, mannish cologne invades my senses, its spicy subtleness intoxicating me. He smells clean and oddly comforting, like the way someone else's home might smell—safe, inviting, yet unfamiliar.

I have to speak. I have to say something to get his attention. I can't just be the ghost girl who lurks. I draw breath to say something, anything—and then nothing comes.

He has a cup of beer in his big, strong hand. He studies it pensively. *This is your moment. No one else is around. You even have the perfect excuse: you're new and you're meeting people. Introduce yourself.*

No better gift than right now; it's why they call it the present.

"Hi," I offer, using my sweetest audition voice.

He doesn't even flinch. After too long a moment, he takes a sip of his beer, then stares into it like he's disgusted with his own reflection. *God, he looks so hot when he makes that face, scowling at absolutely nothing.*

I try again. "I'm Dessie." A beer is in my hand and I don't even remember getting it. Its contents shake because my hands do. "I—I'm a transfer here. Second year. Are you an actor? You look like an actor."

Still nothing. He even turns his head upstage, looking off as if something far more interesting than me caught his attention. Y'know, like a *fly*.

That's when I notice the seriously sexy, dark tattoo running up the base of his thick neck, making me wonder what else he's hiding under that tight shirt.

"Listen, I'm new here, and ... and I'm just trying to meet people," I go on, feeling more desperate and dumb by the second. I set my beer back down on the table. "It would be rather nice to talk to someone who actually *acknowledges* when he's being—"

Then, the asshole walks away.

I watch, completely taken aback by his rudeness. It was clear as hell who I was talking to, wasn't it? He had every opportunity to just simply tell me he wasn't interested in getting to know me. Except, isn't that the point of this damn Theatre mixer thing? To ... mix?

"*Prick*," I mutter at his back, drawing the attention of a couple girls at the other end of the table, but not from the guy to which the word was directed. I hope they didn't hear me.

Or maybe I do. I suddenly, immediately, wholly don't care about anything. I've been used to this my whole life. Cece gets told "yes" every day. My peers at Rigby & Claudio's got all the praise while I sat back and wondered what the hell was wrong with me. I'm the outcast, the failure, the family joke.

I'm the *guppy*.

I abandon the stage, departing through the wing and the rehearsal room. In a matter of seconds, the School of Theatre is behind me and I'm tramping down the dark pathways back to my dorm, alone.

DESSIE

I don't even know his name.

Yet there he stands in all his perfect glory.

"Hi," I mutter stupidly.

He sees me. His eyes zero in and the world zeros out. Nothing exists but me, him, and the breath between us.

"Can you help me?" I ask him, drawing close, too close, far closer than I thought I'd dare. "I think I'm lost. I know the School of Theatre, and the School of Music, but I can't seem to find the–"

"School of Sex?" he finishes for me, and his voice is like silk against my skin. I suppress a moan just from hearing it.

"Yeah." I feel so confident and beautiful. "I need your help ... in finding ... the School of Sex."

He licks his lips and nods knowingly. His eyes pierce me. The subtle light of whatever room we're in barely colors his gruff, unshaven face, leaving so much of him in the mysterious dark.

His hand slips behind my neck. "What ... What are you doing?" I ask, knowing full well. My heart is hammering against my chest. Heat surges between my thighs and I'm trembling with anticipation. "All I needed ... was help in ... in finding the School of Sex."

"Consider it found," he murmurs, his lips drawing close to mine.

Then I open my eyes, and I'm all alone in my dorm room again.

Evil. My mind is pure evil. The crushing vacuum from my dream's sudden departure leaves a hole in my chest that I literally, physically clutch at. I shut my eyes and beg to return to where I left off. *It felt so fucking real.* I try to imagine his face and it's already gone. I try to feel his touch again and all I feel are bed sheets and my own thumping heart.

Believe it or not, this is the *second* night in a row that I've had this dream. Sunday was an uneventful yet totally necessary day where I got to decompress from the move (still without a roommate), buy my books from the crowded campus bookstore, and then enjoy three totally normal college meals at the Quad cafeteria. I even successfully dodged yet another call from my mother.

But nothing seems to ease the ache I carry for that sexy hunk from the mixer. *Prick,* I had called him.

Ugh.

Then, I hear the turning of a page. I'm not alone. I bolt up, drawing the sheets to my neck as if I'm naked, and I see her. "Who're you??"

The girl sitting cross-legged on the other bed lifts her sullen, shapeless face from the book she reads. A sad pair of thick-rimmed glasses rest at the end of her nose. Her hair, straight and plain as the bristles on a broom, is cropped dully at the neck. An unfortunate pox of red bumps I'll pray aren't chickenpox dance up the side of her short, blunt neck. Her nose is a round bulb of flesh and her eyebrows are thick and black and unsightly. She stares at me with the enthusiasm of a sock, her eyes dead and blank.

"Sam," she answers plainly, her voice two octaves lower than I was expecting.

Sam? Samantha, my roommate? Obviously. "When did you move in?" I ask, flabbergasted. "I ... I've been asleep. I didn't even hear you at all."

"I didn't really move in."

I blink a few times in the semidarkness, waiting for more of an explanation. I don't get one. I stretch my neck up a bit, scanning her side of the room only to find three books on her desk alongside an ancient brick of a laptop and a sad table lamp, the only source of light in the room other than the sunrise coming through the blinds and painting stripes of orange across the back of her head.

I wipe my eyes and stare. "You don't even have sheets. You're ... You're sleeping on the *bare mattress.*"

"It's okay," she decides, looking down at it. Her every movement is as slow as a sloth. She wears sweatpants and a loose shirt that looks scavenged from a charity donation bin. For half a second, I worry she is exactly that: a girl with cents in her pockets, here on the last scraps of money her parents could find. They had to put a second mortgage on the house to afford tuition. They sold their grandma's ashes on eBay. She is her family's last hope.

"So ... we're roommates," I state unnecessarily.

"Yep." She offers me an odd, straight line of her lips, almost like an apology, before returning to the book in her lap, a curtain of hair covering her face.

I stare at her for a while, still clutching the sheets to my neck. I'm pretty sure the worry is obvious on my face and she saw every bit of it. For as little emotion as she seems to show, I might never know whether I've offended her or not.

Well, she's who I got. Might as well make the best of it. "So ... you're a Music major? What instrument do you play?"

Sam lifts her head again, drawing a curtain of her greasy hair behind her ear. "Piano."

The girl sounds like a dude. She seriously sounds like a dude. "Oh. Don't you need to practice?" I let my eyes do another scan of the room. "Did you bring, like, a little keyboard or something?"

"They have private piano-playing rooms at the Music building."

"Oh. Yeah, that makes sense."

"I wanted a Yamaha," she admits, fiddling with the bent corner of a page in her book, "but my mom made me choose between paying for school or buying expensive electronics, and ... well, I'm here, so ..."

"Yes. Right. You're ... You're here."

An awkward silence settles between us once again. I put a smile into that silence. She glances sullenly through the window, stripes of the morning sun drawn across her plain face. Then she turns back to me, her eyes like two spots of mud. "And you are—"

"A Theatre major," I finish for her, hugging my sheets tightly. "I'm Dessie."

"I'm Sam," she repeats, like I'd already forgotten.

And with that, Sam returns to reading, and I let myself lie back down, my eyes catching the time on the clock: not a minute past seven in the morning. That is decidedly too early to be awake, considering my first class isn't until ten.

But try as I might, that damn dream of mine won't resume where we left off.

I don't understand what's so special about one hot guy. Why am I finding myself so ... *obsessed* with him? I'm on a campus full of countless good-looking guys. Engineers. Artists. Architects. Singers. Other actors. Why am I so focused on the one guy who wouldn't bother to turn and acknowledge my existence, even when I was talking directly to him?

A half hour passes. I can't seem to hear anything but the quiet turning of pages.

Another half hour, and that lamp seems brighter than the sun at noon, somehow blinding me through my clenched-shut eyelids. *Or maybe it's the actual sun.*

When I give up and rise at half past eight, I feel like I got approximately zero hours of sleep. My head spins and a queasiness settles into my stomach. Why do I instantly want to blame mister hot-shit from the mixer for my lack of rest?

I help myself to a morning shower. Even with all the soap and the slipperiness and the assumption of privacy, I'm too distracted with what diseases my feet might be picking up to revive the morning's dream. *Mental note: purchase some flip-flops for the shower.* I keep hitting my elbows against the wall every time I turn. The room steams up in a matter of five seconds.

I can't even sing as I like to do in the shower, not when I know an entire hallway of boys and girls will hear me. I try to hum and even that miniscule hint of melody feels amplified to the point of vibrating the tiled walls. I feel utterly silenced when I want to sing.

Outside, the campus is alive with tons of bright-eyed students. I fall right in line, following the path to the School of Theatre Victoria showed me Saturday night, though it looks dramatically different in the day. The buildings look so much taller. There's a glow to the Art building I didn't notice in the darkness. When I pass the University Center, there's a big band playing some tune I don't recognize, but it's catchy as hell. I start humming it as I move along, a smile finding my face at long last. Nothing eases me the way singing does. *Look at me, I'm a college student,* I realize, blending in with the crowd of others who head to their ten o'clock Monday classes.

This is what I've been missing.

Most of my Theatre courses don't require books, so I just carry a small bag with my laptop dancing around inside. The School of Theatre is shockingly bright during the day, its front glass windows reflecting the sun and blinding me as I approach.

My first class of the day—a required course for all: Technical Theatre—is held in the main auditorium. Surprisingly, I spot Victoria right away in the seats. She notices me too, quickly beckoning me over.

"Where the hell did you go Saturday night?" she whispers when I take the seat next to her. "You just up and left! Then, you wouldn't answer any of my knocking on your door all day ..."

"I got tired," I lie. My foot kicks into a red cup from Saturday that was left by the seat. "Yesterday, I was probably at the campus bookstore. Did you know that Klangburg University has its own clothing line?"

"Yeah, it's called college merch. Every school's got it. Do you know what crew you want, Des?"

I frown. "What do you mean?"

"Tech crew. That's the point of this class. You get introduced to the five tech crews and get to pick which one you want to do for the semester. Or, rather, they assign you one based on your preference. If you get cast in a play, it counts for a tech credit. No, I haven't been cast yet." Victoria rolls her eyes, clearly holding back a flood of rants. "Are you all actress? Or do you ever get your hands dirty?"

That'd be Cece who is all actress and can't even be bothered to move a damn curtain out of her way when she enters or exits the stage. *"That's what the stagehands are for,"* she had the gall to say to me once.

And just before I answer Victoria, all of my composure is ruined in an instant.

I see *him*.

The tatted hottie from Saturday night's mixer. The man who still hasn't given me proper directions to the School of Sex. The nameless wonder from the wings with the body of a demigod.

I claw at my bag. *I've never wanted someone so badly.*

He saunters past carrying a Fresnel lantern by the handle, his bicep bulging in the effort as he crosses the stage. His shirt is tight. His jeans, loose and sexy. I've broken out in a sweat just watching him.

"Dessie?"

A smirk finds my lips. "Yeah," I murmur back to her. "I get my hands dirty. Real, real dirty."

Then a lean, bearded man who looks like a wizard in coveralls rises from the front row and faces the auditorium. "Good morning, you bunch of brats, you. I see a lot of new faces out there, so I'm going to assume that most of you are freshmen. Sure, a lot of you are probably hopeful actors, figuring you waltzed in here from a high school that kissed your butt every time you projected loud enough for someone beyond the front row to hear you. Loud voices earned you parts. Well, you're in for a rude awakening."

Rude, indeed. I can't stop watching *him* onstage as he transports lighting equipment from one end to the other. There is very little imagination involved in picturing his naked torso, what with the tightness of his shirt leaving little to be curious about.

He is *ripped.* I could spot his godlike physique from a mile away. His eyes pierce me and he's not even looking at me.

I've never been jealous of lighting equipment before.

"College is your first taste of the real world," the wizard is going on. "Plays only have so many roles, and chances are, you won't get any your first year here. You might not ever get cast. This is a reality you must face."

That man onstage is a reality I want to face. I want to face him so hard. I want him to face me. I'm staring at his bulging biceps as he works, my heart racing so hard I wonder if Victoria can hear it.

"Technical Theatre is *not* for failed actors. These people make a living. More often, they make a better living than you actors ever will because there is *always* work for lighting monkeys, soundboard operators, costume stitch-weaver-people, prop masters, house managers–the list goes on and on. Our program requires only six hours of tech crew before you can graduate. That's six times I'm gonna see your ugly faces in this room. We only meet here today. This Wednesday, you will be meeting at your assigned crew area. Understood? Good."

Hot guy sets down a light, which issues a loud bang that ripples across the stage. He returns to the rack for yet another, sauntering as he goes. *Boy, does that sexy man know how to walk.* He has gloves on those big hands of his, those long leather things that come halfway up his arm, the kind I imagine welders wear.

I can't seriously be the only one staring at him. That man is *fine.*

"The five departments are: costume crew, set crew, props crew, lighting crew, and box office," the bearded wizard tells us.

As he goes on to describe the typical duties of each technical crew, I'm stuck in a daze watching the hottie carry Fresnel after Fresnel across the stage, his arms bulging with each trip, sometimes taking two at a time. His face is slick with sweat. Patches of wetness adorn his tight shirt, causing it to plaster to his muscles more and more by the second.

He stops after his five-hundredth trip and runs an arm slowly across the whole length of his forehead, taking just a moment to survey the house. His brow wrinkles as he looks out at us. He has to be an upperclassmen. His presence is so commanding that I can't pay attention to anything else, not with him in the room.

Some papers are shoved at me. I stare down in confusion at what looks like a stack of forms. "Take one and pass them," Victoria tells me. I do so, passing the stack to a girl two seats away from me. "Now you get to pick the crew you want. Preference one, and preference two, see?"

"I see." I'm very thankful for Victoria's guidance, considering how little attention I was paying to the wizard-person. I stare at the five options for crew and consider them.

Victoria leans into me, her bony shoulder poking into my arm. "Costume crew is a living *hell,*" she whispers to me. "Box office is a total blow-off. I'd go for that one, so long as you're not claustrophobic and can do basic math. Ever work with money?"

My eyes wander to the stage. He's examining one of the lights that still hangs from the rack. The gloves are off and tucked under his arm while his fingers expertly inspect the equipment. I imagine those fingers expertly inspecting *me*, the way they'd feel as they trace up and down my arms, run over the length of my body, and awaken a wave of excited goose bumps across my skin. I feel my toes curling in my shoes just thinking about it.

"Made up your mind?" whispers Victoria.

His biceps flex as he works, his fingers making art out of that lighting instrument. I swallow hard, unable to pull my eyes away, unable to slow my thumping heart, unable to ignore my ache any longer.

Yes, I have, I think to myself, bringing the pen to paper and circling my first choice: lighting crew.

DESSIE

"There's a whole row of restaurants on Kelly street, but they're a bit on the pricy side ..."

"Done! Lunch is on me!" I decide with a smile.

That's how Victoria, Eric, Chloe, and I end up at an Italian restaurant on the *not* criminally-inclined edge of campus for an early evening meal after my first Tuesday morning movement class and afternoon voice class are over. Chloe's the one I met at the mixer with choppy black hair whose eyes bleed eyeliner, and Eric is the one who just a moment ago politely asked me to stop calling him Other Eric. I apologized for calling his homebrew "cat pee".

"Auditions are this Friday," Victoria reminds me between bites of a very aromatic plate of basil pesto chicken fettuccini. "I hope you have two contrasting monologues prepared. Oh, I didn't even ask! Which role are you gunning for?"

To be honest, I hadn't given it much thought. My mind's been circling thoughts of a certain someone so much that I forgot about auditions for *Our Town*. "I was considering the wife, maybe?"

"Myrtle? That's Emily's mother," explains Victoria. "Maybe try for Mrs. Gibbs, George's wife, if you want to play a wife. Oh, you'd be cute as her! Go for whichever you want, just as long as it's not Emily."

"The lead? But she has the look," protests Eric.

"That's *my* role," Victoria insists. "I've waited two years for it, and I shall claim it. Besides, Nina *basically* already told me I got the part."

"Nina the acting prof," Eric clarifies for me.

"I know. I have her for acting class on Mondays, Wednesdays, and Fridays. And it's okay," I insist with a nervous titter. "I don't want any leads. I should really, uh ... reread the play." For all my "Theatre background", I sure feel so uneducated right now.

"Not to mention Dessie's experience," Eric goes on, despite Victoria's annoyed snort. "You'd make a great Emily. You have *world* experience. You've been to Italy and shit."

"Yeah," I admit, "but that was a small black box theater, and it was more of a training camp, and—"

"You studied in New York City," he goes on, despite Victoria's look of disbelief. "You already know the life. You have so much to offer *us*. Really, it isn't unheard of for freshmen to land roles, and you're technically not a freshman, so ..."

"I already said the role is *mine*," Victoria interjects, her eyes playing back and forth between us. "I like you, Dessie, I really do. We're hall mates and we're becoming friends and all that, but I think—"

"I think auditions will determine it," states Eric. "I mean, if you're meant to get the role of Emily—"

"I already have it in the bag," she retorts.

"Then you got nothing to worry about, do you?" With that, he gives a light shrug, then forks another sauce-drenched ravioli past his lips.

I smile at my new friends, hoping the mask of my smile adequately hides all my misgivings. They think so highly of me, just for the ritzy school I half-attended and the fact that I'm from New York City. If they knew who my family was, I'd certainly be ruined. *Spoiled*, they'd call me. *Privileged snob*, they'd think of me. I'd become my sister before their eyes, a girl who's been handed everything she ever wanted.

What'll they think when they learn the truth?

"Your résumé *has* to be a mile long," Victoria jokes with a shake of her head. "I bet you have to leave stuff off of it just to make it fit on one page. Wish I had that sort of problem." The comment earns a chuckle from Chloe and Eric.

The truth is, since high school, I've only been cast in a single production. It was an original two-act play at Claudio & Rigby's called *Quieter The Scream*. By some remarkable twist of circumstance, I was cast as the leading role. Claudio could not easily mask his disappointment in me during every single rehearsal, which led me to speculate how I'd landed the role in the first place. My speculation ended the day Claudio threw his favorite mug and I quit the school.

Even still, the whole situation confounds me. *"You'll be a famous actress someday just like your sweet mother."* That's what Claudio said the first day he met me. My, how quickly *that* opinion soured. The truth is, I never fit the skin my parents and sister tried so ruthlessly to put on me. I needed to find my own.

While the others finish eating and start bantering back and forth, I listen to a tune that comes on the restaurant sound system and catch myself smiling. It's a song I know. Finishing my linguini, which isn't half bad even compared to Chef Julian's masterful cooking, I hum along with the melody. I wonder if normal-people food is growing on me, or if I'm simply forgetting already what it's like to be ... me.

A couple hours later, everyone goes their separate ways and I've returned to the theater to sign up for auditions. In a short, closed-off hall that connects the lobby to the theater, I stare at my phone in my palm, dreading what I'm about to do. This is never easy.

I tap her name. My phone chirps at me. I bring it to my ear.

"Desdemona? Hi."

Already, I'm annoyed by two facts. One: I almost don't recognize her due to the thick English dialect she's putting on. Two: she's the only person in the world who uses my full name. Not even my parents bother with all four annoying syllables of it.

"Hey, Cece. I have a favor to ask. A really serious favor."

"Oh, that is quite fine. I was simply partaking in a lesson with my vocal coach," she answers in an airy voice, her English dialect annoyingly realistic. "Andre, can we take five? My dear sister needs a favor of me. Thank you. Desdemona, what is it you need, dear?"

I sigh. "Can you knock off the voice, please? This is serious."

"This is quite serious as well," she goes on, the dialect remaining perfectly intact. "I must master every bit of idiosyncrasy in the Upper RP dialect, and that entails remaining in-character for the rest of the week at the very least, dear sister. My work is *quite serious*."

"Fine." I roll my eyes, unable to bear one more word than I absolutely have to. "Cece, I need help with an acting résumé. I'm required to have one for auditions this Friday."

"Oh, silly girl, I am afraid I do not do my own. That is the job of Xavier and Iris. I would be happy to connect you, if you so wish to—"

"No, no, no." *I resent that I even have to have this conversation.* "You don't understand. I don't have any shows to put on mine. Other than high school, I've only done the one show at Claudio's, and I didn't even do that to completion. My résumé's empty."

"Are ... Are you requesting my assistance in an act of forgery, dear sister? Oh, how wayward you have become! Oh, stars! I am afraid I cannot—"

"For fuck's sake, Cece, I need your *help*," I hiss into the phone, my hands trembling. "It's just a résumé. I can't go in there Friday with nothing!"

Cece draws a deep breath into the phone. I can even picture her as she does so, her body turning rigid and her long eyelashes batting with irritation as she steels herself for her next words.

"Every actor must start somewhere. It is not my fault that you have no history. To have a history, you must first make one. Life experience makes the actor, Desdemona. Not a sheet of paper."

"I haven't been given the *experiences* you have. It isn't fair of you to act superior to me, treating me like it's *my* fault I don't get the callbacks. You're the one who inherited all our family's *magic mojo* and left none for me. So help me out a little, Cece."

"If I may allow you to stand corrected," my sister retorts, her voice clipped and sterile, "with regard to our family's 'magic mojo', you did, in fact, ask for a journey to Texas to find that very thing, didn't you, dear sister? Why cannot you try and see this as a most precious opportunity to find that very special thing that makes you, you? I guarantee, it won't be by forging a false résumé."

I'm clenching my phone so tight, the muscles in my palm ache.

"Thanks for nothing, Cece. I gotta go. I'm so busy over here having my *life experience*."

I hang up, cutting off her response. I always regret asking my sister for help; she makes me want to act upon violent impulses. With a huff, I turn to the sign-up sheet on the wall and bring a pen to its surface with too much force, scratching on my name.

When I'm about to turn away, I hear a noise from the opened door of the auditorium. I stop and listen.

Nothing else comes.

I move to the door and poke my head in. I don't see anyone in the seats. Coming further inside, I look up at the stage. No one. Nothing.

"Hello?" I call out, like the half-naked bimbo does in the horror movie before she's caught and gutted by the killer. "Hello?"

No one answers. I move down the aisle, curious, drawn by the silence. I ascend the steps and stand center stage, looking out at the seating, which is only half-lit by the spray of stage light above.

A smile finds my face. No one uses the auditorium at all, not until after auditions when the set building and rehearsing begins. This big room is abandoned for the time being, according to my new friends.

This auditorium is mine.

I imagine the seats filled to the walls with people who've purchased tickets. I imagine the hum of an animated crowd as they enjoy the house music and await the first act to begin. I imagine myself standing backstage, wringing my hands and excitedly longing for the drapes to be drawn. This is my moment. This is my show.

On this big stage, I feel a stronger sense of privacy than I do in my dorm. The desire to express myself grows strong, stronger ... until I can no longer contain it. The first thing that comes to mind is a song no one's heard of called "A Palace of Stone". I part my lips and sing:

I have made a palace of stone,
a place of which to call my own.
Here is my bed
to lay down my head
and dream that I'm not alone.

For such a feat, what do I win?
The doors are deceivingly thin.
But I built the walls too high
nearly kissing the sky
so no one can find their way in.

There's no staff to help with the messes.
There's no guests to admire my dresses.
Dinners cook themselves
as I dust off my shelves
and watch as my lifetime progresses.

I'm an actress who shows no fear.
The bravest in my whole biosphere.
And by my painted skin
you see the people I've been
and the people I'll never go near.

It's work to perch atop this throne
made of credit cards and silicone.
Don't dare give your heart
or you'll fall right apart

right here in my palace of stone.

When I've finished, I imagine the room erupting into applause. I face the crowd and take it all in, rejoicing. I wonder if flowers are being thrown to the stage. I can smell them if I close my eyes.

There's a noise from behind. I spin, alarmed by it.

He's standing by the light rack, watching me. His eyes are fierce and focused, his lips parted slightly.

Oh shit. He heard everything.

"I-I'm sorry," I murmur, my face flushing horribly. "I ... I didn't realize ..."

His tight shirt hugs the two hills of his shoulders that lead up to his thick, muscular neck. His big pecs stare at me just as he does, and for a moment it's like he's some statue of a god. I bet his muscles feel like one too, firm and unbudgeable. I imagine the meaty sound his body would make as I tackle him, and the metallic racket of the lighting instruments as they bang together, disrupted by our crashing into them.

Wait. What the hell am I thinking?

"I'm s-sorry," I repeat, ashamed, humiliated. All he does is stare at me. He doesn't say a damn thing. "It ... It wasn't *that* bad, was it?"

His eyes bore into me, *smoldering* me, those deep, powerful eyes. He looks so dangerous ... so tortured ...

So sexy. My heart races. I can't catch my breath.

"Oh," I blurt, my voice shaking. "It *was* that bad. I'm not supposed to be here, am I? I'll just ... I'll go."

And that's precisely what I do, tripping over my legs as I race down the steps. The noise of my feet slapping the tile of the lobby assaults my ears as I flee the theater.

DESSIE

"And this guy ... caught you singing?"

I sigh and lean into the table, mortified, then nod sheepishly.

"There *are* some hot guys in our school," admits Victoria, "but I don't know which one caught you. If you'd tell me more, I might know his name. There's Jerry, short for Jeremy. There's Aaron. Ooh, or Ian ..."

Truth is, I don't want you to know who. "It's okay. I just hope it doesn't get me into trouble. I want to make a good first impression."

"Yeah, save that for auditions Friday." She winks and gives me a nudge. "Lighten up. It'll be fine. Hey, I didn't know you could sing."

"I doubt I sang well. He just stared at me like I was an idiot and ..." I can't even finish, not wanting to relive it yet again. "I need to work on my audition pieces. I didn't realize—"

"That auditions would be the very first week? Yep. We don't mess around down here in Texas. I'm sure you're used to that in New York City too, of course. Hey, we can help each other with our monologues! I could totally pick a brain like yours." She nearly giggles with excitement. "I have a whole bookcase of marked-up scripts in my room. Hey, I bet you could even sing for one of your pieces. I think they're allowing that, on account of the spring musical."

I can't stop picturing his face, the way he stared at me so intently after I'd finished. "We'd better get to class," I say, noting the time on my phone.

"First day of crew! Did you see which one you got? They're posted on the door of the rehearsal room."

Twenty minutes later, we've moved from the food court to the School of Theatre, where I stumble as I scurry down the winding halls to the rehearsal room door. I search the list for my name.

My heart skips a beat.

I'd nearly forgotten which one I signed up for.

"Lighting crew?" Victoria questions, staring at me. "You picked … *lighting crew?* Mmm, honey, I hope you aren't scared of heights."

I bite the inside of my cheek and suck my tongue, staring at my name and reading it over and over and over again. My body trembles. My nerves tighten and my knees turn weak. I know exactly why I picked it.

"I … wanted to t-try something new," I struggle to say through a dry mouth. I have trouble swallowing suddenly. Maybe my organs are all shutting down. I might die before I reach my class.

Victoria gasps in protest when she sees her own name. "Costume crew?! Are you kidding me?! No! That wasn't *either* of my preferences! Damn it! That can't be right …"

I can't even participate in a moment of sympathy for her, too wrapped up in my own predicament, if I dare call it that. *Will I see him today? How many people has he told about what happened yesterday in the theater?* Maybe he's not in the lighting crew at all. Maybe he was just … fiddling with them a lot. Maybe he's part of the set crew. Just like any other student, he gets assigned to different crews each semester too, right?

I'm overthinking this. *Calm down, Dessie.*

"Oh well. Come by my room later," she says to me, and I'm pretty sure I just zoned out on her whole tirade about costume crew. "We'll pore over scripts! I want to show you what I've got prepared. You can critique me with all your *New York City knowhow*."

I give her a halfhearted nod and grimace, then we part ways. I proceed in silence to where the lighting crew is supposed to meet: the main stage.

My heart hammers in my chest as I approach the door to the auditorium. It's so cold that I swear they set the AC to a considerate thirty-below.

The door creaks.

I don't know why I'm so afraid of anyone hearing me or noticing my existence at all.

When I step inside, however, I'm surprised to find only twenty or so sitting scattered among the first five rows. After a quick, nerve-wracking scan, I realize that mister mystery-hot-shit is not among them. Everyone in the crowd seems to know one another, chatting and laughing amongst themselves. Two guys in the back have their feet propped up. Three other guys are hanging over their chairs, chatting with the folk behind them. *Am I the only female here?* Literally zero of the people I've met thus far are in this room.

I sit silently in the fifth row behind the strangers, clutching my bag to my chest and waiting patiently for something to happen.

Ten minutes later, something does. A man comes out of a door backstage, emerging into the light. He's dressed in black with a smear of unexplained green paint on his thigh and he carries a clipboard, toward which he inclines his head and adjusts the thick set of glasses that perch at the tip of his nose. His bald head shines with grease under the blaring stage light.

"Welcome," he says to his clipboard, though I think he's addressing us. "First day of lighting crew. Hi. Most of you know me. Six of you don't. Hi. I'm Professor Dan Trellis. You can call me Dick."

Two guys wearing baseball caps in the seats ahead of me turn to each other. "How do you get Dick from Dan?" one of them mutters quietly.

"You ask nicely," answers the other, and they both break into a fit of muffled snickering.

I roll my eyes.

"This is *not* the slack-off crew," Dick says in a tired drone, though it seems less like a fact and more like he's trying to convince himself. "Most of your life here will be cables and gels and C-clamps. Shit gets stressful the week leading up to dress, just before each show goes up. You *will* be going up Bertha the cherry-picker at some point, so if heights aren't your thing, *make* them your thing. Introduce yourself to Bertha. Learn how to operate Bertha. Love Bertha. You'll be given an assistant when you first use her, blah, blah, life's about confronting fears and shit, right?"

I'm about to make a mental comment on all of the professor's swearing when something else steals every bit of my wayward attention.

Every bit of my delicious, sexy attention.

Another figure has come out of the shadows from backstage. His brawny build is unmistakable, as well as the swagger in his stride. When the light finally touches his face, it's like a gift from the School of Sex. Dark, brooding, fierce ... he always looks pissed off about something. Why do I find that so hot?

"Nice to have you join us, Clayton," the professor mutters with a turn of his head. "Most of you know Clayton, my right hand man with the lights for the last two years. Invaluable to us. Be like him."

Clayton ... Is that his name?

If it is, you wouldn't know it from the way he completely disregards Professor Dick, hopping down the steps and taking a seat in the front row. Just as well, Dick doesn't seem to mind as he lifts his clipboard back to his face and resumes instructing us on what our semester with him is going to be like.

Meanwhile, my eyes drift to the beauty in the front row. *Clayton*. His face taut with concentration, he stares at the professor as the speech goes on and on. Something about sound crew. Something about time management and patience.

Yeah, I know all about patience. Here I am, patiently staring at the beauty who's invaded every one of my dreams since I stepped foot into this very theater. I have never, in all my life, been as drawn to a person as I am to him.

Clayton. The name fits him so well. He's a statue, a hardened clay sculpture, a work of art.

Suddenly, everyone's rising from their seats and filing onto the stage. I must've missed something. I get up awkwardly, following the baseball-capped boys. I avoid eye contact with Clayton and pray that, should he get a look in my direction, he doesn't remember who I am. I realize how unlikely that is, considering the full-on eye contact we shared right after my bold and embarrassing performance yesterday.

"Here's the lighting rack," Dick goes on, tapping a giant contraption made of pipes upon which tons of different lighting instruments hang.

The crowd of us gather around the professor as he starts describing the different types of lights. As I take my place in the back, I don't realize until it's too late who I'm standing right beside.

I freeze. The whole world is gone and all I'm aware of is his body standing to my left.

Oh my god, he smells so good. He could have come from three hours of working out, or from a morning of transporting heavy props and set pieces backstage. Who knows. Who cares. His scent intoxicates me, just like it did that first day at the mixer.

Does he always smell like this?

"There's all kinds of gels," Dick goes on. "See, with them, the lights get colors, or get shapes, or get ..."

Clayton's big, firm body is like a bonfire at my side. I feel his heat.

Does he know he's standing next to me? Is this intentional, or completely incidental that the hottest guy in the room is so close that I could climb him? Oh, damn, I want to climb him.

"Now, if you come in close and look here ..."

Everyone takes a step forward, crowding each other to get a better look at—something—and I find myself pushed by a guy to my right ... which causes me to lean into Clayton unintentionally.

My skin touches his.

I feel the tight, rock-hard meat of his arm. It's as firm as I expected, and then a little more. I don't dare look in his direction. My heart is racing so fast, I wonder if he can feel my pulse through the skin of our forearms.

Dick goes on. Something about lamp houses. Something about ellipsoidal reflector spotlights. And my mind goes on about what I'd do if I found myself stuck in a room alone with Clayton.

He's half a foot taller than me, maybe more. It's the perfect height for me to lay my face on his big, muscled shoulder ... if I just tilted my head a tiny bit. Just a tiny, tiny bit.

I'm so close to him that I'm starting to sweat.

Then the crowd starts to move. Clayton goes with them and, after half a second of despair, I follow to the other end of the stage where Dick starts to explain about something to do with the pulley system—all the ropes lined up along the wall that connect to all the things hanging high above us.

I realize with frustration that there's now a person between Clayton and I. The magic is lost. I stare at the professor sullenly and find I can't even focus on what he's saying. Every word flitters by my face, unheard.

"The counterweight system is dangerous. This is not a toy. Learn to use it properly. Want to give us a demonstration?" Dick asks, giving a wave of his hand.

He seems to have signaled Clayton, who cuts through the crowd and positions himself at the ropes. I'm alive again, just like that. Watching the way his body moves is hypnotizing. Without instruction, he knows precisely what to do, flipping some lever with his big hands ... those big hands that seem to make love to every little thing they touch. Then, he unwinds something else and grips the rope, fingers wrapping around it the way they might embrace a lover. He gives the rope a solid tug, the veins in his thick biceps popping, and something happens behind me.

The whole class turns to watch, but I keep my eyes focused right where they are, already watching the most beautiful thing in the world.

His hands still firmly gripping the rope, Clayton's eyes lower, catching mine.

I hold my breath. I experience a jolt of fear ... or a jolt of excitement. I can't seem to tell the difference between the two right now.

And his eyes change. It's subtle, but it's there. *He recognizes me*, I realize as my heart quickens. Yet still, I don't look away.

The professor must've said something because the whole crew moves to the two long battens—which are steel pipes from which curtains or set pieces or lights are hung—that have been lowered. I finally allow that to break my gaze from the distraction that's Clayton, forcing myself to pay attention to Dick.

That attention is short-lived. Not a moment later, Clayton has returned from the counterweights, and he's right at my side yet again. *I just can't catch a break, can I?* Not that I want one. I've never been so worked up in all my life. I'm in agony standing next to him. I feel my pulse in my neck. I can barely breathe evenly.

His arm brushes against mine.

Total. Fucking. Agony.

"Lighting creates atmosphere. Lighting turns the barren nothing of a stage into the snowy Alps, the lobby of a hotel, or the bowels of a whale. Lighting gives life to the cast onstage," states Dick, our mildly inspired professor. "Without light, we are all a bunch of shit-shoveling nobodies in the dark, aren't we?"

Clayton inhales deeply. Just in that inhale, I hear the depth of his voice. There's something so intimate about it, like I'm already getting to know him even without having shared a single word. Then, he exhales deeply, and half that breath tickles my arm and sends shivers of awareness through me.

I am one seriously obsessed stalker right now.

"Short day. That's all, my little light monkeys. I'm leaving the sign-up sheet at the foot of the stage. Sign up for whichever lighting shift you want, and that'll be your shift every week for the rest of the semester. Crew shifts start next week. There's lots of options to accommodate all kinds of classing schedules, so if your whiny ass needs some special treatment, come have a chat with me and we'll figure something out."

With that, the whole crew scatters and Clayton abandons my side. I'd just grown used to having his heat there that when he departs, I feel a vacuum of need so strong that I nearly topple over.

I walk down the steps and approach the sign-up list. Some of the guys are talking amongst themselves or consulting their phones to double-check their scheduling conflicts. When it's my turn to pick from the list, I consider what's available. Amazingly, five of the six available shifts do not overlap with my classes. There's a shift Mondays that would fit after my acting class, a shift Tuesday afternoons between my voice and movement classes, another Friday mornings, another Saturday afternoons, and then a late Wednesday evening shift. I could pick any one of those that I want. Any at all.

And yet it's on that Wednesday evening shift that I see the only name that matters. It's written right at the top of the list. *Clayton Watts.*

Only two others have signed up for that time slot. The least popular shift, it seems. And driven by some kind of insanity, I bring my pen to that Wednesday list of names and add my own.

Dessie Lebeau.

I look up and find Clayton walking away. I only catch a split second of his muscular backside before he disappears through the backstage door. Oddly, I feel a small sense of relief at his departure. It's damn stressful being near him at all. My nervous system got a work out today.

As I walk back to the dorms, the relief turns to emptiness. It's so strange, to be able to go for so long without being aware of how alone you truly are. You convince yourself that your heart is full with all your interests and hobbies and fiery passions. You fill yourself up with hollow reassurance. You get used to the routine of handling yourself, comforting yourself, and smiling all day long.

It only takes one stupid hot guy to unravel all those feeble efforts of yours, reminding you how very *not* satisfied you are.

I'm lonely. I've been alone for years. I've dated a small number of guys in New York, but none of them worked out. One of them lived in a rat-infested apartment in Queens. One had a girlfriend in New Jersey he tried to hide from me. Another played video games all day and lived in his older brother's basement. Each one left me feeling lonelier than the last. My dating history is, needless to say, a trail of murky water.

Long after the sun's fallen, I knock on her door.

"Dessie!" she cries when she answers, the beads that hang at her closet tapping one another. "I found the *perfect* monologue for you!"

The night progresses into a back-and-forth trade of monologue practice and constructive criticism, in which Victoria offers me many queer looks and some politely-worded suggestions. If she has anything ugly to say about my acting ability, she is kind enough to spare me the words. Her roommate, a heavyset pale-as-death girl by the name of Leanne, sits on her bed in a nest of bed sheets and textbooks, typing away on her laptop and pretending we're not even there. We offer her the same courtesy.

When I excuse myself on account of having my morning movement class, Victoria smiles at me at the door and says, "You're going to be perfect for Mrs. Gibbs, which will complement my take on the role of Emily. You'll *totally* nail it. Can't wait!"

Back in my own room, my roommate Sam types at her desk on that ancient, last-decade laptop of hers. She's wearing the same thing she wore the day she arrived, which both unsettles me and breaks my heart. We exchange halfhearted hellos before I lock myself in the bathroom and enjoy the comfort of my own reflection.

I study my face intently, because whenever I blink, all I see is *his*.

DESSIE

I'm standing at the door to the rehearsal room gripping my obviously embellished résumé. Every line of the dramatic monologue I spent all Wednesday night and Thursday rehearsing repeats in my head over and over like gold fish swimming around the bowl, circles and circles and circles. I can hear the tapping of water as they make laps in my brain.

I'm oddly calm. I haven't seen Clayton at all since shift sign-up on Wednesday, which is strange, as I had gotten used to running into him daily.

It isn't fair. Every little thing I do now becomes all about Clayton. When I decide where to eat lunch, I consider whether or not he might be eating lunch at the same time and place, too. When I walk down the halls on the way to my Theatre classes, I wonder if I'll run into him around every corner, or if we'll bump into each other in the lobby, or out in the courtyard. It's crazy how far an obsession or innocent crush will take you, dictating your day, bullying your mind into submission so badly that even choosing which damn bathroom to use becomes a chore—because at any point in the day, I could run into him. Even on my way to the bathroom.

Yet I didn't, and haven't.

And likely won't.

I don't even notice the rehearsal room door open when the voice catches me mid-thought. "Desdemona Lebeau," it speaks softly, its source being a girl with electric blue hair and a nose ring, one of the director's assistants. "We're ready for you."

Inside, a table's been erected at the far end of the room, at which four visibly coldhearted individuals who have each had a worse day than the other sit patiently awaiting my audition. Not one of them smiles. The only one of the four I recognize is my acting professor, Nina Parisi, a needle-eyed, cold-faced *bone* of a woman whose caramel skin sags at the eyes as if she hasn't slept in sixty-six years.

"Hello," I say when I take my place before them. I don't know how close to stand, so I measure myself at roughly thirty feet away, which still feels too close. "I'm D-Desdemona Lebeau, and I'll be acting in a ... Sorry, no. I'm performing one verse of an original song called 'A Palace of Stone' ... as well as a dramedy—er, dramatic piece from D-D-Damien Rigby's *Quieter The Scream*."

Then, with all due emotion, I perform.

"How'd it go??" Victoria begs me the moment I'm out of the door.

I've returned to the lobby filled with the others who have either gone already or still anxiously wait, practicing their audition pieces to the walls or the stairs or each other. There's a peculiar comfort in watching them go at it while knowing that my own audition is over with and I'm no longer enduring the anxiety that is so visible on their faces and in their wringing hands.

"It went okay, I guess."

"Just okay?" She frowns on my behalf. "It's alright. Nerves get the best of us. Maybe spring auditions will be better for you."

I smile. "And yours?"

"Perfectly!"

Her face bursts with ecstasy. It's like she's been dying to express how perfectly her audition went for the past hour. And she does just that, detailing to me every little nuance she discovered, even in the tiny sixty second opportunity we're given in front of them.

"Oh, Des, you should come with us!" she exclaims suddenly. "We're all hitting up the Throng & Song after this."

I squint at her. "Whose thong?"

"*Throng*. Come with us! It's *the* Theatre hangout."

Considering it's Friday and, now that the audition is over with, I just have a weekend full of freedom ahead of me, I tag along with Victoria, Eric, and Chloe on a trip across campus, down a street, and into a piano bar slash diner called, as previously warned, the *Throng & Song*. The inside is shockingly crowded with college-aged kids, most of whom I'd assume are not old enough to drink. Baskets of fries and wings adorn every table and a thin veil of smoke hovers in the air.

We claim a table near a very small circular stage, upon which stands the most rundown upright piano I've ever seen, and a stool where a guitarist strums and sings unheard in the thick clamor of the room. Victoria is telling me something about her audition and I'm just smiling and nodding, unable to hear a word of it even sitting across the table from her. We haven't been in here for two minutes and I already feel drowsy from the noise and smoke.

A waitress comes by and asks each of us if we want something from the bar. To be heard, she leans in so close she could kiss each of us. Her words tickle my ear, and I wince and answer, "Vodka tonic, please."

I wouldn't have thought it possible, but as the day turns to night, the noise grows even louder. It is so deafening in here that I feel pressure against every wall of my skull, as if it's being invaded by an army of sound and every cell in my body works to defend my cranium castle, resisting the swarm. I clutch my head at one point, convinced that my brain is being rattled inside by the noise.

After three vodka tonics and a round (or was it two?) of tequila shots that the others *insisted* we do, the noise doesn't bother me at all.

"Oh my god, y'all," Victoria slurs, giggling as she leans into me. We've all traded positions over the past hour and now she's nearly sitting in my lap. "I'm gonna need another one of whatever the fuck that was. That shit was *goooooood*." Eric shouts the name across the table. "Huh?" Eric shouts it again. "What?"

The guitarist finishes his song, and the half of the bar who are actually paying attention applaud noisily, a chorus of hooting and whistling cutting through the room. "Thank you, thank you," the musician says with a wave of his hand. "I'm taking a ten, then I'll be back. Peace."

When the guitarist makes his leave, Victoria leans into me. "Confession: I want to have his babies."

I giggle, though I'm not sure if it's because of what she just said or because the room's spinning and that somehow tickles. "There's nothing sexier in this world than a singer," I blurt back into her ear.

"Oh! I want to hear your audition piece!"

I stare at her through foggy eyes. "You already did, silly! Thirteen times in a row, remember?"

"I mean your *song*, dummy!"

"Ooh, right, yeah." I laugh. Flecks of saliva dust the table in front of me and I slap a hand over my lips, inspiring Eric to laugh at me. "Shush! I haven't *drinked* anything since—Uh, haven't *drunk* anything—Uh, what's the word? Drank? Drink, drank, drunk?"

"You should drink more often," Victoria shouts into my ear. "You're so much more fun."

"Are you calling me boring?"

"No! You're just ... *less* boring when you're drunk!"

"You *are* calling me boring!"

"No!"

"You think I'm boring? Hey, Other Eric!" I shout, squinting across the table at him. "Am I boring? Hey, Chloe! Am I boring??"

They shout back answers I can't hear. I slap my hand on the table, causing the drinks to jump.

"Alright, then," I say, assuming their answers. "I'll prove to you how very *not* boring I am. I'll prove you all wrong right now."

I push myself up from the table and stumble to the stage. Victoria's laughter trails me along with a few words I obviously can't make out. When I'm on the stage, the pianist greets my eyes with worry. "No, no," I tell him with a dizzy wave of my hand. "Don't worry. I'm an actress. I have training in these sorts of things."

I have no idea what I mean by that, but I say it.

"Excuse me!" I call into the microphone, then give it five solid taps that cut through the cacophony of collegiate banter and screaming and laughter.

To my utter surprise, dozens of pairs of eyes turn to meet mine on the stage. I see every pair even through the haze of smoke and light. The noise cuts in half.

Holy hell, I actually *did* get their attention.

"My friends think I'm boring," I explain to the room, inspiring even more silence and attention from them. "And I'd love to prove my friends wrong. So while our sexy guitarist is taking ten, I'd like to sing you all a lovely little song."

Three guys cheer from the back of the room. Some girl shouts, "Let's hear it!" followed by a chorus of roars. My friends at the table near this tiny stage wear looks of astonishment, their eyes sparkling with pride and alcohol.

"It's a song I wrote about myself," I tell the room. "A song about how we close ourselves up. A song I hoped would inspire me to break free from my own ... from my own proverbial palace. A song ..."

Suddenly lost in the emotion of said song, I stop explaining and let the music speak for itself. Gripping the microphone, I bring my lips to its black, puffy head, then close my eyes.

And I sing.

The room, which was only a moment ago packed with the deafening noise of so many voices, is now filled with only one: mine. My voice reaches through the room. My eyes search, a strange desire to touch every person in this room gripping me by the throat.

Something magical happens. I feel something in me let go. I'm weightless as I sing to them. If I didn't have such a grip on the microphone, I just might float away. I let the words of "A Palace of Stone" stream out of me.

And then, somewhere between the second and third verse, I see him in the crowd.

Oh my god. He's been there the whole time, I realize.

Beautiful as ever, intense, and wearing a tight white shirt that makes that bad-boy tattoo up his neck pop ... Clayton sits on a barstool palming a beer bottle, and his eyes are alight with fierceness, with yearning, with something I cannot even name.

Or is it the alcohol that makes me see these lovely things? Is it the alcohol singing and not me?

Clayton doesn't seem to care, and his eyes do not avert in the least. *I have him in the palm of my hand.* He watches ... He watches and listens.

This would be the second time he's heard this song. This is the second time I've captivated him. What else could that expression of his mean?

I'm hypnotizing him.

Yes. Finally, the tables have turned. *I'm* the one he's obsessed with now, in this one moment, as long as I can make the song last. I am his siren, luring him with my music.

And then I hear the tinkling of piano notes. I turn to find that the pianist has joined in, following my lead with the melody I sing. The guitarist, who's back from his break, has been watching from the side of the stage, his eyes sparkling with wonder. He picks up his guitar and joins his friend, supporting me with their tunes, totally improvising as they go.

Maybe it's the music that inspires me, as a wicked, naughty little demon takes control of my body.

Plucking the microphone off the stand, I saunter down from the stage, still singing, and slowly cut my way through the crowd—to him. Every lyric I have is now given straight to Clayton.

It's a matter of half a verse before I'm standing right in front of him, singing my music.

His face stiffens.

Is that fear I just inspired in his dark, threatening eyes?

I sing my words to them, my fingers slowly, gently, lovingly, tenderly stroking the microphone up and down.

I'm an actress who shows no fear. With my free hand, I bring a finger to his neck, tracing where that dark ink comes up from the muscular, hidden unknown beneath his shirt. Firm and frozen, he coldly watches me. *The bravest in my whole biosphere.* I brace myself against his table, my hips grazing along his side as I sing up to his wary face.

Clayton's eyes narrow, as if I'm wounding him with my music. *Yes, let me wound you with it, so that you might feel an ounce of the agony I've felt all week ever since I first laid eyes on you.*

As the musicians bring me into the final verse, I pause and bring a hand to that beer in his hand. It slips from his grip easily and I bring it to my lips, my eyes locked on his. I take a swig of it, then set it back on the table. My eyes wrinkle slightly in response; I hadn't expected the beer to be so bitter. His eyes turn glassy and a hint of amusement twists his lips.

It's work to perch atop this throne ... Oh god. That smirk of his is so sexy, I could ditch the song and plunge into him right now. *This throne made of credit cards and silicone ...*

I'm standing so close to Clayton now, I feel heat coming off of him.

I've never felt so exposed, so free ... *Don't dare give your heart, or you'll fall right apart.*

I lick my lips as the guitarist strums and the pianist glides his long fingers. *Right here in my palace of stone ...*

He parts his lips, his face tightening, pained.

My lips kiss the tip of the microphone as I push the last lyrics out. *Yes, right here ... in my palace of stone.*

The music concludes in a contemplative, resolving chord.

Silence swallows the room.

Clayton's eyes.

Me and a heavy microphone in my hand, growing heavier and heavier by the second.

I'm met suddenly with the reality of what I just did. *In front of everyone.* The alcohol's no longer a mask. I just sang the most personal song I've ever written to a room full of strangers.

Clayton breathes.

I can't.

What did I just do?

Then there's a shout of joy from the back, startling me, and then the rest of the room erupts into applause and cheering. I think I'm imagining it for a second, stunned by the reaction. Are they mocking me, or did I really do a decent job?

When I look at Clayton again, I see a question in his eyes. Suddenly, nothing else matters. *I got his attention,* I tell myself. *He knows who I am. He's curious. I caught him.* And in the midst of all my doubt, I feel like I've won some game I didn't know I was playing. The game of cat and mouse. The crush game.

"And *that's* how you do it," I say to him, grinning.

He doesn't respond.

With a coy shrug, I waltz back to the stage, return the microphone to its stand, then give the room a little drunken curtsy before giggling and rushing back to my table, the room revived with the musician's music and loud, chaotic chatter.

"Oh my *god*," moans Victoria when I've returned to my seat. "What were you thinking??"

"You can say I was inspired." I giggle, eye-fucking Clayton through the smoke and banter. He looks so pissed off and sexy. "And now he knows who I am. Oh, how was the song?" I ask my friends.

"You were amazing, obviously," Victoria says.

"Thanks!" I laugh, but when I return my gaze to Clayton, he's abandoned his beer and is walking away.

The joy's lost in an instant. I bend to the side, curious, but only catch a glimpse of his backside as he pushes through the door, gone.

Wow. Did *I* do that to him?

"No, no," shouts Victoria through the noise, her face turning serious. "No, Dessie. You can't go after him. You shouldn't. He's bad news."

Why'd Clayton leave so suddenly? Did I make him uncomfortable? Well, he deserved it ... after all the turmoil he put *me* through by just existing.

"Dessie. Are you listening?"

I frown, annoyed. "Why does it matter?"

But then even Chloe chimes in. "Everyone wants a piece of the Watts boy. Girls go crazy for him."

"And guys," adds Eric with a sneer.

"Every new student that comes through here tries to hook up with that hot piece of ass," Chloe adds with a rueful shake of her head. "I've watched it since my own freshman year. It's tragic."

"Hell, even *I* couldn't help but stare at him when he was in my dramaturgy class," Victoria shouts over the table. "Listen, if it's a boy toy you want, I'll get you a list of ten eligible bachelors, my friend. Clayton is *not* one of them."

I lean forward, meeting her halfway over the table. "He's the one from the theater, *Vicki!*"

"Don't call me that! Wait, what??"

"The one who heard me! The one from the other day!" I shout back. "*He's* the one! That's the guy! Clayton!" I stare after the door, still wondering why he left so abruptly. I'm trying not to let it sour the moment we just shared. I feel like I did something wrong. "Now, he's heard my song," I add. "Twice."

"Oh, Des, no, no," retorts Victoria. "He didn't hear your song, sweetheart. Not one note."

I frown at her. "What the hell does *that* mean?"

"Honey, he's deaf."

CLAYTON

I am so fucked.

Six drinks and six blocks later, I still see her face burned into the backs of my eyelids. Or maybe it was the shitty stage lighting.

I barely survived the last time I let a girl get too close to me. I've been so good at keeping focus. I just brought my grades back up from last semester's poli-sci catastrophe. I can't let another actress destroy me again. Haven't I learned my damn lesson?

Things are looking up, too. I'm feeling weird shit I haven't felt in years—like *hope*. Everything I've worked so hard for since freshman year—while struggling to pay tuition out of my own pocket with the scrappy earnings from my three or four summer jobs—is about to pay off. After my experimental lighting design of Oliver's senior-directed black box show last year, Doctor Thwaite, the Director of the School of Theatre, is finally looking at me. I caught him giving me an approving nod when I passed by him on the first day back. His lips moved to form a hello with my name attached. *My name.* They're starting to see me.

That's why I can't let *her* fuck it all up. I know how I get, obsessing over a girl like her. My weakness. It's the same weakness I had even in the first half of my life when I could *hear* a girl say my name.

My opportunity to be the lighting designer for a main stage production is so close, I can taste it.

What I can also taste is her lips. As she sang, I was hypnotized by them as they moved, imagining what they'd taste like if I brought my mouth to them. Then she came down from the stage and got in my face. Just inches away, I could've fucking tasted her.

I had a similar reaction when I caught her singing to the empty seats of the auditorium the other day. When she caught me standing there, I loved how that made her freak out and bolt. I was so mesmerized by the sight of her, I didn't even pay attention to what she was saying to me. I spent that night pushing away thoughts of her long brown hair, her curvy body, her creamy skin ... and those huge, vibrant eyes ...

Fuck. And now she's gone and sang a song to me. It was excruciating, sitting there in the dense crowd of drunken losers while that girl poured sweet music from those lips of hers ... music I couldn't hear.

My phone vibrates. I glance down to find a text from my roommate.

BRANT

Got a girl over. Hot AF n kinda freaky.

Haven't sealed the deal yet. Need the place for 10 min :)

Every girl my puppy of a roommate meets is "hot as fuck". I swear, Brant could hump fire out of a fire hydrant, that horny dog. So much for going home.

I smirk and type a reply:

ME

U only need 10 minutes?

BRANT

Good point. Gimme 15

Moments later, I'm staring at the blank screen of my phone in the 24-hour diner near my apartment. The thought of Brant getting busy with some chick is amusing at first, but that amusement sours fast, and all I'm left with is a ringing in my ears that may or may not be entirely imaginary.

A ringing where that girl's song should be.

Soon, a curvy blonde waitress with big tits comes to my table—some new chick, not the usual one—and she lifts her flirty eyes. Her big lips move. I grip the menu and point. Appearing somewhat put-off by my brash demeanor, she cranes her neck to read, then jots down my order with a frown. Her lips move again. I pick up my phone, mash thumbs into it, then show her the screen:

Over easy. Coffee black plz.

Her eyes flash as she reads the message. She asks if I have laryngitis or something. I shake my head no. Then she pops the magic question. I nod patiently. The reaction is what it always is. Suddenly, I'm a ghost, and she wonders a few things out loud that she thinks I can't understand. I actually watch her lips form the words, "Shit. Okay. I can do this, I can do this, I can do this," before she steels herself and returns to the kitchen—as if she were on a bomb squad and my order needed decoding or some shit.

It's not just the deaf thing. Maybe it's the ink that crawls up my neck from a mass of swirls and thorns that starts at my right shoulder and spreads out like a black, deadly explosion. Maybe it's the fuck-you look I always seem to be giving. People think I'm dangerous. The less they have to deal with me, the better. I know if my roommates were here, the waitress would talk to me through them as if I was some strange entity from another planet they needed to order for. Hell, one time at an Italian place, I went through a whole damn meal without getting a single refill, check-up, or an offer for dessert. The waiter couldn't wait to slap a check on my table and get me the fuck out; that's how uncomfortable I make people.

Oh, and I fucking love dessert. Bastard.

My mind is a mess and the six drinks I downed at the *Throng & Song* are already gone, my buzz killed long ago. Even the eggs don't cheer me up. They're brought to the table by a different person, some server who meets my eyes worriedly as if I were a caged beast he was feeding. I'm guessing big-tits is over me. I cut into my eggs with a scowl and watch the yolk bleed across my plate.

There's something refreshingly different about that girl from the theater ... annoyingly different. It unsettles me. Everyone down here is the same. All the girls have fear in their eyes when they meet me.

She had something else. Curiosity? Confidence? It's like her eyes cut through all the bullshit and the smoke and the walls of cynicism I built up around myself. She *saw* me.

Or I'm just lying to myself all over again, just like I lied to myself with countless girls before.

It's exactly forty minutes later when I'm slipping my key into the door. The second the cold air of my apartment touches my skin, I feel relief, kicking the door shut behind me and dropping my bag onto the kitchen counter where last night's army of beer cans and pizza boxes still sit. The living room's unoccupied and Brant's door is shut, so I assume he sealed his lady-deal. With a huff at the abundant laziness of my two helpless roommates, I surrender to half an hour of housekeeping before I allow myself to chill.

Or maybe I just want to take my aggression out on these dishes and cups and cutlery. It infuriates me that I can't get that girl out of my mind, which shows in the way I scrub the glass in my hand. The water seeps into my sleeves the way *she* seeps into my every thought. Her singing captivated a room full of drunk morons. Who the hell manages to do that? I could physically *feel* the noise of the room die away when she took to that microphone. The frenzied hum of the place, a hum I could feel through every fingertip and follicle of hair on my body, it grew still, just so she could make her music.

That vacuum of sensation was fast replaced by a beauty I was all too eager to drink in with my eyes. I don't think I knew eyes were capable of drinking until that moment.

Thoughts of her bring me to the couch where I collapse and kick my sore feet up, my eyelids growing heavier by the second. I mash a throw pillow behind my head and let sleep have her way with me, assuming she wants me at all. I've had trouble sleeping lately. That same stupid nightmare keeps creeping into my dreams, the one where I wake up in a house filled with water. My bed's floating, my roommates are gone, and no one's there to help me. Since I've had the nightmare so many times, I always know none of the doors will open no matter how hard I push, and somehow, I can't smash the window. Because I already know I can't get free, I'm more terrified each time I have the nightmare. The room keeps filling up, and for a moment, I always think I see someone outside. I scream for them, begging for help, pounding my fist against the glass, and for once, it's the rest of the world who can't seem to hear a thing. No one comes to save my life.

I hate feeling helpless.

But that's not the dream that finds me on the couch tonight. Instead, it's *her* on that tiny stage all by herself, and the entire room at the *Throng* has emptied itself of all those others who don't matter. It's just her on the stage, and me in front of her.

And all that cold, silent space between us.

I study her. Like a zoomed-in camera, my eyes draw up the length of her smooth legs, over her supple hips, and arriving at her perky, perfect breasts.

My cock's so hard, a moan vibrates my chest.

My eyes arrive at her lips, and suddenly I'm at the edge of the stage looking up at her. The whole room feels ice cold against my skin. Her breath is the only warmth I know, and it touches me in little jagged spurts and I haven't even touched her yet. *She wants me so bad. She wants me to do things to her. "Clayton,"* I can imagine her saying.

Yes, I can imagine her voice. I think on what it might sound like. I feel it, smooth and seductive as her finger tracing my tattoos. Her pink lips dance, singing to me. What else can she do with them?

My cock is so hard. *"Clayton ..."* It pushes against the inside of my jeans. I want to pull it out while her breath keeps touching my face.

I want to look up into her eyes and bury my mouth in her breasts.

I want to know what she smells like so bad. I want to taste her. I want to tear off her clothes and watch her gasp with surprise as the beast within me is unleashed on her.

I reach down for my cock, ready to release him.

Then I feel the subtle shake of a door closing and remove my hand, the dream destroyed. *Fucking hell.* I catch my breath and lift my head, only to find Brant standing over the couch holding a six-pack with a smug grin of victory stretched across his face.

Brant is the tall, slender type with the messy brown hair and blue eyes that all the girls go ape shit for, and he knows it too. He works out a third as much as I do, yet keeps a body that's ripped and lean, no matter how much pizza he packs a day. I don't know how the fucker does it. Brant's come a long way since we were kids, that's for sure. We've been the best of buddies since the day we fought and made up over bloody noses in an elementary school playground.

He wiggles the six-pack and gives me a lift of his eyebrows, offering one. I type, then lift my phone with a scowl:

WTF with the dishes? Im not ur mom

Brant smirks, leans over the back of the couch and says it's all Dmitri's leftover mess from some friends he brought over last night. Then he adds something about how if I listened more carefully, I would've heard their ruckus and kicked them out.

I throw a punch into his arm for that remark, inspiring a laugh from him that I can almost hear with my mind. I've known Brant since long before I lost my hearing and we've cracked so many stupid jokes together that I know his laugh as intimately as my own. He's the only person in the world who can get away with giving me shit for being deaf. Maybe it's the only way we both can cope with it ... even if he's still shit at sign language and doesn't seem able to retain a damn thing beyond the signs for "fart", "poop", "penis", and "Cherry Coke".

Brant comes around the couch and plops down by my legs, nearly sitting on them, and asks me if I'm still planning on coming to his thing. *What I was planning to do was jerk off, you fucker.* Truth is, I'm not even sure that's what he asked; the sleepier I get, the harder it is to read lips. I have to think for a moment before realizing what he means: he's got a bowling tournament next Saturday that he's invited Dmitri and I to come watch. It's an unofficial sort of local thing with the prize being free drinks for a week, but it means a lot to Brant. Also, he happens to be some weird kind of bowling ball whisperer.

I nod at him, which seems to satisfy him more than the supposed lady-sex he just had. I didn't see her leave, but I know he never lets a girl stay over, so either her stealth level is top notch or he made her climb out of the window.

The six-pack appears once again and he rips one off, tossing it into my lap. With a snapping of its lid, I take a long, deep swallow. The cold beer runs down my throat and fills me with a comfort I've so craved. My eyes glaze over as Brant throws an arm over the back of the couch and flips on the TV.

I read the captions for two minutes before growing bored.

It doesn't matter what's on TV. Between the cold, wet can in my fist and the colors flashing over my face from the screen, I let the alcohol numb my incessant, invasive thoughts of that girl I shouldn't be craving ... a girl I can't let stay over, a girl I'm letting climb out the window of my mind ...

A girl still waiting for me on that stage with her jagged breaths ...

A girl who finds me on this couch when my eyes finally close, her soft fingers dancing across my skin and sending currents of pleasure up my arms. A girl whose touch makes me so hard, my cock aches as it tents uncomfortably in my jeans. A girl whose pink, pouty lips hover tauntingly over my face, ready to make a slobbering, paralyzed idiot out of me.

A girl who is carefully, patiently taking me apart ... one agonizing piece at a time.

DESSIE

I can't contain my excitement, not even in acting class. My stomach's doing cartwheels in the grass and my lips keep twisting into a smile that hasn't gone away all weekend.

I don't care if he's deaf. He didn't hear my song? No big deal. He *felt* it. I could see it in his eyes, which burned black with hunger, with need, with *danger* ...

I don't care about my friends' warnings, either. Everyone has a *story* attached to them. Living in the limelight of my parents, I'm used to doubting every piece of gossip or hearsay that drifts past my ears and eyes. I've seen my mother blasted on enough slanted, click-bait articles to know not to trust rumors.

My phone buzzes. I glance down at a text.

NOT-VICKI

OMG Des, the cast list is up.

I gawp, pulled out of my thoughts of Clayton. *Already?* It's only been two days. Who the hell casts a whole season of shows in two days?

ME

I didn't expect it so fast.

NOT-VICKI

Yep. Im stuck in costume history tho :(

ME

I'm in acting. Meet up afterwards?

NOT-VICKI

YES and then lets get some lunch to celebrate !!!

I stow away my phone, worried that my acting professor Nina has caught me when I realize the room's gone silent, but instead it's just one of my classmates performing, being all dramatic and taking long, annoying pauses between his lines.

My mind drifts back to thoughts of Clayton, and the rest of the class period is forgotten.

I leave the black box eagerly. The world brushes past my face as I reach the cast list hanging off the rehearsal room door. A flock of eager students push one another out of the way to read its contents, much in the same way dogs fight over a bone. There is a moan of disappointment to my left. There is a cheer of victory to my right. There is silent pondering everywhere else.

And then there's me. Two heads in front of me move apart, and through the sea of whispers and groans and hair, I finally see the names. I rub my eyes and stare, reading the name at the top a dozen times. I don't believe what I'm reading.

"Congrats," murmurs Eric, who I didn't notice at my side.

I shake my head. "But I didn't think—"

"You obviously earned it," he says, offering me a smile. "And hey, look. I'll be playing the town drunk, Simon! But we don't have any scenes together ..."

"That's great," I tell him distractedly, still reading and rereading my name on that list.

"You know what the secret to acting drunk is? It's to try *not* acting drunk." Eric laughs hollowly. "I'll see you later, D-lady."

I still can't believe it. It has to be a mistake, right? "Bye," I say belatedly, then realize that Eric's already gone.

And it's not only that I was cast; it's the *role* I was cast in. I shake my head, unable to comprehend it. Maybe this is an error, surely. Maybe there's another Desdemona Lebeau in the Theatre department.

To make matters worse, not twenty seconds after Eric's ghostly departure, Victoria replaces him at my side. "Oh my god, oh my god, oh my god," she sings excitedly, her eyes eagerly scanning the cast list.

I get the pleasure of having a front row seat to observe my friend's face as it slowly, gently collapses in disappointment.

"Wow," she mutters after some time, the pain evident on her face. Then, she squints, something occurring to her. "Lebeau ..." she reads.

Oh, fuck.

She turns to me, a look in her eye. "Lebeau?" She's piecing it together. "Any relation to—?"

"No," I blurt a little too quickly. *Of course she'd know my family; she knows everything.* "There's lots of Lebeaus in New York. Like, tons."

"Hmm." Though the dubious glint remains in her eye, she gives a shrug and says, "Congrats, Dessie. Honestly, I didn't know you were going for the role of Emily." She tries her best to sound composed. "Of course, you totally fit the role. I mean, you're pretty and all."

Now I can't tell if she's sincerely complimenting me or just being a bitch. "Thanks," I say anyway.

"I gotta get to class," she blurts, although I know her next class isn't for another two hours. "I'll see you back at the dorms later." Then with a tiny smile that looks like a grimace, she's off.

So much for our lunch plans. I'm about to shout after her, explaining that I wasn't even going for the part, that I didn't indicate "Emily" as a preference on my audition form, but saying that would probably just make things worse, admitting I got a part I didn't even want. The part *she* wanted. The lead role.

The ... lead role.

Suddenly, that fact hits me as if it weren't already made plain. *The lead role.* Oh my god. I just got the lead in the first main stage production of the year. That's how good they thought I was. *This has to be an error,* my mind keeps telling me, but a sudden whirlwind of confidence seems to take over instead. Maybe I'm still riding the high from my show on that tiny circular stage last Friday night.

Quite suddenly, whatever wrinkle of guilt I was feeling is long gone.

"I got the part!" I say elatedly into the phone when I'm by myself in the corner of the lobby, just outside the auditorium doors.

"Of course you did, doll," sings my mother's fluid voice. I hear wine glasses and silverware tinkling in the background, wherever she is. "Now, it's important that you put in an actor's worth of work. No, I'll take another chardonnay. Please, with some brie."

I smile as I stare out the tall glass windows of the lobby, letting my mom talk to whoever else it is who's got her attention. I'm watching some sweaty guys throwing a Frisbee back and forth in the courtyard outside, too happy with the news to be bothered by my mom's distracted attention to it.

As a side thought, I genuinely wonder if Cece would be happy for me and have some nice words. She's not used to *me* having any sort of success. Maybe I should call her up, too.

"An actor's worth of work?" I prompt her when it sounds like she's free. "What do you mean?"

"Oh, you know, doll. Listen to your director. Make interesting choices. Don't upstage. Excuse me, this is *not* the chardonnay I drank earlier. Where's the good stuff, sweet thing? Get Geoffrey, he knows what I like. And don't forget the brie."

"Thanks, Mom."

"Brie, yes. *Brie*. This'll be good for you, doll," she says, returning to me. "You really need to find that special voice in you. Put in the work and you'll get as much as you give. Call me after your first rehearsal."

Silence greets my ear when she hangs up abruptly. I see a flash of my mom's headshot on the screen before my phone goes dark.

I feel so damn invincible suddenly. I could take on a hundred auditions, even with my tiny little nothing embellished piece of crap résumé. I'd brave any tiny circular stage at any random piano bar and sing my heart out. I can do anything.

And then I see Clayton's face in that piano bar. I recall how I made him *squirm* on that barstool—and then how he left so abruptly after I made my move.

A heaviness settles right on top of all of my joy. He couldn't hear my singing. Maybe he didn't know what I was doing. Maybe he thought I was mocking him. Maybe he hates attention. Who the hell knows what he was thinking after my little performance?

I want to make things right. Excitement invades me again. An inspiration, if you will. My heart grows lighter just thinking about it.

I can make this right.

Driven by my idea, I rush to the computer lab at the library just down the road from the School of Art. It's pretty crowded for a Monday, but I manage to find an unoccupied computer right in the middle of the madness. Typing quickly, I log in and run a little search in the browser. I study the pictures that come up, curious. With a click, a video fills the screen. I move my hands, carefully trying to imitate what I'm seeing. There's a few students nearby whose attention I've caught, but I pay them no mind, the performer in me ignoring the unintended audience.

The smile returns to my face. Today is just the best day ever.

The sun beams on me as I cross the campus later, heading for the University Center for a bit of lunch. Since Victoria forgot about our plans, I opt to eat by myself. I'm far too happy to feel bad. It's not my fault I got cast and she didn't. If I could give my part to Victoria, I totally would, but what would *I* have, then? The whole point of attending this university is to get a normal college experience and hone my craft. I'm sure Victoria will understand; she just needs time. Hell, maybe in a few days' time, she'll even help me with my lines. Victoria's a good, kindhearted person.

After I pay for my turkey sub sandwich, which comes with a bag of baked potato chips and a soda I didn't want but accept anyway, I search for an empty table. Noon is just the *worst* time to eat; this place is so packed, I can't even hear my own thoughts.

When I come around the corner, I spot a booth with a familiar face. Sam, my roommate, is eating all by herself. Or, rather, she's not eating at all. She's seated there with a textbook spread out in front of her, looking bored as ever. Those ugly thick-rimmed black glasses swallowing half her forehead, she looks up, her beady black eyes finding mine. Her lips stretch into a long line, which I think is her trademarked version of a smile.

I plop down across from her. "Hey there, Sam!"

"Hi." Her eyes drop down to my sandwich.

It doesn't go unnoticed. "What're you studying?" I ask, opening the crinkly wrapping to my turkey sub.

"Theory."

Since my sub's cut in two pieces, I lift the first half to my mouth and take a bite. "It's so freaking busy in here," I whine through a full mouth. "And so loud!"

"Yeah." She swallows, staring at my hands.

"Have you eaten already?" I ask her.

"Yeah. I had ... breakfast."

I don't know how, but I suddenly suspect that my roommate skips meals and saves every penny she's got. Maybe her parents' weekly-ormonthly allowance is regrettably meager at best. Maybe she *didn't* eat.

"Y'know, I'm not gonna be able to finish all this," I confess. "Want the other half of my sub?"

"Oh." Sam shifts in her seat. "No, it's ... it's okay. I'm not that hungry."

"Well, guess that second half's gonna go to waste."

She stares at it dubiously. I nudge the remaining half of the sub I was totally planning on eating toward her. After a moment of hesitation, she picks it up and takes a bite. From the way she eats, it's clear how very hungry she was indeed.

Not to say the sight of her scarfing down the sub is the prettiest thing I've ever seen. I suffer staring at a speck of mayonnaise on her chin for a solid five minutes before she wipes it and licks it off her finger.

Just before I put the last bite past my lips, I see Clayton through the mess of people in the cafeteria.

Fuck. *He's here.*

I never see him anywhere on campus except for the theater.

My insides seize up. The last delicious bite of my lunch is left on the table, forgotten. My eyes zero in and the only thing that exists in the world is his muscular frame as it slowly strolls by in the distance. Just at the sight of him, my legs squeeze together.

I can't explain that last reaction.

"What's wrong?" asks Sam flatly.

"I'll be right back."

I ditch the booth and cut through the masses, my feet flying as if there were no floor beneath them.

I maneuver around all the annoying tables that stand in between Clayton and I. My feet nearly catch the strap of some guy's backpack that rests by his feet. My elbow knocks into some girl who shouts a protest at my back that I don't hear.

I find Clayton standing near the double glass doors at the entrance to the cafeteria, the sunlight cutting through and painting his face in shades of white and yellow, making his dark demeanor glow like some beautiful, otherworldly being. He stares down at his phone, his biceps bulging from holding the screen to his face. The plain black shirt he wears hugs every contour of his body, tapering down to meet his sexy jeans, which are torn at the knees.

He is sex in the shape of a man. *God ...*

He looks up, and when his eyes meet mine, there is electricity there. *Kill me now.* His face changes, and his heavy-lidded, dark stare penetrates me. All that bright confidence I had a moment ago is sucked into my throat, rendering me unable to breathe. *He's so sexy.* He's got that distinct, bad-boy handsomeness, his cheeks dusted with a five o'clock shadow and his eyes catching the light from outside, making them appear like two shimmering chips of glass.

My heart hammers against my chest.

It's performance time.

I lift my hand up and wave, offering a smile.

After a moment of staring, he returns a tiny nod.

You're doing good, I coach myself. *He acknowledged you. Keep going!* With a jolt of excitement coursing through me, I bring a fist to my chest, then slowly rub it in a circle—*Sorry.*

He doesn't respond to that, his eyes glued to my face as if he didn't just see what I tried to sign to him.

Just keep going, Dessie. I bring a flat hand to my chest—*My.* I take two fingers from one hand and tap the two fingers of my other—*Name.* Then, I carefully form what I hope to be the correct letters with my right hand—*D, E, S, S, I, E.* When I've finished, I clasp my hands together, proud of myself, and smile again.

His face hardens. His lips purse, causing his sexy cheeks to suck in as he considers me. *Oh, crap.* Did I do it all wrong? Did I just call him an asshole, or insult his mother, or accidentally tell him I'm a purple frog? Maybe I should have gotten a second opinion before practicing sign language for the first time—*that I learned from a Google search*—on Clayton.

Then, without relaxing any of that hard attitude on his face, he nods again, then redirects his attention to his phone, where he seems to be typing for a short moment. He shows me the screen:

I' m Clayton

I breathe a sigh of relief. "I know," I say out loud, then find myself struck with the horror of the fact that I don't know any more signs. I looked up how to say some other things, but they've gone completely out of my head.

Crap. I'm out of conversation.

It doesn't seem to matter. Clayton, his jaw flexed, gives me another tight nod and a short, halfhearted wave before he turns and departs the building. The glass doors close behind him.

I stare after him, my pulse throbbing in my ears.

Then, all the fear and doubt is replaced yet again with unapologetic glee. I just conversed with Clayton. Wow. I just conversed with Clayton *using my hands.*

There's a few other ways I'd like to communicate with Clayton using my hands.

Feeling twenty times lighter than I did before, I return to my booth and pop the last bite of sub into my mouth, a giggle wiggling its way up and down my whole body. I can't believe what I just did. I can't believe that actually just happened.

"Is he a friend?"

I look up at Sam, who has yet another speck of mayonnaise on her face, right by her lips. I don't care. It's even adorable, suddenly.

"You could say that," I answer with a dumb grin.

"Is he deaf?"

"Yep."

I open the bag of chips I didn't even want. I pop one into my mouth, then scoot the bag across the table to my roommate, who doesn't even have to be asked, helping herself to one.

"He looks like someone I knew in high school," she says. "He could be part of a heavy metal band."

"A sexy drummer," I say, dreaming on. First thing I'll do when I get back to my dorm is research every sign I possibly can. "Guitarist," I go on, wondering how to sign the phrase: *I want you to push me into the wall and stick your cock inside me.* "Sexy, sexy guitarist."

"Him being a drummer would make sense," Sam reasons. "Vibrations and everything ..."

"Vibrations," I agree, dreaming about what sort of *vibrations* I want to feel between my legs tonight, if I can get some time alone. I think about what signs I'd need to learn to tell him: *Bend me over the table and pound me until I forget my own name.*

Imaginary signs and hand-shapes keep spinning around my mind as I share the rest of the potato chips with my roommate, lost in dreams of *him* ... and what other kind of magic I can do with my hands.

CLAYTON

What the fuck was that?

I can barely concentrate even when I'm backstage sorting stage weights and fucking two-by-fours, as if I've suddenly doubled as the set crew, too. Dick was so damn efficient with his lighting crew this morning that there's barely anything left to do tonight or tomorrow, which leaves my body in a perpetual state of busywork and my mind trapped on that girl.

Dessie.

Not a name I've heard before.

I'm so distracted by her that I let a stage weight go too early and the heavy fucker drops on my foot like a brick. After a shriek of pain, I kick the damn thing fruitlessly and study my foot, thankful I wore some sturdy boots today. When I take a glance at the others who are messing with the counterweight system, I realize I might've shouted louder than I intended to. I give them an annoyed nod, then continue about my work, determined to keep my toes unbroken.

That Dessie girl signed to me. Great. Fucking great. It's obvious she either never used sign language before or just learned those few signs for my benefit. I don't know which feels worse. I hate the attention that signing in public gives me. The only person I sign with is my other roommate Dmitri, who met me in an astronomy class last year when he noticed that I had an interpreter present. He's got a deaf sister, so he was already fluent. Fuck, he's even more fluent than I am.

But that girl signed me her name. She obviously gave enough of a shit about me to introduce herself. I feel that horrible flutter in my chest. The girl I've been obsessing about ... *she fucking signed to me.*

It makes me insane. Who the hell is she? Why did she appear out of nowhere this semester and fly right into my line of sight and pull me off my tracks?

I'm doing so well. Things are so fucking perfect.

I know the cost of my obsessions. I know what happened last year. I know how girls can ruin me.

I can't do this again.

But I want to so fucking badly.

Someone comes up to my side and I watch his lips ask me if I'm okay. It's some freshman I don't know. I just ignore him, minding my duty in organizing these stupid set pieces and flats that were left for me, and I find myself thinking about signs and hands and that girl's sexy fingers.

She had sexy, sexy fingers.

Just that small moment at the University Center with her, it revived feelings I'd long left buried since my freshman year, which was a total nightmare. I hated interpreters back then, and maybe I still do. For some reason, I wanted to prove to myself—and maybe to everyone else—that I could do this all on my own. I wasn't any different than my hearing classmates, and I wanted to prove it. Some leftover high school arrogance had me caught in its know-it-all web.

Defiantly, I downloaded a voice-to-text app on my laptop that I used in all my classes to convert each professor's speech into words on my screen before my eager eyes. Trouble is, the stupid thing would constantly miss key phrases, misinterpret words, or just plain fuck up. It was like living in an autocorrect nightmare. Still, I was so stubborn and determined that I sat in the front row of every class and *stared* at my professor's lips, determined to read them like a hawk.

But, unbeknownst to most, lip reading is, in fact, a very flimsy and inaccurate means of communication.

After too long a time, I finally surrendered to the University's interpreting services and got myself some school-appointed nerd named Joe, who occasionally sent a girl named Amber in his place, and either of them would interpret the lessons to me each class. I got to know their hands so intimately, they became my own. They seemed used to people who were born deaf, so I had to slow them the fuck down until they got used to a speed I was comfortable with.

As for the attention, I'd just deal with it. Soon, I stopped noticing the people in class staring.

So when this girl Dessie shows up out of nowhere, sings some song at me, grips my heart right out of my chest and then brings it back to me during lunch with a cute expression on her face and her fingers making clumsy words before my eyes, what the fuck am I supposed to do? My heart turned into a racing drum that shook my ribcage apart.

I want to tell her to stay the fuck away from me. I want to tell her that I'm bad news for her. I want to warn her the way a good friend should ...

And I want to pin her to a wall and fuck her until she can't walk.

A shadow drops over me, pulling me out of my thoughts. Standing to my side is the towering shape of Doctor Marvin Thwaite, the Director of the School of Theatre. He's a staggeringly tall, round man whose steps I normally feel coming as he shakes the stage with each one. He has no hair, save a ring of grey that runs from one ear around the back to the other. His nose is a needle of flesh and his lips are pencil-thin.

He says he'd like to talk in his office, if I can pull myself away from what I'm doing. At least, I hope that's what he said. I look over at Dick who stands with the others near the lip of the stage and, having heard Doc's request, Dick lazily waves at me. I nod at Doctor Thwaite, then follow him out of the theater.

His office is as warm as an oven, its windows facing the sun all day long. Despite the AC running at full blast, it never seems to bother him. He takes a seat at his desk and motions to a chair where I sit. Doc faces me, then asks if I'll need an interpreter or if I can understand him without one.

I give a patient shake of my head, then type into my phone and show him the screen:

If you speak slowly, I' m good.

Doc smiles and nods amiably.

I know what this meeting is about and can hardly contain myself. *He's going to offer me to do the lighting design for the main stage show.* That has to be it. Maybe the lighting designer has some conflict of interest or discovered a scheduling issue and isn't available. *It's your time of reckoning, Clayton.* My stomach turns into steel and I find my hands attached to the armrests with anticipation.

His lips start to move.

I watch with every fiber of my being as my mind converts each lip movement into words. "*...invaluable to our program...*" He rubs his nose. "*...and respect for your hard work and dedication...*" He swallows between sentences, licking his long, thin lips. "*...for someone with your capability...*" His teeth are so white, they blind me with every consonant. What's his point? Get to the point. I'm so impatient, I could break the armrests off this chair. "*...lighting designer...*"

I nod and mumble my consent. It's the closest I've ever come to using my voice in front of any of the faculty. Yes, yes, yes. I'll do it. The hint of a smile finds my face as I continue to watch his mouth move.

"...from New York City, and I want him to..."

My brow furrows. Something isn't clicking. I find myself falling behind whatever it is he's saying. Doctor Thwaite seems to notice, because he stops and asks if I'm following. I shake my head no, frustrated with the sudden break in communication.

Wait a minute. Did he just say something about a lighting designer from New York City?

He types at his computer for a second, then twists the monitor around. I'm shown the headshot of some handsome, dimpled, thirty-something douchebag. His name's Kellen Michael Wright. Professional Lighting Designer from New York City.

Never heard of the fucker.

I glue my eyes to Doc's lips as he goes on. *"...can bring the School of Theatre some good publicity..."* My heart sinks. *"...as you know the department better than most, and can show him everything..."* Blood pumps into my ears, into my cheeks, into my every fingertip. *"...and make his transition here as comfortable as possible."*

As comfortable as possible. His transition here.

I've gathered everything he needs to say to me. I'm sure my face is a reflection of the turmoil inside. Not that Doctor Thwaite will care to acknowledge it, as he is known to avoid confrontations and pretend like nothing's ever wrong. I swallow that thick pill he just popped into my mouth with an astute nod.

When he gives me the final smile, I dismiss myself. I'm sure I left imprints of my thumbs in the armrests of his lovely office chair.

Back at the auditorium, I ignore the inquiring stares from the others and return to my work, my face burning with anger. Sometimes, being deaf has its perks, like having an excuse to ignore the world when I want to shut everyone out and fume all on my own. If anyone tries to enter a conversation with me, I'm sure they won't leave it with their head still attached.

No, he didn't want me to do the lighting design for *Our Town*. No, I'm not some special flower. No, my hard work hasn't finally been recognized. Instead, Doctor Thwaite's flying in some big shot from New York City to design the show for us, and he wants *me* to show this guy the ropes.

Me, of all people. What the fuck is Doc thinking?

I'm overlooked enough as it is. Now, as if to push salt into my gaping wounds, I'll get to experience the joy of watching someone else—who isn't even a part of this damn school—do the work that *I* should be doing. I had so many ideas for *Our Town*, too. I've read the play ten times. I had a vision for the funeral scene, for the different homes, for the church ...

Fuck. And there isn't a single other person in the whole department whose sole interest is in designing lights, and Doc knows that. That's *my* dream.

When I get home an hour later, the door slams so hard behind me that I feel the floor shake. I ignore the mess in the kitchen and shove through the door into my bedroom, ignoring the squinty glances from Brant and Dmitri on the couch, who seem lost in the middle of playing some first-person shooter game I don't recognize.

Dropping my bag under the windowsill, I fall back on my bed and shut my eyes. The AC turns on a moment later. I can feel the pull of air as it tickles my skin. Something about that sensation centers me, and I find myself looking up at the bare ceiling as my mind wanders somewhere else entirely.

Dessie. I wonder what her story is. She shows up out of nowhere this year. She's also from New York City, if what I caught from a buddy in the lighting crew is correct. Does *she* know the douchebag who's coming to steal my glory? No one knows anything about her, yet she's on everyone's radar. And now she's been cast as the lead in the first play of the semester.

And she learned a sign or two and told me her name with her sexy hands. *Dessie* ...

I feel a thrumming on my bed and twist around to find Dmitri standing there. With a squint of his eye he signs to me: *What's up? You okay?*

I shrug and lazily lift my hands: *Shitty day.*

He sits on the edge of the bed, which makes it impossible to see him, so I sit up and turn around. He signs to me: *We're going out for a bite. Want to come with?*

I shake my head: *Not in the mood.*

Dmitri smirks: *What's going on? Is it a girl?*

In an instant, I realize I don't want to talk about the haughty dipshit lighting designer from New York. Dessie ... That's someone I'd much rather spend time and effort in moving my hands to discuss.

I shrug, playing up my nonchalance: *Someone new at the theater*, I sign. *Yes.*

Dmitri laughs, then signs back: *A girl wants your nuts?* Instead of the actual sign for nuts, he just grabs his junk and smirks leeringly at me.

I shake my head and snort too hard, the vibration going up my skull, then say: *Verdict's still out on that.*

His hands are oddly long, which makes him extra expressive when he signs. It's almost the equivalent of shouting in sign language. But that's the only thing about him that's long. Dmitri is otherwise a short guy, barely five-three, with a boyish face, rosy cheeks, and jet black hair. He has a red and blue tribal tattoo running down his forearm, a sunburst tattooed to the back of his neck, and a diamond stud in either ear. He's bisexual, but he doesn't ever bring anyone home and, more or less, seems completely uninterested in sex, despite chiming in whenever Brant and I check out girls. It's really nice having someone around who I can easily communicate with, even if I refuse to sign much at all in public; I hate the attention.

He signs to me: *Don't let a girl ruin your day. She isn't worth it, no matter how pretty.*

It's so much more than how pretty she is. Fuck, I wish I could've heard her music. I sign: *She's a singer and actress from New York City. And she signed to me.*

Dmitri's eyes go wide. *Oh*, he signs. *You're fucked.*

Fucked, I agree.

He slaps my shoulder, then moves his hands: *Come out with us. We're getting tacos. It's Brant's treat.*

I smirk knowingly: *Does* he *know he's treating us?*

Dmitri grins: *He will when he gets the check.*

I think the company of my buddies is just what I needed. The whole way there, I sign to Dmitri, telling him about Dessie, how she sang to me, how she ran into me at the food court and fucking signed to me. Dmitri relays a lot of it to Brant, then keeps signing: *You're fucked.* Brant agrees by mimicking his signs, except it keeps looking like the signs for: *You fell.*

When the three of us arrive at the diner, we take our usual booth in the back. Brant tells us about this new girl he met in the psychology building and how he's got this fantasy about her hypnotizing him to do things. When he makes a face to imitate how she'll look when he's diving between her legs, I laugh so hard that I spill my sweet tea across the table, soaking Dmitri's pants and causing him to curse loudly, drawing the attention of nearby tables. In the midst of his tantrum, I sign to him: *Would you mind signing all that? I can't quite make out what curse words you're shouting.* That makes Dmitri mouth the very distinct words of *"Fuck you"* before he laughs and throws a tea-soaked wad of napkins at Brant.

When Dmitri excuses himself to the bathroom to dry up, Brant leans over the table and asks me about the girl. I shrug, mumbling and looking away. He taps my hand to draw my attention back to him, then asks what I'm going to do about it.

I frown. What the hell does he expect me to do?

His eyes turn serious—something I don't see in Brant very often. His lips move slowly: *"I don't want you to be alone forever. I care about you. You have to do something about this girl."*

I shake my head, dismissing him again. There's no use pursuing her, no matter the signs she learns. She won't be able to handle me. They all run away.

He smacks me over the head. I catch his hand, threatening to crush it if he does that again, but he only responds with a superior smirk, leaning across the table. He reminds me that she signed to me, then mimics her by making dumb motions with his hand, ending randomly with his favorite sign: *fart.*

I snort and shake my head, the humor not hitting me. The more I think about her, the more frustrated I get. I punch my thumbs into the phone, then show it:

What' s ur point??? I' m too much work. I' m fucked up. She' s beautiful. she' ll run off the second she gets close

Brant nods. *"Yeah,"* he says slowly, *"she* will *run off because you gave up."*

I glare at him. I start typing again, but Brant's hand covers mine. He says something else.

Then, I get so fed up that I do something I almost never do: "It won't work out," I tell him.

The sound of my voice takes him aback.

My face flushes, angry. I can't stand talking. I can't stand not knowing what I sound like. I feel so fucking insecure about it. I remember hearing and making fun of the slurred S's and the weird vowel sounds that other deaf people made when I was a kid, and here I am, having become the butt of my own childhood jokes. I was such a little shit when I was a kid ... when I could hear ...

Sometimes, I wonder if this is my punishment.

Brant flicks me in the chin, nabbing my attention. He tells me: *"You'll never know unless you ..."*

He thinks for a moment, brow wrinkled. Then, he creates fists with the thumbs poking out between his fingers and twists them in the air.

It's the sign for "try".

DESSIE

"I want you to fuck me. Fuck the doubt out of me. Fuck the ex-boyfriend out of my head. Fuck me until there's nothing in my mouth but your name, over and over again, in screams."

Her name is Ariel. Yes, like the stupid mermaid. And she's beautiful. And all the guys stare at her and she bats her stupid eyelashes and she's the perfect actress. And even when she says a word like "fuck", she makes it sound like poetry. Her hair is a golden, wavy waterfall of wonder and her face is oh-so angelic.

And apparently she and Clayton had a thing a year ago or so. Yeah. That *mermaid* up there is his type, and that's a type I will never be.

"Great," says Nina, the acting professor who never calls anything great or good or lovely, ever. She sits in the audience seats among us, observing Ariel who stands proudly in the acting area awaiting critique. Miss Nina Parisi adds, "You gave just the right amount of care, and just the right amount of nothing to each 'fuck'. Great."

If there's one thing I don't regret about college acting compared to high school, it's the sudden permission to read and act from scripts that have an overabundance of the word "fuck" in them. Hell, it's encouraged. Fuck this. Fuck that. Fuck me and you.

And Fuck Ariel. I'll never look like that. She has the same pretentious glassy-eyed face as my sister Cece, the one that never seems to change when she steps off the stage. Whether standing before an audience or all by herself, the actress acts, the face lights up, and every word that vomits out of those lips is seasoned with pretense and packaged with the pristine care of three weeks' meticulous rehearsal.

And Clayton wants *that?* I roll my eyes and chew grindingly on my thoughts—which may or may not be my teeth—embarrassed that I ever gave that man the time of day. That beautiful, striking, incredible man. That heart-stopping, slab-of-beef, gorgeous-eyed solid *demigod* of a man.

That beautiful man I signed my name to.

I'm fooling myself, aren't I?

Nina rises from the seats and crosses half the length of the black box theater we have our acting class in, the heels she wears stabbing the stage floor and echoing off the rafters and the four plain walls. Quietly, she says, "I want you to do that piece again. Bravo." She faces us, her eyes alight. "Pay attention to the little things she does in this monologue. What she does with her hands. Her eyes, just the story in her eyes alone. The focus she gives to an acting partner who doesn't even exist. Take notes, people."

Ariel lifts her tiny chin, stares up at an imaginary beam of heaven-light, then recites her line: "I want you to fuck me."

Go fuck yourself, Ariel.

When class is dismissed, I gather up my bag as fast as I can and hurry across the black box, only to find Ariel's tiny figure stopping me at the exit doors. "Desdemona, right?"

My heart races. I blink. *What does this bitch want?* "Yes, that's me."

"Oh, awesome." Her eyes sparkle. She extends a tiny hand. "Ariel Robbins. I'm the T.A., as you know, and I just wanted to say that I am really enjoying your work in this class. You're going to blossom with your role in *Our Town* when rehearsals start next week. You give such remarkable attention to nuance!"

Oh, this is just lovely. The bitch turns out to be all nice and crap after I spent the class despising her. "Thanks."

"No, really. I don't say this about many freshmen," she insists, batting her eyelashes, "but you've got a special something, Desdemona. I know real talent when I see it."

"It's Dessie, and I'm not a freshman," I murmur quietly, unable to process her annoying compliments. Really, it's Chloe's fault I feel like this; she's the one who spilled all about the *mermaid* here. It was Chloe and I in the lobby surrounded by cafeteria snacks and scripts while discussing Clayton's supposedly long history of girlfriends and flings. I believed about ten percent of what she said, tossing the rest into the rumors-and-embellishment bin.

"Oh! Yes, of course," says Ariel with a feathery chuckle. "I was told that. I'm so silly. Transfer, yes?"

"Right."

She smiles warmly. That smile lasts for about four seconds before it turns to ice. "So I heard about the song, Dessie. At the piano bar."

I swallow, steeling myself for whatever it is she wants to say. "Song?" I prompt her innocently, but knowing exactly what she's talking about.

"You sang a song to Clayton. Clayton Watts," she clarifies, tilting her head so all that angelic, blonde hair drifts to the side like a curtain of snow. "I don't mean to step on any toes, or to come off any certain way, but ... just friend to friend, woman to woman ... you need to be warned," she tells me, her eyes soft and glassy. "I don't know what you've heard, but—"

"I'm usually of the mindset that it doesn't matter what I hear," I retort as politely as I can, despite the sharp edge to each of my words. "I judge a person based on how *I* think of them, not others."

Ariel's sweet smile hasn't left her face, though it tightens considerably at my words. I'm not fooled. Of course the ex would want to scare everyone else away from Clayton; this bitch just doesn't want to picture his sexy lips anywhere near mine. Possessive, much?

"You are a very sweet person," she tells me, and despite how I'm feeling, I can't tell whether she means it or is just being snarky. "I wish everyone had as open and caring a mind as you. Well." She tightens her smile yet some more. "It was certainly a pleasure. I have to be off now to help grade Phonetics papers for the voice prof. Have a nice day, Dessie! And ... *do* take care," she adds. "A rose always looks lovely from a distance, but their thorns will *prick* you just the same. It's in their nature."

With that, she dives back into her little river, her legs turning into half a fish, then flitters away.

I spend the afternoon alone, bitterly eating Ariel's words and spitting them out of my mind. She'd totally do well to have a sea hag rip *her* tongue out. No, I didn't get a text from Victoria, nor did she answer when I knocked on the door to her dorm four separate times. Sam wasn't there either, presumably at the library or something, so I enjoy a dinner alone in the University Center food court. My meal is a half-wilted salad with nine-thousand calorie dressing. Boy, have my standards plummeted. If my mom and sister could see me now ...

My dad would probably cheer me on and laugh. He was always the cool one in the family who encouraged me, even when I had my five-year-long tomboy phase in junior high, which completely humiliated my sister. You wouldn't be able to tell from looking at me, but I'm actually quite handy with a switchblade. I also know how to tie eleven different knots and am not afraid of mud—which I always made fun of my sister for, considering stage makeup basically *is* mud that you put on your face.

When I'm back at the School of Theatre for my Wednesday evening lighting crew shift, my heart rate is so high, I seriously feel like I might faint before I reach the door. I don't know why my confidence is so finicky; it's blazing one minute, dead-cold the next.

I push through the door of the auditorium.

Clayton is seated on the edge of the stage.

Alone.

He doesn't look up. He seems intent on staring at the seats. Surely he isn't avoiding looking at me.

I force myself down the aisle to the stage. When he *still* doesn't look up at me or acknowledge my existence—even with me clearly being in his peripheral view now—I give up, sitting on the edge of the stage too, but keeping quite some distance between us.

I fight an urge to fruitlessly say hello, then roll my eyes at how dumb I am. *I shouldn't have signed to him. I had no idea what I was doing.*

I still don't.

"This is just *lovely*," I mumble under my breath, picking my nails despondently.

"What's lovely?" comes a voice from behind.

I jump, turning around to find Dick standing there.

"Hello, D… Dick."

"What'd you call me? Just kidding." He sits down between us, legs dangling off the stage. I wonder if he was saving up that joke; I can picture him practicing it into mirrors. "Some guys switched around, since I had openings for more people Monday and Tuesday. So, it looks like our Wednesday crew is now … just you two. Which really means it's just you, Dessie."

"Just me," I echo.

"And you've been cast in *Our Town* as Emily," he reminds me unnecessarily, "and they will be starting rehearsals next week."

"Yes, right."

"So, it seems that we have a bit of a sudden scheduling conflict."

I frown. Clayton seems to be in his own world, his hands braced on the edge of the stage in a way that tightens and accentuates his big, muscular arms. He stares down at the floor. I wonder if he was somehow told of this conflict already. Despite knowing he's deaf, I can't help but feel like he's overhearing this whole exchange. It's weird to me to think that he's there, yet not a part of this conversation at all.

"What are we going to do, then?" I ask.

"We have a number of options. You can work today. Clayton can show you the grid one-on-one. I trust him, just have your phone handy so you both can back-and-forth that way. I presume you know he's deaf," he adds quietly, as if it's necessary to whisper. "I have a serious stack of paperwork to catch up on in my office, otherwise I'd take you around myself. Also, the Monday and Tuesday crew kinda finished all the work I had planned for you guys this week, so ..." Dick runs a hand over his oily head, as if there were still hair there. "Work tonight, and next week we'll discuss whether rehearsals can be worked out to exclude Emily's scenes on Wednesdays. That, or we'll have to find you another shift."

Heaviness sets in my chest. I hadn't realized how much I was looking forward to being near Clayton every Wednesday night. And alone, at that. Now, it sounds like I won't be anywhere near him after today.

"I liked this shift. It fits into my schedule," I tell him, pushing the words out despite knowing full well that I'm completely free for most of the rest of the times available.

Dick nods. "I'll talk with Nina and we'll figure something out." And with that, he gives Clayton a big slap on the back, the sound of which is meaty and firm, like he just slapped a mountainside. Clayton slowly turns his head to meet Dick's eyes with his dark, half-lidded ones. "I'll leave it to you, Clayton! Show Dessie the *grid*," he says, overpronouncing his words. He even points up for emphasis. Then, he turns back to me. "He'll introduce you to Bertha, the cherry-picker. If you guys tip over, just scream; the Wednesday night set crew is working beyond the double doors and should hear you," he says with a nod toward the backstage. "Just teasing about the falling over. Really, you'll be alright if Bertha's legs cooperate and lock today."

"Bertha's legs?"

"My extension is 330," he whispers, then hops off the stage and departs the auditorium.

The silent vacuum of the enormous room crushes in on me. Then, through that silence, I hear Clayton breathing. I turn my face. He seems to be scowling at the floor like it did something wrong to him. So, what's the plan now? Are we just going to sit here?

Tentatively, I give a small wave of my hand. Either it does not get his attention, or he's ignoring me. "Hey," I say, then feel dumb the moment the word comes out. Would it be rude to get his attention by slapping the stage? Screw it. I tap the flat of my palm against the stage three times, inspiring three small vibrations, and accompany the gesture with another thoughtless, "Hey, Clayton?" Nothing.

I clench shut my eyes. *I shouldn't have signed to him. I ruined everything. What a dumb idea.* Even now, I'm reliving that moment in the UC food court with a tinge of humiliation, reimagining the annoyed look on his face. He was annoyed, right? Or am I projecting my own doubts onto a perfectly innocent memory?

I'm here for three damn hours. I'm not going to spend them sitting on the edge of the stage playing ignore-me games with Clayton hot-as-fuck Watts.

Fighting a blush that's quickly spreading over my face like a firestorm, I climb to my feet and search around for something to do. A pile of cables, already neatly coiled up. I check to ensure that they're sorted by length and color. They are. *Lovely.* I approach the lighting rack where all the lights dangle by C-clamps. They're organized by type. One of the Fresnel lanterns is crooked, so I do the important and necessary work of pushing a finger into its side, righting it.

All in a hard day's work.

Footsteps approach from behind. When I turn, Clayton stands there, dark and foreboding. His shirt is especially clingy today, giving me an impressive display of his gorgeous pecs. His thick, unforgiving shoulders torment each sleeve of his poor black shirt, which stretches to embrace the mass of his arms.

I sigh just at the sight of him.

"Up here," he murmurs, nearly inaudible.

I blink, then meet his eyes. Did he just ...? Did I just hear him ...? Or did I imagine that?

"You can talk?" I ask inanely.

"My eyes ... are up here," he repeats just as quietly.

I thought I was blushing before. Nope. My face is burning like a fraternity beach bonfire now.

And his voice ... The sound of his voice is *electric* to me. I don't know what I was expecting, but his every word is like silk against my skin. Isn't that exactly how it sounded in my fantasies of him? I wonder if he realizes how softly he speaks, how sensitive he is to the vibrations of his own voice. Regardless, I could listen to that man all day long. The gentle cadence of his speech is sex to my ears.

I clear my throat, then enunciate each of my words with great care. "I take it ... you can *understand* me?"

His heavy-lidded eyes regard me with a mountain of patience as he looks down on me. With the tiniest of smirks playing on his sexy lips, he nods once.

"Okay." I offer him a tiny, smug smile of my own. "*So*," I say, punching each word, "do *you* ... want to *introduce me* ... to *Bertha?*"

"Talk normal."

I study his eyes defensively. "I am," I argue back.

The tiny smirk becomes an amused one. "Don't have to shout," he says. "Doesn't help me hear your pretty voice any better."

With that, he turns away, heading for backstage. I watch his muscular back as he goes, gawping after him. *I was shouting??* How the hell can he tell, anyway? My eyes drop down to his perfect ass. He's wearing a loose pair of tattered jeans that hang low on his hips, yet somehow are capable of hugging his hot, sculpted buns in a way that is annoyingly distracting. My urge to tackle him and hear the meaty sound of his body crashing into the wall as I have my way with him has not diminished at all over the past week.

Stop staring at his ass, I chide myself, then follow.

His biceps flex gloriously as he grips and pulls the handle of an enormous blue lift machine that has the name "BERTHA" written across the base of the cage in thick black marker. The monster rolls slowly on four squeaky wheels, Clayton grunting slightly as he tugs it to the center of the stage. I wonder if he knows he's grunting. Miss Bertha has got to weigh a *ton*.

Once it's placed, he pulls out four long metal legs from some compartment in the base, then sticks each one into their matching slots, locking them in place with a twisting, rotary handle-thing. The legs stretch out about five feet or so in each direction, giving the machine balance. He runs its cord along the stage to an outlet. A moment later, he's in front of Bertha and pulling open the little door of the two-person metal basket thing that we'll be going up in.

He pats the scary apparatus, which rattles horribly in response. "Giddy-up."

The last thing I want to look like is some scared girl who can't handle a little bit of height. Throwing my chin proudly in the air, I saunter over to the machine, determined to—as the lovely Dick put it—become intimate with Bertha. *I'd really rather become intimate with the man who plugged her in.*

Stepping into the basket, my shoe slips and I catch myself on the door. Clayton's hands shoot out instinctively, grabbing a hold of my hips, and for a moment, we're locked in place, staring at each other's eyes. He lets go quickly, seeing that I've clearly caught myself from falling, and I feel my face flush again as I climb into the basket, gripping its railing so tightly, my knuckles bleed white.

Clayton steps into the basket with me. This is not the biggest machine I've ever been in, and I suspect its elevating platform we're standing on was meant for only one person, or two small people at best. His body is nearly on top of mine when he shuts the gate and locks it.

I inhale his scent. My body shivers, consumed by the way Clayton smells—it's like sawdust, sweat, and a hint of spice. The heat he exudes touches me as potently as his aroma, and I fight an urge to lean into him and just rake it all in.

This is madness. This is torture.

He turns to me. His face is so fucking close to mine, I feel his every breath on my forehead. "Ready?"

I nod.

He pushes a thumb into a console I didn't notice until it's too late, and the basket jerks, startling me, then slowly begins to rise. The vibrations tickle my feet. *Bertha's an old bitch*, I think to myself. Clayton doesn't even bother gripping the railing for balance; he just stands there, his lazily planted feet doing all the work of keeping him upright as we ascend.

He watches me the entire time. I can't meet his eyes. The blushing in my cheeks stubbornly persists, refusing to calm even for a moment. I start to breathe in and out through my mouth the higher we get. *I'm not afraid of heights*, I remind myself, then take a peek down.

Big mistake. The stage is so, *so* far away. This machine is so damn rickety, it sways left and right as we go, giving me the impression that the whole basket we're entrusting our lives with is secured to Bertha by two screws and a strip of tape.

"Nervous?" his soft, sultry voice asks.

I face him defiantly, despite my fears. "Petrified," I answer sarcastically, then wonder if I actually meant the word.

To be fair, my fiercely gripping hands have not let go and my palms are starting to cramp.

That knowing, cocky smirk plays on his full, plush lips again. I involuntarily lick my own, thoughts of what I'd do with him alone in a room racing across my mind and rendering my face vulnerable for a second. *I bet he can see my thoughts ... these thoughts.*

Then I realize I *am* alone in a room with him. A very, very big room. I glance down again. *Fuck, I clearly don't learn from my mistakes.* My stomach spins and the machine keeps going up, up, up. How tall is this damn stage? This is the biggest auditorium I've ever been in. Texas. Everything's bigger, or something.

"Here," he says.

I look up at him, then notice what he's indicating, following his nod. We've reached the hanging pipes of the fly system where curtains and certain set pieces are hung. There appears to be a flat, painted sun—or something—that hangs in the middle, likely left over from a summer production if I had to guess. Lighting instruments can also be hung here, or in the grid, which is even higher up.

"Do you ever ..."

His voice startles me, as I was focusing on the flat-sun-thing so as not to be so damn aware of the basket swaying side to side. I lift my eyebrows. "Do I ever ...?"

He swallows suddenly, appearing frustrated. The look comes out of nowhere, his abrupt change in mood casting a shadow over his face. Then, with a scowl, he whips his phone out of his pocket and starts typing. I think he's texting a friend when he suddenly lifts the screen to my eyes:

Do u ever work in the grid? Ever hung a light?

"Oh," I mutter. "No. Not really."

"No," he mumbles, repeating my word. I wonder for a second if he's aware that he echoed me, and then he plunges his face back into the phone, typing away. He shows the screen again:

U're not gonna die. U're safe w me.

I still haven't let go of the railing. "*Bertha's* a bit *shaky*," I explain, then catch the fact that I am, in fact, yelling and overpronouncing my words. "A bit shaky," I repeat a touch more naturally. "B-Bertha."

He nods, then types some more:

We can go back down if u want

Why did he stop talking? I love the soft sound of his silky, sexy voice ... but does *he* hate it?

An idea hits me. As it's just the two of us here, I find the confidence that had totally abandoned me in the food court a couple days ago. I have no idea where this confidence comes from, considering that I'm ten seconds from peeing my pants out of fear right now; the basket's swaying in all four directions, like some child's arm reaching up to grab candy from an out-of-reach candy jar, bending left, bending forward, then right, then left again. If I can get through this without losing my dinner all over Clayton's tight, muscle-hugging shirt, I'll call it a win.

Removing my hand from the railing for the first time, I lift a shaky, sweat-ridden fist and knock on an imaginary door in front of me, as if my fist were a nodding head—the sign for "yes".

He frowns as if my sign hit him in the face. Then he shakes his head, his lips pursed and annoyed.

Shit. Figuring I'd done it wrong, I bring a fist to my chest and draw a circle, repeating the sign for "sorry" that I'd done before. What was that other one?—the sign for "please"? It's similar to "sorry", oddly enough. My hands hover in the air as I try to remember it.

Then Clayton grabs my hands, stopping me.

My eyes flash.

Neither of us move. I stare at him, stunned, and he stares back, though I can't get a read on his eyes. He's almost angry. His brow is wrinkled, pained, as if I just wounded him. He seems to be gnawing on his teeth, his jaw drawn tight, his cheeks dimpled with tension.

The air between us is so still, I wonder if either of us are breathing.

Then, his grip relaxes, but he doesn't yet let go. With a face as hardened as stone, he says, "Don't."

I was just trying to talk to him in his, uh ... native language. How is that wrong? "Am I *that* bad at it?"

The corner of his lips bend into a scowl.

"That's a yes?" I press on, my hands still caught in his powerful yet strangely gentle grip. "Horrible? I'm just horrible and awful at sign language? Is that it?"

His eyes run all over my face, as if searching for something. Did he get lost in my words? Did I speak too quickly?

I keep going. "Am I really that bad with my hands? Do I look dumb?"

Still, the beast before me stares wordlessly.

"Should I start typing on my phone?" I ramble on, unable to will myself to shut the hell up. "Would you prefer that over reading my lips?"

Then he jerks on my hands, pulling me in, and our lips collide.

My eyes cram shut as he takes over, his warm mouth consuming mine. Clayton's hot, jagged breath dresses my face, his powerful hands still clasped over mine and keeping me in place, trapped in his kiss.

Holy fucking shit.

Then it's over, just like that. He pulls away and lets go of me in one fluid motion, jabbing the button to bring the basket slowly back down to Earth.

And I'm just staring at him with what might be the biggest *what-the-hell-just-happened* expression on my face. I don't even notice us swaying, nor feel a trace of the fear of heights I just had. All of my attention is one hundred percent Clayton Watts and those lips.

Seriously, though ... what just happened?

The basket shudders when it hits the stage abruptly, and Clayton swings open the cage, escaping Bertha as fast as if his pants caught fire.

"Clayton?" I call after him pointlessly. He's off the stage in seconds, headed down the aisle into darkness. The auditorium doors open, flashing his beautiful silhouette at me for a moment before they shut gently behind him, closing me in with the cold silence and the warm sensation of his lips still on mine.

Chapter 10
CLAYTON

I can't do this again.

Fuck, she tasted so good I already want another taste.

No, this can't happen. I'm not losing my head over a girl, not right now.

But her eyes ... Standing that close to her, I could have poured myself into them and made a home.

What the fuck am I talking about?

She's a sophisticated city girl from New York. I'm the dirty scum of a poor Texas nobody. She can do so much better than me.

Why did I kiss her?? Why would I fucking do that to myself?—or to her? I'm sending the wrong message. A kiss means "come here" when I should be teaching her the signs for "get the fuck away from me".

And she learned signs. She learned them so she could talk to me with her hands.

I can picture her now, looking them up online and mimicking the hand motions in front of the screen. *She did that for you, Clayton.* I'm so fucked.

I stop at a giant abstract sculpture made of wire and glass panels just outside of the School of Art and collapse onto one of the benches that encircle it. On that bench for an hour, I stare at the horizon as it ignites with angry shades of orange and pink before being chased away by deep blues, then darkness. That sunset pretty much sums up my mood: up in the air with Dessie's mouth on mine, I was ignited, and back down on the ground, I'm the shadows.

I pull out my phone and text Brant, asking him what he's up to. I desperately need to distract myself. My phone shivers twenty seconds later, Brant asking me where we keep the chocolate syrup because he's got a girl in his room and they "have ideas". With a sigh, I inform him that we have none, then shove my phone back in my pocket, ignoring his response. That was more distraction and imagery than I needed.

Two girls pass by, and the conversation they were clearly having is paused as they sip the straws of their beverages suggestively, but it's their eyes that do all the drinking, staring me down as they pass. One of them, a pretty brunette with curls down to her boobs, gives me a wiggle of her long fingers, sporting blood red nails.

I look away, annoyed. Girls like them used to be my thing. *I* was the expert. I had the skills that Brant was jealous of, even back when we were kids and our voices were still changing.

It's the strangest thing, for the last memory of your own voice to be that of your twelve-year-old self, an unreliable voice that cracked at the worst of times, a voice that turned rough one day of the week, then boyish and squeaky the next.

But that squeaky voice couldn't dare stop me from going after all the pretty girls. Little Clayton knew how to talk to them. He wasn't afraid.

It was little dorky Brant who had all the trouble, and I was the one who coached him that day at Laura's party. "You can't think of a girl as someone you want," I told him—my cocky, know-it-all self who acted like I had all the answers a dumb twelve-year-old would ever need. "You have to see *her* as someone who wants *you*."

"I feel like I'm gonna puke," whined little Brant. It always annoyed me how much he complained.

"Walk up and ask her why she hasn't offered you some punch yet," I teased him, nudging him with my elbow. He pushed me off, annoyed, and I saw the fear in his eyes. It didn't make me sympathize with him; it made me want to laugh at the scared little fucker. "You're such a chicken, Brant."

"Shut up, I'm not."

"Watch me," I told him, puffing up my chest. "Watch and learn, little bro."

We weren't brothers, but I loved acting like the older brother Brant never had, in all the best and worst ways.

I walked up to that girl he'd had his eyes on ever since fifth grade. It was that easy. I strutted up to Miss Courtney and enjoyed the conversation Brant was meant to have. And at nine o'clock that night, it was me kissing Courtney in the closet under the stairs while everyone else's fingers turned orange eating Cheetos and playing Twister in the living room.

I'd done some pretty sick shit back when I could hear. I was on top of the world and acted like I owned it, no matter how poor I was, no matter how I felt after Dad took off before my sixth birthday with some blonde bitch he met online, no matter how bad Mom's hoarding problem got for those three months before he came back. I wouldn't let anything stop me, even when Brant was furious with me for taking Courtney from him. "Snooze you lose," I recall telling him in my room before he hurled a PlayStation controller at my head and pounced on me. In the heated struggle, Brant sliced open his arm pretty bad, and a trip to the emergency room earned him twelve stitches and a crescent scar he still has to this day.

He didn't forgive me for a while. The last time I ever heard his voice, it was in the hallway at school right in front of my locker where he shouted, "I'm sorry I ever looked up to your selfish, coldhearted ass! You're not my friend! Fuck you, Clayton!"

Not two months after that exchange, I lost my hearing forever.

And Brant's loving, final words to me would be thereafter locked in my mind. When he saw me next, the only apology I received was in the form of his lips moving, creating words I couldn't understand. Then I couldn't even see the lips anymore as they began to blur behind a sheen of my tears.

I blink away the memories, startled to discover how dark it's gotten. The only light that touches me now is the nearby lamppost. I pull my phone out, the screen blinding me, and type a message to Brant:

We DO have caramel sauce, tho.
Behind the salsa, back of the fridge

I grin to myself, a chuckle pushing past my lips before I rise from the bench. Hands in my pockets, I stroll into the calm, breezy night, the moon my only guide, and consider what the hell I'm going to do about a certain beautiful Theatre girl.

Chapter 11
DESSIE

The water in the shower is just perfect, turned up almost too hot, bathing my skin in its liquid fire. His face is still burned into my brain. His breath touches my skin like we're still trapped five zillion feet above the stage in that shaky metal basket. I can imagine it so vividly, so I think, why not go for it?

I slide a slippery hand over my breast.

"Oh, God," I can't help but moan.

If he were in this shower with me, it'd be as tight a squeeze as standing in that rickety basket. I can see the water soaking his shirt, picturing it in so much detail, it's like he's really here with me. The more the water drenches him, the more his firm muscles reveal themselves.

My nipples are so sensitive. I can't stop moving my hand over them, up and down, then in circles.

"Fuck," I breathe, quivering.

The water is almost too hot to bear, and so is he. My fingers run lower, tickling down my stomach. I keep myself on edge, anticipating the sensation I want to feel so badly. I deliberately take my time, torturing myself. My fingers are Clayton's. My touch is Clayton, evilly crawling his fingers down my body too slowly.

"You're so bad," I whisper into the water, echoes of my own voice hissing all around me in the white noise of the shower. "You're so, so bad."

Then my slippery hand plunges between my legs. No muzzle or hand or gag can possibly hope to snuff out the moan that escapes my trembling lips now.

Clayton Watts is down there working a cruel sort of magic on me.

"Don't stop," I beg him.

He doesn't. My fingers that are *his* fingers start to move quicker. I sway so badly, I catch a stream of shower water in my gaping mouth. One hand down below, I keep a set of fingers working my increasingly sensitive nipples. I'm so horny I feel sick. My insides are coming undone fast. I know I'm about to come.

Clayton ... Clayton wants me to come for him.

"Yes," I agree, the word turning into a sizzle on my tongue, my face scrunching up in sweet agony. "*Yes.*"

The impending waves of ecstasy chase up my body as I race over the cliff of orgasm. I lean forward into the wet wall of the shower, face flattened against the tile as I plummet off the edge, my fingers working me into a state of delirium as I moan my release through the steam and the water and the heat.

It's not often that you can say you feel dirtier *after* a shower.

I breathe deeply, recovering as I press against the shower wall. I suck in one lungful of air after another, my hands stuck right where they are, half hugging the sensitive parts of my body.

As the thrill of orgasm departs, reality makes a quick replacement of the joy I was chasing, and I realize that I'm all alone. That kiss we shared while we swayed in the air two days ago, it's already so far gone that I'm having doubts it ever really happened.

Clayton Watts, you teasing asshole. You're driving me insane. *I'm so obsessed with you.*

Then, my moment is further stolen from me by a loud knock at the door that leads to my suitemates in the adjoining room, followed by the words, "I need to pee! For the love of God, can you hurry up??"

I kinda thought I was alone. I was so lost in my fantasy, I wonder self-consciously if she heard any of my moaning or whispering dirty things through the noise of the shower.

Shutting off the water, I dry off—which is literally impossible in this tiny chamber that fills up with steam in a matter of five minutes—then dismiss myself to my room wearing just a towel as the desperate, squirming suitemate barges her way into the bathroom. No eye contact is made and my door's shut and locked before any due awkwardness can ensue. Still, that doesn't save me from the deadpan stare I get from Sam sitting cross-legged on her bed, who I didn't realize was here either. *Did everyone in the world return to their rooms during the one shower I take in which I chose to get myself off?*

No matter, I hide in the closet and dress myself for tonight's read-through. Even though rehearsals don't start until Monday, they've scheduled a reading of the script with all the cast and some crew heads tonight before we all break for the weekend to learn our lines.

The whole way to the School of Theatre, I find my heart thrumming heavily between my footsteps. I don't know if it's because auditions happened last Friday—exactly a week ago today—or if I'm somehow channeling the bold recklessness that a few drinks gave me before I sang my heart out at the *Throng*.

I enter the rehearsal room and dozens of eyes are on me at once, the noise of chatter cut in half by my arrival. I'm stunned by the reaction, worrying for a second that I'd gotten the time wrong and I'm late. There's a set of long tables arranged in a U, around which actors and designers are seated with scripts set before them, ready.

"D-lady!" calls out Eric, who magically appears, waving. "Got a seat for you!"

I smile mutely at the others in the room, then put myself in the empty chair at his side. When I look up at the person seated across from me, I'm stabbed in the chest.

Clayton stares down at his script, his mess of hair casting a shadow down his face. He knows I'm here. He saw me and now he's avoiding all eye contact.

Yeah, this is all about you, Dessie. I roll my eyes.

But I can't help myself from staring at his thick, round shoulders in that red-and-black plaid button-down he's wearing, how it tapers up the trapezoidal shape of his neck muscles where that coil of black ink runs up his neck like a deadly, poisonous vine. Two buttons of his shirt are undone, giving me a cruel and tormenting peek at the top of his pecs. Clayton's face is still drawn tightly to his script. I doubt even an earthquake could pull his attention up to *pretend* to acknowledge me.

What is he even doing here??

"Sorry," Eric whispers to me.

I jerk, turning my face. "For what?"

"It was the only seat," he murmurs quietly, barely heard in the noise of the room even sitting right next to me. "I got here seconds before you did. Besides, the view isn't that bad, eh?" He gives me a wink.

I smirk, narrowing my eyes. "No idea what you're talking about, *Other Eric.*"

"*Gay* Eric would be more accurate," he amends, "and that makes me twenty times more interesting than the Erik-with-a-K. Really, that's what we should call him. Ugh."

Oh. I hadn't realized, since no one said it outright. "Well, then," I mutter back. "You can have all the fun you want staring at Clay-boy. He's all yours."

"I wish," he breathes with a rueful glance.

Right then, Nina Parisi enters the room, and all the chatter wilts away in the same manner as paper shriveling up to nothing in the presence of fire. She seats herself at the head of the table, then flips open her script and coldly welcomes us to the first reading of *Our Town*. She proceeds to give us a speech about what she hopes to accomplish with this brave, unique production and her "big picture".

And it's taking everything in me not to look up and drink in the delicious sight of Clayton across the table from me. *Why does he have to make things so hard?* He's the one who kissed me and ran away. He's the one who's acting all weird, not me. Also, I'm pretty sure if I dare to look at him, he'll know instantly that not an hour earlier, I had my fingers up my hoo-hoo getting off to fantasies of him in my dorm shower.

Just the thought makes me sweat.

Soon, Nina has us run down the line and briefly introduce ourselves. "I'm Kat, the stage manager. The *actual* stage manager, not to be confused with the role of 'Stage Manager' in the play, to be clear," says a curvy, olive-skinned woman to her left with a mop of red and black hair gathered in cute nests by her ears. "Astrid here, assistant director," announces the girl next to Kat, a pale thing with twenty braids piled up and pinned to her head. "Alice, or Ali, costumes," says the next, listless and sleepy-eyed.

As the intros move down the line, I betray all that resolve I built up, daring myself to look at Clayton.

He's staring right at me.

I look away at once. *Damn it.* The person to my left shifts in their seat. There's a fraction of a second of silence before I realize it's my turn. I rise suddenly for my intro, despite the fact that no one else did. "I'm Dessie, playing my ... playing the role for ... of Emily."

My face red, I clumsily drop back into my chair as Eric rises from his, endearingly following my lead. "Eric Chaplin O'Connor here. I'll be playing Simon Stimson." He sits back down, then gives me a wink of encouragement, which only makes my face redder.

I look up to find Clayton still staring at me, except now there's a hint of amusement in his wicked eyes.

I scowl at him, despite my incessant flushing, then mouth the words, *"Stop staring at me,"* across the table.

To that, his smirk only widens, now touching his dark eyes, and then he slowly shakes his head no.

He is so infuriating.

The introductions have come around the table, and the round man to Clayton's right rises, who I belatedly recognize as the orange-bearded guy from the mixer, except with glasses. "Hey! I'm Freddie, your lucky sound designer, and this here's Clayton Watts, assistant lighting designer. And ... please audition for my spring show. Auditions are Tuesday in the black box at six, with callbacks Wednesday. Uh, thanks. Appreciate it." He awkwardly sits back down, and then the person to Clayton's left continues the round of intros.

Clayton keeps watching me with that wolf-like, hungry glint in his eyes.

I don't know whether to be turned on or scared.

"Great," says Nina, the intros finished. "Let's get right to it. Act one, scene one."

Is this some sort of game to him? Kissing girls he likes, then running away and expecting them to chase after him? I've had my fair share of game-playing guys in my past. Sure, I dated very few of them, but I never had one that I could properly call a boyfriend. Everyone in New York City was shopping for the next best thing. Everyone knew a hundred other people. Games, that's all the men there could play. Whether on the stage or off, everyone was an actor, even if they never stepped foot on a stage.

I hate to think of Clayton like that. In fact, I can't. There's something so different about him. *Maybe this isn't a game,* I consider, chewing on my lip in thought. *Maybe this is his way of ... showing interest.*

Like when you're a kid on the playground and you shove your crush into the sand and make them cry.

The read-through begins. I patiently wait for my lines to come, reading along with the script. The Stage Manager role has a crap load of lines before anyone else even speaks, introducing each family to the audience and painting a picture of two houses on an empty, deliberately set-deprived stage, setting the scene for the audience's imagination. *What a weird play,* I tell myself.

Really, I do know this play, I swear I read it long ago. But the roles are all confused in my mind, and I don't even really remember how it ends. Of course, this doesn't help the nugget of guilt that sits in my chest, wondering what other highly deserving actors could be sitting in my place right now, as I wait for Emily's first line. Victoria hasn't spoken a word to me since the day the cast list was posted. *That was at the beginning of the week, five days ago.* Eric swears she's just been busy, but I know better.

Finally, after an eternity, it's my first line. I draw breath and recite it plainly, as if I were reading from a textbook. *Ugh.* I feel so stiff. I read my next line, and again, I might as well be reading advanced algebra equations. I can't help but feel self-conscious, worried that everyone in the room is thinking the same thing: This *is the person Nina cast as Emily, the lead?* This *is the one who beat out all the others?*

I'm certain there's even people in this room who wanted the role of Emily, but got cast in other parts. It's not just Victoria, I realize; *all* the women wanted my role. Some of my competitors are in this room right now listening to me, comparing themselves to me, scoffing inside their heads.

As I read the next line, I glance up to survey the table. I see the costumes girl yawn. I see the face of someone else near her appearing utterly bored. I catch the assistant director who tiredly meets my eyes, smirking.

I suck.

I suck so much.

When my scene is over and the character of Emily has exited the stage, I let go a little sigh, which doesn't seem to go unnoticed by Eric, who gives me a little pat of encouragement on my thigh.

Then, I feel someone softly kick my foot under the table, so I retract my foot a bit, figuring it to be in the way. Then, my foot's tapped again, more deliberately.

I look up.

Clayton's gone back to staring at me again. *It's his foot.* He smirks, his eyes narrowing as his shoe taps mine again.

A rush of excitement surges up through me.

What a game-playing, mind-toying asshole.

I pull my feet under my chair, far away from his. Then, I pretend to pore over my script and ignore him utterly, despite my stomach-tumbling desire to do the exact opposite.

I am exercising some serious discipline here.

I push through the next scene, also making it a point to ignore the others in the room. I can't be judged by all of them; I judge myself badly enough.

The role of George—who is Emily's love interest, wedded to each other in act two—is played by a guy I haven't met before. He's a decent-looking man, most likely an upperclassman. His well-groomed hair and plain, coppery face make for a fitting George and male lead, if you discount the Stage Manager role and his twenty-or-so billion lines I don't envy.

When it comes to the scenes in which Emily and George flirt, I look up and try to say the lines across the table to the actor who's playing him—whose real name I've already forgotten from the intros earlier, or perhaps never paid attention to in the first place. A few times, I lose my place in the script due to looking up and stumble over the words.

"Just read for today," Nina cuts in, startling me.

I look up, my heart slamming against my chest in the not-so-pleasurable way. "Sorry?"

"It's a read-through," she explains patiently, as if I needed to be told—in front of everyone—what we're doing here today. "You don't need to connect with the other actors. At least, not with your eyes. We'll have plenty of time for that in rehearsals. For today, just read." She offers me a cool smile and a nod.

Some others around the table meet my startled eyes. I feel the flood of judgments and silent sneers coming from my castmates.

How embarrassing is that, to be called out like some amateur by the director and told to "just read" during a read-through?

I can already hear my sister scolding me, were Cece in this room.

"Of course," I answer Nina, the stiff-necked, rigid-as-an-icicle director, then resume my lines.

The rest of the read-through is far less enjoyable. I make the wedding in act two sound like the funeral in act three. Even reading the lines, I trip over the words, pushing them out with the enthusiasm of a slug.

The read-through can't end fast enough. After it's all over with, the director thanks us, then dismisses us with a forewarning that the first act of the play is due to be off-book by Monday, which gives me exactly two days—my weekend—to learn my first act's lines. I give very little attention to the rest of the room, closing up my script and rising from the chair. Eric asks me something about hanging out at the *Throng*, but I decline—perhaps too quickly. I very suddenly want to just go back to my dorm and forget that the rest of the world exists. Even Clayton, who would have a totally different opinion of me if he heard any of that awful, horrible excuse for "acting" that I just did.

I push through the rehearsal room doors. I walk quickly down a half-lit hall to the lobby, finding the darkness of night through the tall glass windows. A group of students are rehearsing a scene by the chairs in the lobby, and they stop when they see me.

"Dessie."

I turn around. Clayton stands there, his sharp eyes locked on mine and his script tucked under his big arm. Oh. Maybe it was *him* the students in the lobby stopped to look at.

But my patience is long gone. All my emotions are high and flustered and hot, my nerves tight as wires. "What do you want, Clayton?"

After a moment of studying the obvious distress on my face, he frowns. For a second, I feel bad about snapping at him. Then, with his free hand, he brings a fist to his chest and draws a circle.

Sorry, he signs.

My mood softens instantly. I wonder for a second what he's apologizing for. The kiss on Wednesday? The shitty read-through just now? The foot-thing?

"What for?" I ask.

He brushes the knuckles of his right fist against his left fist, then sweeps a hand to the side, palm-up.

I sigh. "I don't know what that means."

He shrugs, then quietly says, "Everything."

I hear whispering from the lobby, likely from our little audience of actors who've shut up to pay witness to this whole exchange. I fight an urge to shout at them to mind their own business.

I don't know why I'm so mad at Clayton. It's not like he owes me a damn thing. He kissed me during lighting crew. So what? It's not like I didn't enjoy it too. Besides, if I'm really honest with myself, maybe I'm just pissed about getting cast in this dumb show, cursed with the very thing I begged the gods for ever since my older sister gulped her first tasty teaspoon of success: a lead role. Now the gods laugh at me, giving me the role without the due talent needed to perform said role.

I'm no good for Clayton, regardless of whether or not he's any good for me. "I should go," I tell him dejectedly, though I'm really not so sure I want to.

"Why?" he murmurs in his small voice.

The students in the lobby whisper to each other.

"I don't know," I admit, hugging the script to my chest. It feels heavier with each second that goes by. "I just need to go. I need to be by myself."

He sucks on his tongue for a moment, frustrated, his jaw tightening. Then he pulls out his phone, types, and shows me the too-bright screen:

Want to hang out tomorrow night?

I'm stunned. My heart races up my throat as I read the words five times in a row. I look up to meet his eyes. He's searching mine, desperate for the answer.

He wants to hang out with you, Dessie. You'd be crazy to say no. Don't you dare say no. I will never, ever forgive you if you say no.

But can I say yes? I was feeling so defiant a week ago when my friends enthusiastically advised me to stay away from the Watts boy, telling me he's bad news. Chloe even gave me his romantic history. Ariel even pitched in her two unasked-for cents. Now, I wonder if I should have heeded all their warnings. Is this the game he plays, luring a girl into his little trap, having his way with her, then tossing her aside like a used towel? I'm not going to lie; he looks exactly the type to do just that. I mean, he's *gorgeous.* He's got a killer body. And he's aggressive as hell, despite the soft nature of his voice.

Can I really trust him?

I take a deep breath, shake out my hair, then face the beautiful beast with a pinch of confidence.

"Where?" I ask nonchalantly.

He types again:

> Bowling alley on Kingston Blvd. Right off campus. Walking distance, ten minutes tops. My roommate has a competition thing and I' m going, thought you might like to come too

With that, he meets my eyes as I read the words a few times. The look in his eyes is ... hesitant. It's like he fears my answer. *Is he as afraid of rejection as I am afraid of his intentions?*

Even if I agree to this, I can still be in control. It'll be a public place with other people around, and I don't have to kiss him again or do anything I don't want to do.

Not that I don't want to kiss him, because I do.

A lot.

Oh, hell. I'm so screwed. *Look, Dessie, you can bolt at any time. You owe him nothing.* Right?

Or maybe my fear is that I won't want to bolt.

What am I so afraid of?

DESSIE

Okay, so I said yes.

Something about a man like Clayton standing over me and asking ... with his dark, hungry eyes and his smooth, sexy hands and his plush, perfect lips ... is somewhat persuasive.

Annoyingly persuasive.

I haven't been to a bowling alley since I was a kid. Yet somehow, I instantly remember the smoky, sweaty stench. No, I'm not a fan. There's only one reason I'm suffering it tonight.

And that reason isn't here.

I stand awkwardly by the entrance. The front counter, where a man has annoyingly asked me four times if he can help me, is to the left. An arcade filled with the likes of the Alpha Kappa Louda-As-Fucka fraternity is to my right. Ahead, the loud clanking and banging of the bowling lanes awaits.

I stare down at my phone and curse myself for not getting his number. At least then, I might've received a text that he would be running late, or that the thing was cancelled—who knows. Instead, I'm standing here wondering if I should bother getting a drink, or maybe making the ten-minute walk back to my dorm before it gets dark. After all, I was warned by Victoria that our campus sits between crime-land and fortune-land, and I can't with any confidence say which one I'm in.

Someone rushes up to the front, leaning across the counter to speak to the man there. He's a slender, tan, good-looking guy, full of energy, with tight jeans torn at the knee (is that a Texan thing?) and a grey fitted t-shirt with a frog plastered on the front. Upon second inspection, a joint hangs out of the frog's mouth and its big eyes are bloodshot. This carefree, cheery dude-bro wears a pair of bowling shoes, one fingerless glove on his left hand, and a backwards cap squishing down a head of messy brown hair.

He turns. His eyes flash when they meet mine.

I look down at my phone suddenly, pretending to be occupied with a very interesting text message. In reality, I'm staring at the reflection of my own worried face. *Crap, is that what I look like?*

"Hey."

I look up, startled. It's the carefree dude-bro.

"Hi...?" I return warily.

He brings the blue and orange marbled bowling ball up to his chest with one hand, his bicep bulging in the effort. "You look lost. Are you lost?"

He's got a slight Texan drawl to his voice. I offer an apologetic smile, then shake my head. "I'm not lost. Thanks for your concern." I look back down at my super interesting phone.

"Do you go to Klangburg?"

I nod without looking up. He's pretty cute, I'm not going to lie. But if I were to take a guess from his easy demeanor and slick charm, he's had about eight girlfriends this week alone, and he's likely sizing me up to be his ninth. I know a player when I see one.

"What's your major?" he asks, leaning against the wall and tossing his bowling ball gently from one palm to the other.

"Theatre."

"Oh, sweet. My roommate—ah, um ... Anyway, you here to bowl?" He shuffles uncomfortably, which draws my attention back to him, wondering why he changed the subject so abruptly.

"Just to watch," I answer, then glance down at my phone for the time. Almost thirty minutes late. *Where the hell is he?* "What do *you* study?" I ask distractedly.

"Boobs. Just kidding. Titties. Just kidding. Uh ..." He grins as he looks off, flashing a pair of perfect teeth, then hugs the bowling ball to his chest and answers, "I'm thinking architecture."

I don't know why, but I find myself amused by this totally cocky horn-dog. I swallow a laugh. "You're *thinking* architecture? Still undecided?"

"I've ... ah, I've changed my major about four times since my freshman year. Don't judge." He gives me a warning look, his blue eyes flashing. "I like to take a little taste of everything, if you know what I mean."

I'm quite certain I know exactly what he means.

"Nice," I say, feeling smart. "So, since freshman year, you've switched majors from boobs to titties to lady bags ... and finally settled on architecture."

He grins. I think he appreciates me throwing his humor right back at him. "I like a ... *hands-on* major."

"Your mother must be *so* proud."

"You sure you aren't lost?"

"Nope. Just waiting for someone. I know exactly where I am."

After a second, his expression changes. Then, with a new, almost alarmed look in his eyes, he shifts his posture and says, "You wouldn't happen to be *Dessie* ... would you?"

I stare at him and blink. "Yes, I am."

"Oh, fuck." He lets out a laugh, his face flushing, and then he whistles and hoots loudly. "Right on!" he finally says after he's recovered. "I should've known. I'm such a dipshit! So, you're Dessie." He extends his free hand. "You're Clayton's friend, and I'm rude."

Now it's my turn to blanch. "And *you* are?"

"Brant," he answers, his hand still extended, as I haven't yet trusted it with my handshake. "I'm the reason you're here. The one who's bowling tonight. Tournament. Clayton's favorite roommate—just, ah ... don't ask him to confirm that."

"Brant," I echo hesitantly, shaking his hand.

He seems to cling to mine, fascinated. "Your skin is soft as fuck."

"You're cute," I tell him, "but I'm not interested."

"Sorry." He lets go, then nearly drops his bowling ball as he recoils—like some magic barrier just formed around me after learning who I am. "You're ... you're a lot prettier than I was expecting."

I choke on a laugh, unsure how to react to that. "Were you expecting a swamp creature?"

"He said you're from New York City," Brant goes on, a hint of uncertainty in his voice, "so I kinda presumed you'd be, like ... I dunno. Rough-looking? Edgy? Nose-ring and purple hair and kinda rude?"

"Is that what you think everyone from New York City's like?"

"I've lived here my whole life, born and raised," he explains, a twinge of southern accent playing in his words. "I don't get out much. You can just tell me to shoo at any moment, seriously, and I'll just go and bury my head in an ice bin or something."

"Good thing I came down here to Texas," I say, toying with him right back. "I totally thought you all ride horses to the supermarket, dodge tumbleweeds on the highway, and wear spurs to your best friend's wedding."

"Wedding? Oh, no. Clayton's never marrying," he says with a hearty guffaw. "That dude's been ..."

And then as quickly as the joke occurred to him, it dies on his tongue, his eyes glossing over. I wonder for a moment what he was about to say, then find myself staring down at his shoes awkwardly, struggling to give Clayton the benefit of the doubt and assume that his "best friend" Brant here wasn't about to spill some magic beans I might want to be privy to, if I had any interest in pursuing Clayton seriously.

Which I don't. I'm here to hang out. That's it.

"Let me get you a drink," he says suddenly. "What do you drink, Dessie? I'll get it for you. On the house. I know people. Just name it, they got everything."

I smile mutedly. "Tea?"

He frowns. "Except that."

"Water, then."

"I mean a *real* drink. The bartender who's working tonight, mmm, she makes a mean martini."

"Just a water."

He studies me for a second. "You don't drink?"

I fondly recall the hangover I enjoyed last weekend after my night at the *Throng & Song*. "No."

Brant nods, appraising me with smiling eyes. "I think I like you. I hope Clayton keeps you around."

I fight one of my stubborn blushes that's coming on. "We're just friends," I insist, checking my phone again. Thirty-five minutes late. *What the hell, Clayton?*

"Well, hey, why don't you come over to our lane?" He beckons me with a wave of his hand as he backs away. "Dmitri and I are hanging out. Oh, you haven't had the pleasure of meeting Dmitri, Clayton's *least* favorite roommate. He isn't drinking tonight, either. His major is poetry and general arty-fartiness, so you two will get along just fine."

Figuring it to be safe, I give a mild shrug and follow him into the noise. The bowling alley is packed tonight with people of all ages, from families with children to college students. Even a pair of elderly couples occupy lane fifteen.

It's lane twenty near the wall where the guys are set up. Dmitri rises from his seat, a short, chalky-skinned guy with black spiky hair and thick glasses that remind me so much of Sam's, I'd think I was staring at her if it weren't for the blue and red tattoo running up his arm. He wears a black tank top and dark grey shorts that cut-off just below the knee.

"This is the one," Brant says in half a whisper to Dmitri, though I hear it perfectly.

They lean into each other. "What one?"

"The girl."

"Clayton's?"

"Yup."

Dmitri pulls away from his friend and shoves his hands in his pockets, facing me. He even smiles the same as Sam, his lips flat-lining. "Hi. I'm Dmitri."

"Dessie," I return.

Brant sighs. "Oh, hell. The fuckers are here."

Dmitri squints through his glasses. "The who?"

"My dipshit opponents from Sigma Phi Dildo," he answers, "whose asses I'm gonna whip into Saturday."

"It *is* Saturday."

"Sunday, then. I'll get your water, Dessie," he tells me suddenly, then hops away through the crowd.

The benches opposite us are quickly filled by the loud frat boys I saw in the arcade. Two of them give me a more-than-obvious once-over. I turn away, not appreciating the attention and growing more and more annoyed by the second at Clayton's absence.

"You okay?"

I look up at Dmitri. "I'm just wondering where Clayton is, to be honest."

"I could text him," he offers, pulling a phone out of his pocket. "Not like him to be late to anything."

"Thanks." In stark contrast to Brant, he has no southern drawl at all. "You're a poetry major?"

"That damn Brant! I'm a *creative writing* major."

"Oh, okay."

"And I've probably told him twenty or thirty times and he just blanks out. Poor guy can't process a damn thing past his wiener, I swear."

I laugh, then cross my arms and glance at the frat boys who've occupied the other half of our lane. There is at least ten of them, but only four seem to be changing their shoes. I wonder for a moment who else is on Brant's team, as the only other one who seems to be here is Dmitri. Isn't this supposed to be some kind of tournament or something?

"It all goes down at nine," Dmitri explains to me.

I nod. "And Brant's team is ... where?"

"Who knows. I'm only here to support him. Oh, I forgot about Clayton. All that about Brant calling me a poetry major got me distracted." He starts typing into his phone. "Clay ... ton ... exclamation point ... Where ... the ... hell ... are ... you ... question mark," he narrates as he types. "And *send*. There we go. I bet he'll walk right through the door any second."

CLAYTON

It all starts at the corner store.

I go to pick up some drinks and a couple other things we're out of. I don't want to be presumptuous or assume I'm bringing Dessie back to our place, but just in case we *do* hit it off, I want our apartment to be in a good state and adequately ... equipped.

When I get up to the counter, the clerk asks me a question. I don't catch it, leaning forward to read his lips better. He asks it again, then points at my pile of stuff. Is he asking for my ID? I pull out my wallet and show it to him. The clerk rolls his eyes, then asks me the same damn question. *I don't know what the fuck he's asking.* I point to my ears and shake my head; usually that gives them the message.

And that's when the asshole behind me taps my shoulder with more aggression than you give a person you don't know.

I turn, annoyed. It's some chunky dude in a polo, the russet skin of his face wrinkling as he glares at me under a mess of sandy-brown hair. He's got two buddies with him, each carrying a six-pack. This kid spits a question of his own at me.

And I read his lips perfectly: *"You deaf??"*

No, he's not actually asking me. He's just being a little prick. I turn back to the clerk, ignoring the kid, then pull out my phone to type to the clerk, figuring it the best way to communicate.

The fucker behind me disagrees, grabbing my arm and spinning me around. His face crushed into a scowl, he waves his hands at my phone and spits more words and curses at me. I'm guessing he thinks that I am actually texting some buddy of mine and holding up the line deliberately.

I show my screen to the clerk while glaring at this dude, a second away from pushing a fist through his fucking face. Then, I return my attention to the clerk, whose attitude seems to have changed now that he knows I'm *actually* deaf. Whatever he was concerned with, he seems to not care anymore, ringing up and bagging the items. I pay for the goods, then swipe the bag off the counter.

And on my way out of the store, I push open the door with my back, facing the fucker that was behind me, and give him the finger.

People can be such pricks. Some don't want to see the truth that's right before their eyes; they'd rather see their own truths and live in a world full of things that agree with their own beliefs. No one wants a challenge. No one wants to learn anymore. Once they graduate school, they act like all their learning's over with and, for the rest of their lives, the world has to bend to their limited understanding of it.

The worst part is, I wonder if I would be just as much of a prick as that dude behind me in line was ... had I not lost my hearing. I wasn't a good person as a snotty, fuck-head twelve-year-old. I was selfish. I was greedy. I was dishonest. I had no honor, no sense of justice, and little compassion for others.

And maybe, just maybe if I hadn't lost my hearing and spent my high school years enjoying a lesson in humility, maybe *I'd* be the prick behind someone in line who says, "Hey, dipshit, you deaf?"

Hey, dipshit, you deaf?

Can you hear me?

Listen up, dumbass.

The fuck is wrong with you?

I don't make it halfway home before something blunt and impolite clubs me over the head.

I stumble, the ground turning uneven suddenly and my feet becoming unsure of where to be placed. I turn too slow and watch the bony knuckles of some mystery attacker as they rush forth to marry and divorce my left cheekbone in one clumsy swing.

The pavement is next to meet my face. No matter how many times I blink, I keep seeing stars. It's no joke; when you get hit in the face that hard, all you see is a fucking solar system, and somewhere through that mess of twisted galaxies and unnamed planets, you get flashes of the street you're kissing, barely lit by a setting sun and an unhelpful streetlamp nearby.

I turn onto my back and lift my hands, expecting something else to hit me. When nothing does, I blink twenty more times until I realize there's no one there.

I sit up and turn, catching sight of three figures as they disappear down the street.

Three to one? Hitting me from behind? What a dick move.

Furious suddenly, I scramble to my feet and shout after them, tearing down the road and determined to put my fist through each of their skulls.

But my left leg gives, a wicked cramp working its way into my hip joint, and I tumble over, collapsing and allowing the road itself to punch me yet again. When I try to rise, a whole new family of pain makes a home in my leg.

I shout out, cussing at the dumb fucks. I shout so loud I feel spit on my chin.

All of this shouting. All of this silence.

After some time, my skull reminds itself that I was bashed in the head a few times. Pain lances through my brain, somehow stinging my eyes. I bring a few fingers to my cheek, then pull them back. *Blood.* The fuckers split my cheek open with one lucky hit. He must've been wearing a ring or something.

I take a deep breath and get back to my feet. With a slight limp, I make my way back to the bags I'd abandoned at the spot I was attacked. One of them is toppled, the one with the drinks. Something clearly broke, a stream of dark liquid drawing itself across the pavement like long creepy fingers.

Fucking great.

I'm so pissed. And the more pissed I get, the more my cheek throbs, as if punishing me for my anger. I suck in air, then blow it all out, ignoring the ache that washes over my face.

I take home whatever I can salvage from the bags, the fuckers dripping the whole way. I'm fuming about the incident, refusing to feel sorry for myself or see myself as some victim. *Fuck that.* I keep picturing that prick from the store. *"Are you deaf??"* Even though I didn't get a clear look at any of them, I know it was him and his buddies who attacked me.

They better hope they don't go to Klangburg. If I ever see them on campus, the end of my fist will be the last glorious sight they enjoy before I blind them.

I check myself in the mirror before I leave the apartment, then let out a healthy "Fuck!" as I survey the damage. I wet a washcloth and run it over my face, caring for the wound on my cheek, which is just an inch below my eye. If the fucker hit me just a touch higher, *I'd* have been blinded. I wonder suddenly if I have a concussion. To be honest, I can't say whether it was fist or weapon that hit me first.

I use the washcloth over the back of my head, unsure if I'm bleeding there too. Soon, my whole face is a mess of wetness, and I have a bandage slapped over my cheek, which stings when I apply it. I run a hand through my hair and stare at my reflection, the bitterness and the fury sizzling beneath my eyes.

After I lock up the apartment behind me and make my way down the road, I curse the fact that I forgot to check the condition of my own room. It's probably a fucking mess. I was too occupied cleaning up my face, lost in my boiling anger and picturing a hundred and twenty alternative ways that encounter could've gone—all one hundred and twenty ending with me standing over their bloodied bodies. Still, even wearing my anger as armor, I find myself looking over my shoulder twenty times on the way to the bowling alley. Better safe.

Just before I reach the glass doors, my phone gives a shake in my pocket, startling me. I wince as I reach to grab it, some totally new and annoying ache in my shoulder making itself known. I free the phone and lift the screen to my strained eyes:

DMITRI

Clayton! Where are you?

I sigh, ignoring it since I'm already here. I push my way in, the stench of the place dancing unwelcomed up my nostrils. The guy at the counter waves, then flashes me a number of fingers, his hands opening and closing two times to indicate lane twenty. I give him a nod of thanks, then make my way.

Brant whips around the corner out of nowhere and grabs me for a hug. I snort and wince in pain, caught off-guard by him as he thanks me profusely for coming.

Then his face changes when he gets a good look. *"The fuck happen to you?"* I think he asks. I shrug and wave him off. He grabs my arm, stopping me as I try to move past him. Reeling me around to face him again, he asks, *"You fall down the stairs?"*

I could laugh if I didn't know it'd hurt like fuck. I lick my lips and say, "I'm fine," with my voice sending tremors up my jaw and to my cheek. *Even speech hurts.*

He frowns, then beckons me over with a shake of his head. I follow him to lane twenty where I see the opposing team has set up shop. Through the crowd of them, I catch Dmitri with the rest of what I take to be Brant's team: two Hispanic chicks—who, if I recall, are an on-and-off couple, but no one talks about it—and a computer nerd black dude named Josiah who's a head taller than me and always seems to be smiling.

Dmitri rises from the bench the second he spots me, rushing up to my side. *What happened?* he signs.

I use as few signs as possible: *Nothing. Fell.*

He shakes his head: *You should clean up. Bathroom. You're bleeding through your bandage.*

I huff irritably: *It's not* that *bad.*

Dmitri lifts his eyebrows, which carry his glasses up a bit with them: *Yes, it is. Dessie is in the bathroom. Fix yourself up before she returns.*

The spelling out of her name sobers me at once. Of course she's here already. I'm late. I move my hands: *How long has she been here? How long has she been waiting? Do I really look that bad?*

When Dmitri's eyes avert, I realize I'm too late.

I turn to find Dessie standing there. My god. She gets more beautiful every time I see her. She's wearing some cute white peasant top thing over a pair of jeans that hug her sexy, curvy shape. They hang low on the hips, leading my disobedient eyes straight to them—and my imagination straight to what smooth sexiness resides underneath.

And her pretty face ... it's evident from the subtle makeup and the pink of her lips that she fixed herself up a little for our hanging out tonight. Even with the smog of our regrettable environment, I swear I can smell her through it—lilac and fruit and something else I can't name, something fresh and inviting.

I can't trust myself in a room alone with her. I would rip off that innocent-looking white top and strip down those hot as fuck jeans.

Fuck ... what I'd do to her ... I'd own those lips for longer than just one fleeting moment in a cherry-picker, that's for sure.

So mesmerized by her, I belatedly realize her lips are moving. *"What happened?"* she's asking.

I shake my head, then murmur a word to her.

"What?" she says, leaning in closer.

I guess the place is louder than I realized. I tell her, "It's nothing. I'm fine." But the words rattle my jaw and I wince against the pain.

Dmitri steps in, puts an apologetic hand on Dessie's shoulder, then signs: *Maybe you two should go back to the apartment and hang out. I'll stay and support Brant. You'll have the place to yourself for at least a couple hours, maybe more.*

I feel my face flushing. I don't know if it's because of the attention Dmitri's signing is earning us, or if it's because of the pain, or if it's because he's basically giving me permission to take Dessie back to our place and have ample time ... *alone together.*

He seems to be relaying the message to Dessie, as he leans into her and says something. I feel my heart jerk awake, hopping around inside my ribcage as I wonder frustratedly what he's saying to her.

She gives a shrug in response, then says something back to him. I look at her eyes questioningly. She spreads her hands, then says something to me. I don't quite understand until Dmitri signs: *She said yes. You two can hang at the apartment. It's too loud here.*

Too loud. What a concept.

I lift a brow at her. "You sure?"

Dessie nods, the waves of her long, brown hair dancing when she does, and her cheeks seem to flush the same shade as her beautiful, kissable lips. Fuck.

Behave, Clayton.

Chapter 14
DESSIE

Oh my god. We're going back to his place.

This breaks about ten of the rules I set for myself before agreeing to this whole "innocent hanging out" thing with Clayton Watts.

My hands are sweating.

My mouth has gone so dry, I'm sucking on my tongue.

I can barely put one foot in front of the other without threatening to trip myself on the way down the street to his place, which is apparently a couple blocks over from the *Throng*.

"So ..." I say out of habit as we walk, then shake my head, feeling dumb. It's not like we can talk on the way. *This was such a stupid idea.* When I turn to look at him, however, he seems to have noticed my mouth move. "Sorry." I laugh, feeling dumber. "I, um ... So ... You fell?"

Clayton nods slowly.

"Dmitri told me," I explain, speaking slow. I don't know if he can see my lips in the semidarkness that well. I deliberately time my remarks for when we pass each streetlamp along the road. "And Dmitri said he doesn't believe you."

Clayton chuckles dryly, though he doesn't smile. *He looks in pain.* My heart crushes in.

Even as we walk, he keeps his eyes on me. I get the feeling he's trying not to miss a word of what I'm saying. Instead of feeling self-conscious, I feel oddly touched by the gesture.

"I didn't realize everything was so close," I tell him. "Bowling alley, just down the street from the *Throng*, which is just a block or two from *your* place, which is right across the road from *campus* ..."

He smiles. I'm not sure he got what I said, but I smile back anyway and continue walking alongside him in the quiet. I try to ignore how nervous I am.

We reach his apartment complex. His place on the first floor faces the main road, visible through a tall, wrought iron fence. He pushes a key into the door, then holds it open for me. I walk past him and catch a hint of his cologne. *God, he smells like sex.*

"Thirsty?"

The sound of that one soft, sexy word tickles me, sending chills up my neck. "I could maybe use a little something," I admit after turning around to face him with a muted smile. "Yes," I answer with a nod, just to be more clear. "Whatever you have."

He walks past me, the door shutting loudly at his back, then pulls open the fridge. He turns, lifting a questioning, expectant eyebrow.

A spike of confidence hits me, inspiring me to straighten my back and take one step toward him. "I'll help myself. How about you take a seat on the couch?"

His brows pull together. "Huh?"

I grip his arm—*oh my god, he's so fucking meaty*—and guide him around the kitchen counter to the living room. He stares at me the whole time with questions in his defiant eyes. "As far as bandaging your own wounds," I tell him with a smirk, "you suck at it."

He frowns, his eyes narrowed as I lead him to the couch, letting him sit. I'd almost call those eyes cute if he didn't look so damn dangerous all the time.

"Sit here," I tell him plainly, pretty sure he didn't catch what I was saying on the way to the couch. "I'm going to rebandage your wounds."

"No."

"Yes. But first, a drink." I leave him on the couch with a frustrated expression, helping myself to his fridge and searching for something safe to drink.

My eyes land on the tequila.

I return with the bottle and two shot glasses. He eyes me suspiciously when I set them on the coffee table in front of us. "To relax," I explain to him with an innocent shrug. "Where's your bathroom?"

He meets my eyes late, distracted.

"Bathroom," I repeat.

He points to the hallway by the kitchen. When I enter it, I pull open the medicine cabinet and find a first aid kit. Upon closing it with a bang, I see my face in the mirror. I look so ... tense. Who am I fooling, trying to act like I'm in charge? *I'm about to rebandage Clayton Watts's face. I'm in Clayton Watts's apartment and I'm about to have my hands all over his face.*

I take a deep breath in and blow it out.

When I return to the couch, I find Clayton sitting there with the two shot glasses in his hands, filled. Jaw tightened, he looks up at me with a severe look in his eyes, then offers a glass.

I sit on the coffee table across from him, take the glass, then clink it softly against his. "Bottoms up!"

He kicks his back in one animal gulp. I ... slowly sip mine until it's empty. Holy hell, that shit is strong. I turn my head to cough, my eyes watering instantly. *It's not going to take much,* I realize. *One's enough.*

But by the time I've recovered, he's already poured us seconds.

"Oh." My eyes widen. "I was just—"

"Bottoms up," he says with a smirk, cutting me off, then kicks his second one back.

I give mine one rueful look, then slowly knock it back. Hissing afterward from the back of my throat, I find myself laughing and blinking away the burn. "Wow!" I shout.

When my eyes meet his, I'm instantly sobered. The intensity in his stare reaches deep into me.

Focus, Dessie. I set the shot glass down a skosh too hard. Popping open the little medical supply kit, I fish out a butterfly bandage and a tiny antiseptic wipe.

When I reach to take off his bandage, he recoils. I give him a warning look. His eyes flash challengingly. Is that a snarl on his lips?

When he finally relaxes, I gently peel the bandage off. *Why does this feel like I'm negotiating with some wild beast?* I frown at the ugly gash underneath. I have this strange blessing of having an iron stomach; nothing makes me sick, not the sight of blood, nor vomit, nor even big gaping wounds. Maybe I'm supposed to be a nurse. Maybe I've missed my calling.

"This'll sting a bit," I warn him when I've taken the antiseptic wipe out of its package.

Clayton lifts a confused brow, having missed my words. Then I touch the wipe to his cheek and he hisses, flinching away.

"Clayton!"

He glares at me, then surrenders, relaxing himself back into position and letting me clean the wound.

I wonder if maybe my effort is totally insufficient and he should, in fact, see a doctor or get stitches. I'm no medic. The most of what I know is from movies and plays I've seen, like that one about the nurse in the ER where her love interest dies in the end from rust poisoning.

The thought freezes me. *Let's not kill Clayton.*

"Bandage," I say unnecessarily, applying it.

His eyes haven't left mine, I realize. Suddenly, my confidence crumbles again. Now that I've finished the business of properly bandaging him, I suddenly find I have nothing left for my hands to do.

We're just staring into each other's eyes, and that look of wariness in his has been exchanged for something far more sinister ... something dark and needy ...

Something hungry.

"Thank you," he says suddenly.

The words tickle me somehow, a smile finding my face, perhaps to break the tension. In response, I bring a flat hand to the front of my chin, then let it fall outward—*Thank you*.

Now it's Clayton who smiles. After a second, he repeats the sign back to me, except a little differently.

"Oh." I watch him. "I was doing it wrong?"

He repeats it again.

I mimic the gesture back to him.

"No," he says, then takes my hand.

The touch of his fingers running over mine sends electricity up my spine, touching the hairs on the back of my neck.

"This," he murmurs so quietly, it's hardly a word at all.

He brings my hand to his chin, slowly, then directs my hand outward, demonstrating the sign using my own hand. Even when he's done, he doesn't let go.

"I swear, that's what I'm doing," I tell him, my heart racing so fast, so potently, Clayton *has* to feel my pulse in my fingertips.

"Again," he orders.

Instead of signing it, I take the fingers of his left hand and bring them to my chin.

Then, I bring them a bit higher, touching them to my lips.

His eyes lock onto mine. Oops. Have I awakened the beast?

Not yet. I part my lips, letting one of his fingers slip inside. It tastes salty. His skin is rougher than I expected, too. Seeing his reaction makes my heart race even more, how *his* lips part and an unblinking look of shock takes over his face, paralyzing him.

I gently nibble on his fingertip, staring at his dark eyes challengingly.

A growl, deep and wolf-like, escapes his lips like a warning.

A warning I don't heed.

Then in one swift, powerful movement, he grabs my wrist with that hand I was tasting. I gasp, but I don't stop him. *I welcome him.*

He jerks me forward, and our lips collide, catching one another's clumsily, then locking.

His breath bathes my cheek, jagged and furious.

A hand reaches behind my head, tangling itself in my hair there and trapping me in place, holding me against his kiss. My arms are caught between our heavily-breathing bodies. I'm a prisoner to his mouth, and I'm not going anywhere.

Oh my god, he's so strong and dominant when he kisses me. I have never felt anything more powerful. The way his lips make work of mine, it's so like eating your favorite dessert that you have craved and been denied for so long. The power of his jaw alone ...

And then his tongue ... The taste throws me out of my mind, how perfect it is, how inviting he is ...

My trapped hands find his chest. He is so firm and smooth that even through the tight shirt, I feel every ripple of muscle on his sinewy body, especially as they flex in his effort to destroy my mouth with his kiss. He is a mountain of meat and fury, and I want to explore every inch.

My fingers graze over his nipples daringly.

He moans in response, bucking under my touch.

Then his big hands grip me at the hips and, in one powerful thrust, he pulls me off the coffee table and throws me to the couch. I gasp against his kiss just as he pulls away, his animal eyes observing mine.

Is he asking permission?

Clayton Watts, you have it.

As if I need more convincing, he straddles me, then grips the bottom of his shirt. *Oh god.* He slowly tugs, sliding the material up his torso and giving me a show. Inch by inch, I'm exposed to a spread of abs—yes, there's six of them, the whole sexy pack is there—and then his two hills for pecs that are simply perfect. The tattoo that crawls up his neck also crawls down his chest in a thorny nest of ink that makes him look exotic and dangerous.

He casts the shirt to the side, and the sight of a shirtless Clayton atop me is too much to behold. This kind of stuff doesn't happen to me. This isn't real.

His slender, dimpled hips disappear down into his loose-fitting jeans, drawn tight over the meat of his big thighs, which trap me in place on the couch.

I am utterly pinned and totally at his mercy.

Then he bends down and nibbles on my neck, sending shivers of joy up and down my body as I squirm against him in pleasure.

The weight of his body presses down on mine, nearly taking the air out of me. I'm so dizzy with what he's doing to my neck that I hardly notice. In fact, I welcome it, clinging to him in an animal effort to somehow fuse our bodies together.

Pressed against him, I experience a split second of wondering if we're moving too fast.

The next split second, I'm crying out, "*Oh my god!*"

Clayton's worked his way up to my ear, his tongue tracing my jawline. When he reaches my mouth again, the animals are reunited and I throw my arms around his shoulders, crushing his face into mine.

"Dessie," he whispers when he pulls away for one fleeting breath.

"Clayton," I agree to nothing in particular, each of our breaths blasting against the other's face, before plunging our mouths back together.

Our lips locked, he lifts his chest and runs his hands down the length of my body until they reach my hips. His fingers tease under my top, tickling the sensitive skin there.

Oh god.

Slowly, cruelly, his mischievous fingers work their way back up, taking my top with it.

I sit up for one moment.

My top's gone the next.

His face hovers over me as his hand trails down from the top of my lace bra to my exposed stomach, then traces the waistline of my jeans, flirting with the buttons. I feel a quiver of anticipation below. My legs squeeze together and I feel a jolt of excitement.

"Wait."

Clayton saw my lips move. He lifts his eyebrows, breathing heavily.

"Wait," I repeat, placing a hand on his warm, bare chest. "Wait, wait, wait."

He obeys, his dark eyes locked on me and waiting, for whatever reason, he doesn't yet know. The only sound in the room is our erratic breathing. I watch my hand rise and fall as his chest does with his every breath. His body is so perfect, I can't even compare it to anything or anyone. The shape of his pecs, the definition of his abs, the subtle ripples of muscle that work down his sides, his artful tattoo ... There's just too much for my eyes to drink in all at once.

"Too fast?" he breathes.

I nod once, warily looking into his eyes.

What I see isn't frustration. In fact, he seems to agree, like a thought or two has worked through his brain. He holds himself up with a hand pressed into the cushion on either side of my head, his face over mine as we each catch our breath.

His lips twist into a smirk. "Can't handle me?"

I laugh, despite our circumstance. "You are a lot to handle."

He pulls away, giving me room to sit up. I fetch my top from the floor and slip it back on. It doesn't escape my attention that Clayton watches my every move. At some point, he had managed to undo the top button of my jeans, so I fix them up as well.

I give him a smirk of my own. "Quit staring."

He shrugs. "I like what I see."

After a moment of staring into his eyes, feeling oddly powerful, I grab his shirt and throw it at him. He catches the sleeve with his teeth, biting it like a dog and growling at me.

I can't help but laugh.

Clayton holds up the shirt. "Put this back on?" I nod in response. "That's a first," he says teasingly.

I love the way his teeth, tongue, and lips form the word "first", a hint of Texan accent in it and the "s" muffled slightly.

"Well, unless you want me to hold a conversation with your *chest* ..." I tease him.

He throws an arm over the back of the couch, the shirt dropped to his lap and forgotten.

I sigh with pleasure, unsure if he heard me or not. My eyes are helplessly glued to his muscles. "Fine," I say breathily. There are worse things I've been subjected to. "You going to tell me how you got that thing on your face?"

Clayton's forehead screws up. I assume he didn't catch what I said, so I indicate my own cheek, then point at his expectantly.

He sighs and looks away, biting his lip. I slap the couch, drawing his attention back. "I know you didn't just ... 'fall'."

He shakes his head no, confirming my suspicion.

"So?" I prompt him.

It seems to take a measure of effort for him to even think about it, which casts a lightning bolt of worry through me. Finally, he pulls his phone out, taps a bit on it, then shows me the screen:

Some punk assholes from the corner store
followed me out n jumped me.

"Oh my god!" I blurt out as I read it. "Why??"

"Bad attitude," he answers quietly. "Dumb." He shrugs, all the muscles of his shoulders moving with him. His eyes linger on my lips.

I remind myself that he's staring at my lips for the functional purpose of grasping what I'm saying and urge myself not to be so damned turned on by it.

"You don't like to talk much," I observe, though I meant it as a question.

His eyes detach from mine, caught in a thought. Then, with a short sigh I'm not sure he meant for me to hear, he types into his phone again. I watch his face work through a bunch of different word choices as he struggles with how to say whatever it is he's typing. With a pinch of reluctance, he shows me the screen:

I've always been weird about talking out loud
since I can't hear myself.
Been this way since I lost my hearing :/

I nod slowly, then take his phone from him, earning a snort of protest as I delete what he typed and write my own message. I reveal the screen:

I like what you sound like. Not that you need
any more boosts to your insufferably large ego.

He grins, and half a laugh escapes his lips, all his pearly whites shining. He meets my eyes with his head still tilted down to the screen, his forehead scrunched up in an adorable way.

"I like what you sound like," I repeat, shrugging.

His eyes harden. "I ... wish I could hear what *you* sound like."

"My voice is pretty boring," I assure him. "You're not missing much."

"I doubt that." His eyes brush over my face, a hint of curiosity in them. He reaches for the tequila and pours two more shots. When he offers me one, I shake my head and gently push it away. To that, he shrugs and downs them both, one at a time. His face visibly loosens, his eyes turning watery. "There's a lot about you I'd like to learn, Dessie."

I put an arm over the back of the couch. Utterly incapable of enforcing discipline on my hands, I find myself curious about his tattoo. The moment my finger touches his neck, he seems to freeze in place, staring into my eyes intensely as I observe his ink, tracing the shape.

"Why the tattoo?" I mouth to him, hardly using my voice.

"Mmm." He gives it some thought. "Tattoo," he mumbles, his mind seeming to go somewhere far away. "Had to watch my back all through high school. When I turned eighteen, I ... I decided I wanted to look like a bad-ass no one should fuck with. So I ... wanted to ..." He sighs and takes his phone out of my lap, typing into it as I continue to trace the ink on his neck. I wonder what that's doing to him, if anything.

Then, he shows me the screen:

Ur finger is driving me nuts

I grin. He glares at me playfully, but I see the tightness in his jaw. *I might be waking the beast again.*

My finger reaches his earlobe. I study it curiously and find my mind arriving at a question I'd wanted to ask for quite a while, the most obvious question.

"How long have you been deaf?"

He squints at me, the humor in his eyes traded quickly for solemnity. I wonder if he understood the question, due to his lack of response. I let go of his ear and take the phone back, typing into it:

How long have you been deaf?

He hardly looks at the screen before he murmurs, "Since I was twelve."

"How?"

"Measles." He mumbles the word so bitterly that I almost miss what he says. "It spread to my ears, shitty parents, lack of medical treatment, lucky to be alive, blah, blah."

The sensitive topic seems to have brought him to a dark place. Maybe it was that *and* the tattoo. I regret ruining the mood, if that's what I just did.

"Sorry," I murmur. "I was ... I was just curious."

"It's okay." He takes a quick breath, his eyes not leaving my face. Then he forces a smile. "Touch me all you want. Another drink?" He reaches for the bottle.

"No," I say at once.

He freezes, studying my face. "You sure?"

A flutter rushes through my stomach. For some reason, I find myself thinking of all the warnings people have been giving me. Is Clayton trying to get me drunk so he can continue having his way with me? Am I just tonight's girl, and tomorrow there will be someone else on this couch being talked out of her clothes? His roommate Brant nearly slipped, laughing at the idea of Clayton ever settling down with one woman. Is that because he sees all the tail Clayton catches?

Am I an idiot for staying here, entertaining some idea of a relationship with him?

"What's wrong?" he asks softly. He obviously reads the tension in my face. He's remarkably observant, even when buzzed.

I type another message, then show it:

So you said there's a lot about me
you want to learn? Like what?

He studies my eyes long and hard. After a second, he reaches and gently takes a tangle of my hair, then brings it to his face demonstratively and sniffs. "Like what shampoo you use," he moans.

I slap his hand away and laugh.

He looks at me. A brief moment of gravity hardens his face, and then he reaches for the tequila. "I'm gonna need another," he says without looking at me.

I touch his wrist, then pinch the fingers of my other hand in the air twice by his face, sort of like the universal gesture to indicate a person talking.

He squints at my hand, reading the sign. "No?"

"Too much," I say, to which he snorts. "I don't want you falling asleep on me."

He lifts a brow. "You want me to sleep with you?"

"That's not what I said!" I know he's teasing me, but he stares at me as if that's really what I asked him. I make the pinching sign again—*No*. "Am I doing that right?" I murmur, repeating the sign by pinching two fingers against my thumb twice.

A devilish smirk crosses his face. "Isn't this how we got into trouble earlier? Sign language lessons?"

I blush, then lean back on the couch, crossing my arms. He laughs, then pours himself a single shot. After giving me a quick, daring look, he downs it. His eyes turn to water and he slams the glass down on the table too hard and hoots. He wipes his mouth with the back of a wrist, connecting his eyes to mine as he leans back into the couch himself.

Then, he asks, "So why Texas?"

I shrug. "It looked like a good Theatre program."

He doesn't seem to be looking at my lips. He leans the side of his face into the couch, inclined toward me with his hands in his lap and his dark eyes zeroed in on mine. The way he watches me, I feel like he's penetrating right into my thoughts. I lay the side of my own head against the couch too, mirroring him and gazing at him.

Then, in a moment that's so fast it startles me, he swipes the phone out of my grip, types on it, then shines the screen at me:

> What was so bad in New York City
> that u had to run all the way down here?

His question makes me sit up, as if the words on the screen hit my face. I can hear Claudio screaming again. I see my sister's disapproving look. I picture my mother filling another damn glass of chardonnay and ignoring me. I imagine the empty rows of seats in the theater, dreading the day they would be filled.

Then I think about the knot in my stomach that's there because of the secret I'm keeping. The secret I've kept from every single person I've met so far. How can I make any real friends here if I can't even be honest with any of them? I'm a liar. I was a liar the moment I stepped foot on campus.

Clayton is something of an outcast too, if even a hair of the rumors are true. We are both, in our own ways, running away from what people think—or *could* think—of us. I feel like there's so much more about us that's alike than I expected. I feel oddly safe.

"I want to tell you something," I murmur, my eyes averted, "but ... you can't tell anyone."

"Can't tell anyone?" he asks, to be sure that's what I said.

I meet his eyes sternly. "Yes. A secret."

"Secret," he echoes, his own eyes turning severe.

I press my lips together, then take his phone from his lap again. I type it all out. I mention my parents and who they are. I type that I got here because my dad knew someone in the department and pulled a string. I type that I feel embarrassed by it, that all I wanted was a normal college experience, no special treatment. I didn't want anyone to know who my family was. After typing it out, I stare at the message for a solid minute, debating whether or not to delete the whole thing and not show him the screen.

Then, after a deep sigh, I clench shut my eyes and hand the phone back to him, looking away.

I dread his reaction so much. I don't know why, but I feel like this little factoid about me could ruin everything. Sure, he wanted to know more about me, but maybe he'll change his mind now. That, or things will start to get weird.

After too long a moment, I dare to open my eyes, peering at him. He seems to either still be reading, or rereading my mini-novel. After a second, he looks up, letting the phone drop to his lap.

"I'm sorry," I blurt right away. "I wasn't trying to lie to anyone. I just wanted to start fresh. I just—"

"Start fresh," he echoes in a slurred murmur. "I wish ... I wish I could start fresh."

His words fall on the ears of all those misgivings inside me, rousing them. What isn't Clayton telling me? What life, if any, do all those stupid rumors have? Why won't anyone be upfront with me, least of all Clayton himself? I wish he would just volunteer the information, the same way I just did. *Please, Clayton, don't make me drag it out of you.*

"I won't tell anyone," he says to me, his dark eyes locking with my worried ones. "Our secret." Then he makes a fist and taps the thumb-side of it to his lips twice.

I repeat the sign back to him. "Secret?" I murmur.

"Secret," he confirms.

I smile appreciatively, despite the worry that's still doing somersaults in my belly.

"So," he mumbles, "you're ... famous?"

I snort. "My mother is. Maybe my sister someday. Not me. I'm nothing. I'm nobody."

"No," he says, frowning. "You're Dessie Lebeau."

"Desdemona," I say, overpronouncing the name. "That's my full name."

"*Desermona,*" he repeats slowly, though the word is shapeless in his mouth, the vowels bleeding together.

I type it quickly into his phone, then show it to him. "Desdemona," I repeat when his eyes return to my lips. "Shakespeare's Desdemona. From *Othello*."

"Shakespeare, right," he says, following.

"They named my sister Celia," I go on. "You know, after Shakespeare's *As You Like It*. So she's named after a woman who falls in love and has a happy ending, and I'm named after a woman who's smothered to death with a pillow. But, you know, of course I am."

Though his eyes hover at my lips, I get the feeling he didn't catch all that. He seems to be getting sleepy, or else the alcohol's doing its number on him. The way he studies my lips, it makes me feel like he wants to kiss me again.

I'm one hundred percent positive that I would let him, and one hundred percent positive that it would lead to a second round of couch-wrestling that I'm quite sure I wouldn't have the strength to resist.

"I should go," I murmur to him.

At my words, the tiniest pinch of frustration runs across his face. Then, he lifts his head and says, "You sure?"

"It's late," I say, not bothering with checking the time; I'm sure it's hardly even eleven o'clock yet. "I have lines to learn before Monday. Like, a lot of them."

He doesn't seem to follow what I'm saying. Now, the frustration in his face seems far less easy to hide. The alcohol is betraying him, showing all those truer feelings that he keeps trying to keep out of my view.

"I gotta go," I repeat.

"Don't go," he mumbles, hardly intelligible.

"Sorry." I push myself off the couch.

He's on his feet as fast as I am, though his knee hits the coffee table in his effort of getting up and the shot glasses clatter loudly. "You sure?"

That would be his second time asking. And no, I'm *not* sure. In fact, I *do* want to stay. I want to tackle him to the floor as well. I want to eat this man alive.

"Yes," I say instead.

"Can I walk you back to your dorm?" he murmurs suddenly, his voice strained.

Between him getting jumped today and Victoria's warning my first day here, I give him a quick nod, and that seems to wash away all the frustration in his eyes.

We cross the campus in silence. No ninjas jump out from behind bushes, and no ski-mask-wearing thugs emerge from around corners with guns. I was reluctant for a moment before we left his apartment, judging whether or not he was drunk or just "a little buzzed", but as we stroll across the disconcertingly unpopulated campus at night, I find myself incredibly thankful to have him walking by my side. I couldn't have a better escort than Clayton Watts, who does not look like someone you would want to mess with.

We reach the Quad too soon. I wish the walk had lasted for hours.

I pull out my phone and type out a message, then aim the too-bright screen at him, causing his eyes to squint as he reads it:

Thanks for escorting me, Clayton.

He scowls at me after reading, then plucks the phone right out of my hands and types on it for quite a while. I'm about to ask what's taking so long when he finally hands the phone back to me. I read:

I gave you my number and took yours.
Hope that's OK. Text me sometime?

I feel my heart lift up into my throat. I can't fight the dumb grin that happens on my face. I nod at him with a bit more enthusiasm than I intend.

"Good night, Dessie," he murmurs, giving me the gift of his soft, velvety voice.

"Good night, Clayton," I return, giving him the gift of my moving lips in silence, then slip into West Hall, the doors slamming behind me with a big *boom*.

Chapter 15
DESSIE

I texted him to make sure he made it back safe.

When my phone buzzed with his reply, I giggled and cuddled the phone on my bed like a dumb, crush-obsessed teenager. The script for *Our Town* was long forgotten for the rest of the night as Clayton and I texted back and forth until one in the morning.

I learned what his favorite food is (teriyaki ribs), the name of his high school (Yellow Mills High), how horrible he is at math, that he's an only child, how his mom's a chain smoker and his dad's a sex addict and somehow against all odds they're still together, and how he had to take two semesters off because he couldn't pay tuition during "a rough time" and that's why he's only starting his third year when he should be graduating this year.

I also got a detailed description of how he'd light the stage if he was given the chance for *Our Town*, with a clever idea or two for how he pictures the funeral and graveyard scene to look in the third and final act of the play. I grinned stupidly for hours and, lost in a digital world full of Clayton, already couldn't wait until the next time I would get to see him.

When Sunday came, I had a quiet breakfast with Sam, who was all aflutter (read: almost undetectably less deadpan than usual) about a music composition project she's been assigned by her Theory prof. I congratulated her absentmindedly, wondering how long I should wait before texting Clayton again.

It was in the afternoon that I finally caved and sent him a text. The phone rested on my lap while I studied *Our Town* on a bench by the Art building, memorizing Emily's lines distractedly while shooting glances down at my lap to see if he'd responded yet.

He never did.

I went to sleep that night with a scowl on my face. Sam had gotten some cheap composition software for her ancient laptop and wanted my opinion on a song as I was lying in bed trying to go to sleep, and I pretended not to hear her, turned away toward the wall and staring at the blank screen of my phone, waiting for a reply that never came.

So after a miserable Sunday like that, why would I expect Monday to bring me anything good?

On my way into acting class, I see Victoria. She stands in front of the box office chatting with Eric at the window. They draw silent at my arrival. My stomach dances in the bad way at the sight of her. It's the first time I've really seen her since the cast list was posted. How she's managed to avoid me for this long is a total mystery, considering she lives directly across the hall from me.

"Hello," she says coolly.

Between Clayton not answering my texts from yesterday and my own inner frustrations, I find myself in a state of having little to no patience. "Victoria."

"Desdemona Lebeau," she murmurs, crossing her tiny arms and tilting her head. "Daughter of Winona Lebeau, Broadway star and film actor, and Geoffrey Lebeau, world-renowned lighting designer."

My heart stops. "Listen ..." I try to say.

"It's called Google, honey." Victoria scoffs at me, shaking her head. "Unless you're about to proclaim that there's actually *two* Desdemona Lebeaus—"

"Please," I beg her and Eric, rushing up to the window. "I didn't mean to lie to anyone. I just didn't want to be given any ... special treatment, or ... Listen, I just want to be another normal student, just like you guys, and—"

"Ugh, I feel so *normal*," groans Victoria mockingly. "Don't you feel that, Eric? Don't you feel that sting of *normalcy*? Gosh, we're so bloody *normal*."

"Don't tell anyone," I beg her anyway, despite how quickly all trace of hope for her to respect my wishes is evaporating. "Please, Victoria ... Eric ..."

"Who would I tell? Who would care? You think we have nothing better to do with our days than sit around and talk about The Dessie From New York?" Victoria smirks. "Get over yourself. I have an audition at a community theater in-town tomorrow and an audition for Freddie's play in November. I'm an *actor* and a *big girl*, Desdemona. When I don't get cast, I get over it and move on. It's an actor's life."

Her words do their intended job of pummeling me in the stomach. It isn't lost on me that she's calling me by my full name deliberately. That almost bothers me more than anything she's already said.

Also, it hardly sounds like she's moved on. "I'm sorry for lying to you. To both of you. I really am. Victoria, you were the first person I met here. Please, don't let this ruin our—"

"I'll see you later, Eric," she says, turning to him at the window. "Lunch, maybe?"

He smiles tiredly, but it looks more like a grimace.

Then, Victoria saunters off, departing through the front glass doors. When I look back at the window, Eric's on the box office phone helping a customer, his eyes going everywhere except to me.

What a lovely start to a lovely day.

I text Clayton while I have lunch with Sam sitting across from me in the UC food court. I've already dumped all my frustrations on Sam, subjecting her to all my worries as of late, from Clayton's refusal to answer my texts, to Victoria's complete one-eighty (sans the whole who-I-really-am thing), to the fact that rehearsals start tonight for *Our Town* and I am still swimming in fractures of lines that I do *not* have memorized. Not to mention a voice class routine I need to have ready to perform by tomorrow. Or a Thai Chi group-thing for my movement class I'm assigned to do Thursday. All the stress has me passing a banana and another half of a sandwich off to Sam, insisting I can't eat it and meaning it this time.

When I finally get to the rehearsal room at six, my stomach feels hollowed out. I sleepwalk through the most of it, watching listlessly as the Stage Manager character is given the blocking for the opening scene—which basically means he's told where to stand and who to direct his lines to and so on.

For a solid hour, I wonder what the hell I'm doing here. I stare at the screen of my phone and consider all the logical reasons for why he's not responding.

I didn't have sex with him. I put on the brakes.

He's bored with me. He's moved on to some pretty chick he met in a math class, a chick who's tutoring him and showing him exactly how to solve for X.

He drowned himself in three more bottles of tequila and slept all day Sunday and simply missed my messages.

He made a sudden career change and he's an astronaut now. I'll find him on the news walking the surface of Venus and insisting that it's totally not as hot as scientists say, his flesh boiling and his hair bursting into flames.

Then the voice of Nina cuts through all the turmoil of my head. "Desdemona."

I lift my eyes from the screen. Every actor in the room is staring at me. I've missed something.

"Yes?" I say in a nearly inaudible choke, yet the word still carries perfectly in the dense silence.

"Care to join us for this scene?" Nina's patient voice rings through the room like a spear made of ice and stinging resentment, skewering me to the spot.

I swallow hard. "Yes, of course. Sorry. Yes."

The script drops from my fumbling hand. I shove my phone away and pick up the script off the floor, thumbing through until I get to my first scene.

"Stage left," she dictates.

I move, taking my place at where I guess to be the approximate entrance.

"Your other left."

"Sorry." I walk across to the other side of the room, my every footstep slamming against my ears. I feel the weight of every pair of eyes on me. Suddenly, I catch myself wondering if Victoria's told anyone else what she discovered. Am I being paranoid? How many people in this room know who I really am?

The rehearsal goes as rigidly and as horribly as I would have ever expected it to, regardless of mood. Every line I say is stiff and emotionless. Every place I walk to on the stage feels uncomfortable. I ask Nina to repeat her directions, feeling stupider each time I do. The cold, patient, half-lidded stare she gives me my whole time onstage makes me feel an inch tall.

Rehearsal ends at ten and I can't pack my things fast enough. When I throw my bag over a shoulder to go, a shadow drops over me. I look up to find Eric.

"You look tense," he notes with a grimace.

I sigh, leaning against the wall. As most everyone else has left and it's only us and a couple of stragglers chatting at the other end of the room, I drop my bag back down on the ground and blurt out, "I suck."

"Well ..."

"I suck so much, Eric." I let it all out, exploding with every ounce of frustration these past couple days have packed into me. "Nina *hates* me. Ugh."

"Nina cast you. She doesn't hate you."

"And Victoria hates me. And *you* hate me."

"No, no. I am *not* Victoria," he tells me, wagging a finger in my face. "We are very separate people."

"You didn't say anything when she went off on me in front of the box office," I point out. "I just figured you agreed with her and—"

"Victoria's ... touchy. She's always been like that. Don't think about her. And as for your sucking," he goes on, "*everyone* sucks in rehearsal. That's the point of rehearsal. The point is to suck. Did you even *hear* the Stage Manager's twenty-thousand opening lines? He sounded like a cucumber with a mouth. So suck away, Dessie. Suck lots. Now is the time to suck."

I try to sigh, but it turns into a chuckle. "Is that what this is, then? *Our Suck?*"

"*Suck Town*," he agrees.

I pull my phone up to my face. Nothing. "Maybe I'm also letting a little ... something else ... get to me."

"Wanna spill about boys at the *Throng* together?"

"Eric, I'm exhausted."

"Me too, and I have an early morning class. But we're still going to the *Throng*."

"Ugh. We are?"

Twenty-five minutes later, Eric and I are sharing that same booth near the tiny circular stage at the *Throng & Song*. Being a Monday night, it's far less noisy than it was before. The same musicians are playing—that sexy guitarist Victoria's obsessed with and his piano sidekick—while Eric and I vent over our respective boy troubles.

"So I told him, 'Listen, I'm not into anal,'" Eric goes on, "and he called me a 'gay anomaly' and said I needed to give it up or else give *him* up. Who the hell makes an ultimatum like that?"

"And here I am," I say, spilling my problem at the same time he's spilling his, "waiting on texts from him after we had an *amazing* night Saturday ... I mean, what the hell? It went well. It ended well. And now I'm staring at my phone like some lovesick—"

"I wouldn't put up with that for a *second*," Eric spits back. "Do you even know how many guys have asked me if you're single? Guys that I wished played for *my* team? You lucky bitch."

"The only one I want is him," I complain, mashing my face into my hands and sulking.

"Hey, you."

The voice echoes through the room, startling Eric and I out of our conversation. I glance to the side and notice the musician staring at me, his guitar resting in his lap and the microphone bent to his mouth.

"Yeah, you," he says, grinning. "I remember you. Full of the feels. You got any new music for us?"

Eric and I share a look before I turn back to the musician. "I'm not really a singer."

"The hell you aren't," he spits back, half his face shadowed by the beige bowler hat he's got on. "You got a pretty set of cords on you."

"No, really," I say after sharing an amused chuckle with Eric, "it's just a hobby. I'm more of a sing-in-the-shower type of gal."

Gal. Listen to me, sounding all Texan already.

"Come on, girl. I know you got some tunes in you. Don't hold out on me." The guitarist smacks a chord on his guitar for punctuation, inspiring a couple cheers of encouragement from somewhere in the back of the room. "We all got some blues in us we gotta get out. Some feels. Some pain. Don't you want to get that pain out of you?"

I take a breath. "Well, when you put it like that."

A moment later, the guitarist scoots over and I stand in front of the microphone, facing an audience that's one tenth the size I had before—an intimate crowd, far more preferable.

Though Clayton is clearly not here, I pretend to see his face, focusing on an empty table in the middle of the room. Then the song comes, some new thing I've played with in my head, and I let it all out to that empty table while the musicians improvise, following my lead. No rehearsing. No judgmental stares. I just open my heart to the room and let the music go.

On the last note of my song, my phone, quiet as a fly, buzzes.

CLAYTON

I stare at the text I just sent her.

My insides shiver. Every nerve in my body is all knotted up and shit.

Brant and Dmitri play Xbox on either side of me, sandwiching me on our couch, and I feel every shift and jerk and annoying jump of their bodies.

I take another long swig from my beer, then stare at the phone intently, desperate for a response.

Dmitri taps my arm and I ignore him. He tries to get his hands in my face, signing: *You want to take a turn? I need a break.* But the last thing I feel like doing is playing more Xbox against Brant; he's a fucking prodigy at gaming and no one ever stands a chance.

Sunday was such a mess. Monday was no better. I knew I shouldn't have let a girl do this to me. How many times did I warn myself?

That's my best and worst quality: I never learn.

But Brant and Dmitri kept pushing me at her, as if they know what's best for me. If they knew anything at all, they'd mind their own fucking business and let me suffer in peace.

I decide to text her again. I'll text her until I get a damn response.

Over the course of the next hour, Brant goes off to bowl, which I learn through a few rushed signs from Dmitri after he gives up playing Xbox and tells me he has a short story due tomorrow that he needs to finish, then closes himself off in his room to jerk off; even without ears, I know what the fuck he's really doing in there.

Or maybe I don't know anything. Maybe I made a huge mistake by blowing Dessie off.

But when I woke up Sunday, reality had sat on my chest and made me its bitch. It wasn't just the mild sting of a hangover; it was the feeling like I'd just woken up from an amazing dream that I couldn't climb back into. I felt frustrated, lost, and obsessed.

I still feel frustrated, lost, and obsessed.

Suddenly I'm seventeen again and being laughed at by Lacy Torrington in the cafeteria when I tried to ask her to the homecoming dance. The dude she went with, some wrestling captain dickhead named Jerry, confronted me in the hall after fifth period. I couldn't understand what he was saying, but judging from the laughing faces that surrounded me in the hallway, he wasn't complimenting my shoes. The confrontation ended with a coach pulling me off of Jerry's bloodied, sputtering face. The hall wasn't laughing anymore.

The interpreter in the principal's office gave me all of Principal Harris's words in a bunch of hand-shapes and finger wiggles that my parents were hearing. He tells my parents that I have an anger problem and they should consider routine counseling for me. I watch as the interpreter gives me my parents' reply, my mom groaning about how the fuck they're going to pay for something like that, and my dad pointing a finger at the principal, asking him what the hell he plans to do about Jerry and the other assholes who pick on his disabled son for being hard of hearing.

No matter how many times I tell my dad that "hard of hearing" isn't the correct term and that I am, in fact, completely fucking deaf, he never learns.

But maybe that's where I get it from. I never learn. My dad's fucked enough random women during his marriage to give me seven hundred siblings. Every time he'd get caught in public going somewhere weird or playing peeping-tom at the pool or doing fuck-knows out in the city until three in the morning, he'd come home and give my mom the same remorseful rhetoric he'd given her since I was ten, and I'd be standing in my little Spiderman PJs in the hallway when they thought I was asleep, hearing every damn word.

He never learns. I never learn.

The next week, I was snuck up on by some idiot I didn't even know during gym class who thought he'd make a joke out of me. I made a funnier one out of him when I slammed his face into the locker.

I clench shut my eyes, remembering the dazed, glassy look in his eyes when metal met skull.

I was not a monster. I felt remorse. I felt the pain of every fucker I beat up. I felt their pain because I could feel a little bit of my own leaving me with every swing, kick, and bloody nose. Still, no matter how many dumb kids I beat up, no matter if it was them provoking me or vice versa, the pain never went away.

Why is he so angry? This was the lovely question the principal had for my mom and dad. *We need to get to the bottom of this. Clayton's been suspended twice. I really don't want to expel him.*

The interpreter, some twenty-something college babe, looked sadder and sadder each time we had one of these meetings. She shifted so much in her seat. I would stare at her moving hands, watching her sharp green eyes, watching her cross and uncross those long, slender legs of hers.

Do you have anything to say for yourself? I watch the interpreter's smooth fingers, signing for the principal.

In response, I signed to her: *Want to fuck in the supply closet after this shit is over?*

She swallowed hard, slowly faced Principal Harris, then said: *"He says he's very sorry."*

An hour later, I showed the interpreter just how sorry I was by ramming her against a rack of shrink-wrapped sponges, scouring rags, and mop-heads, my jeans at my ankles and her skirt hiked halfway up her shuddering, porcelain back.

I am my father's son.

Out of nowhere, Brant comes around the couch, the sight of him pulling me mercifully out of Yellow Mills High. I look up at him, confused. *"Forgot my lucky glove,"* he mouths, swiping it off the coffee table. He freezes, noting the expression on my face, if I had to guess. *"You alright?"* he asks, his brow furrowing.

I shake my head no.

Brant abandons his lucky bowling glove like it means nothing to him, plopping down on the couch. *"What's going on?"* he asks.

"Dessie," I mumble.

He swipes my phone away and types:

Didn't you bang her the other night?

I snort and grab my phone back, then shake my head no. "We talked," I mumble sourly. "It was good."

"Good??" he asks, not caring to mask his disbelief.

To him, a night of sitting on the couch with a hot girl like Dessie and just ... *talking* ... is probably the most boring thing he's ever heard.

"I'm tired of ..." I start to say, then swallow my words. Something about remembering all the kids I've beaten up, all the girls I've dicked around with, all the mistakes of my parents I've blindly—or perhaps even freely—repeated ... I feel so shitty suddenly.

Brant waves his hand, urging me to go on, his bright blue eyes flashing at me with urgency.

I try again, but with a different tack. "That anger problem my dad says won't go away. My inner demon. My bitterness. I'm so tired of using it to ... to just keep all the ... to keep girls away, or ..."

Brant slaps a hand on my shoulder, which shuts me up. He leans in and says something I don't catch.

So I ignore the words and push on. "But I'm afraid I can't help it. I feel like I piss on everything I care about. And I barely know her. We just started getting to know each other, but I feel ... I feel like ..."

Brant moves his lips again. *"You're talking a lot,"* I think he says.

I am. I meet Brant's eyes, realizing that he's one of the only things that kept me sane during all of my worst years. Between those visits to the principal's office, there was Brant throwing his arm over my back. Brant, telling people to fuck off. Brant, my pair of ears when I had none. Brant snuck into my house while I was suspended, even skipping a day to spend it with me behind my parents' backs. Brant may very well be the reason I'm still alive.

If I didn't have him in my life ...

"I want ... I want to talk more," I push out. "I have a ... I have a fucking voice."

"You have a fucking voice!" he repeats back, a smile spreading across his face as he grips my shoulders and shakes me.

Dmitri pokes his head out of his room, shirtless and sweaty. He signs at me: *What the fuck about a voice?*

"Nothing," I say back to him, pushing the words out despite my discomfort. "Just that I have one."

Dmitri squints, confused, then signs: *Oh.*

I smirk. "You can go back to jerking off, Dmitri."

He flips me the finger, then shuts his door.

Brant slaps my thigh, bringing my attention back, and he tells me I'm not going to hurt her. Or maybe he's trying to convince me that I won't. *"You don't piss on everything you care about,"* he tells me, mouthing the words so distinctly, it looks like he's shouting. Maybe he is. *"Now message her and go get some dinner!"*

I shake my phone. "I did. She won't answer."

Brant pats my leg, then flips on the TV and grabs an Xbox controller. I stare at him quizzically. He lifts a brow at me when he notices. *"What?"*

"Your bowling thing," I mumble at him.

"Fuck it," he says, then adds something about the team being doomed because the lesbians are going through something and are gonna break up any day. Or maybe that's not what he said at all. He shrugs, then mentions something about catching one of them giving him *"the eyes"* and how he's pretty sure she goes both ways. *"And also, I want to be here for you when Dessie answers,"* he says, nudging my phone with his elbow. Then, he faces the TV and starts playing.

I grab the other controller. When Brant notices, a grin spreads across his face.

"Oh, it's going down," he says, his teeth flashing.

CLAYTON

An email from Dr. Thwaite puts some extra speed to my getting-ready routine early Tuesday morning.

Mr. Kellen Michael Wright, our Official Lighting Designer Douchebag, has flown in early from the big apple to work with us here in the rotted grapefruit and he wants me to meet him at seven at the theater.

So fucking blessed.

And still not a peep from Dessie.

My eyes half-open, I pull a shirt over my head before I'm completely dried off from my shower, droplets of water wetting down the back in spots. I'm racing to get ready not so that I'm punctual for this Wright fucker, but because I need to do this right to impress Dr. Thwaite. It's *his* opinion that matters to me, and being late receiving this lighting designer will reflect poorly on the whole department.

But most of all, me.

I push through the doors of the theater in record time, even before the box office has opened. No one's in the main office except for Ramon who answers the phones, so I assume the big shot isn't here yet. I make a trip to the bathroom to check myself in the mirror, rubbing the sleep out of my eyes and fixing my hair. I haven't been to the gym in almost a week and I can tell; I get so irritable so quickly when I don't go. All that aggression doesn't take long at all to build up inside me, and add to that the frustration of how I'm fucking things up so bad with Dessie, it's a wonder I haven't busted a vein in my forehead.

I doubt she's up this early, but I have nothing to do until the designer arrives and I need to occupy my head with something other than wanting to put it through a wall. My phone's out in seconds:

ME

Hey Dessie. Really sorry about being MIA. I hope u're OK. I keep thinking about u. A lot. I'm at the theater early waiting on someone. Kinda feel bad about leaving you hanging. Plz message me back?

With a sigh, I run some water over my face, then stare at my phone and wonder if she's actually awake and might answer back. I stare for ten full minutes.

Suddenly, I feel a presence at my side. Turning my head, I find another student at the sink next to me. I ignore him and study my face again, especially the ugly wound on my cheek. I bandaged my face twice, but it's not as good as when Dessie did it. I might as well wrap my face in duct tape for as unsightly as it is.

The dude taps me on the arm. I turn, lifting a brow. He's a bit older than I realized at a first glance, maybe thirty or so. He's my height and he wears a short-sleeve salmon-colored button shirt and jeans. His left wrist is thickly decorated in leather bands, wristlets, and wooden-beaded bracelets. He has a thin build and designer glasses. I have never seen this dude before, and clearly he doesn't know who I am because he starts talking at my face, his mouth so little, I can't understand a fucking word.

Until he says three words I *do* understand: Kellen Michael Wright.

Fuck, are you serious? I straighten up at once, my eyes flashing open, and I extend a hand. "Clayton Watts," I get out, feeling my voice shake, which sends a surge of insecurity through my body that I instantly resent.

He shakes my hand and smiles, then confirms precisely who he is with a few words, the last of which being "New York", I think. Did Dr. Thwaite not warn him about me, or ...?

I type into my phone quickly that I'm deaf, then show him the screen. He reads it, then nods and pulls out his own phone, holding up a finger to tell me to wait as he types one-handed. Then he flashes me his own screen, telling me he's looking forward to a quick tour once he takes a leak.

I smirk and let out a chuckle, then nod at him and say, "I'll be outside," before dismissing myself from the bathroom.

Well. So far, he's not the dick I was expecting. Instead, he's all nice and normal and shit.

I sit on a bench in the hallway, waiting for Kellen to do his business in the bathroom while I stare down at my phone and beg telepathically for Dessie to answer my text and put me out of my misery. To be fair, I'm certain I subjected Dessie to a misery of her own when I was lost in a swamp of bitterness all Sunday, refusing to answer her texts.

I'm such an idiot. I deserve this.

I clench shut my eyes and squeeze my phone until my hands cramp. Behind those eyelids, I feel the pull of the dream world as I imagine Dessie and I back on that couch, slowly pulling each other's clothes off. *Why did she stop us? Why did she put an end to something that was so fucking perfect and real and hot?* I hadn't been that intimate with anything other than my right hand for so long, I felt like a fucking horny teen again.

That's what Dessie does to me. And Dream Dessie is about five times as cruel as doesn't-return-my-texts Dessie. She pushes me down on that imaginary couch and opens her bra to me. When her breasts emerge in front of my face, I feel my cock stiffen in my pants so much, it aches.

There's something about being sleepy that makes a guy so susceptible to having a raging-hard boner.

I press the phone down into my lap, eyes still closed, and grunt against my hard-on that grows bigger and harder by the second.

Dessie's tits are in my face and I can't shake away this fantasy. *"Clayton,"* I imagine her whimpering in a voice I've never heard before. *"Put your cock inside me, Clayton. Deep inside."* Fuck, Dessie, I want to so bad. She's squirming on top of me, gyrating those sexy, tight hips of hers against my junk. *"Fuck me. Oh, Clayton, I'm so fucking wet for you."*

She'd probably never talk like that.

It doesn't matter in dream land. I can't grind my cock through my pants any harder. What if she texted back right now? The vibration would race through my cock like it was her actual hand, gripping it. *Please, Dessie,* I might as well beg. *Please text me. I need to feel you in so many ways right now.*

A hand on my shoulder shakes me from the dream. I flick my eyes open.

Kellen's looking down at me, drying his hands with a paper towel. His lips move: *"You okay?"*

Scrunched up as I am, I probably look like I have a cramp or something. For a split second, I honestly debate whether I should slip back into the bathroom and choke one out real quick. "Yeah, I'm good," I say instead. "Is ... Is it okay if you type what you ... what you say so we can—?"

He nods curtly, holding up a hand as he, again, types one-handed into his phone. Kellen must have one speedy-ass thumb. He lifts the screen, telling me he's ready and excited to see what he's got to work with whenever I am.

I shift my legs, praying my stiffy is strangled into submission enough not to tent my jeans, then rise from the bench and lead the way to the main stage auditorium.

After an hour or so with Kellen Michael Wright, I have made the unfortunate discovery that he is, in fact, a very knowledgeable, talented, and personable guy who is patient as hell in communicating to me through texts on his phone. I respond with voice as much as I can, pushing myself to talk despite my unremitting insecurities.

I hate to say it, but I can probably learn a shitload from this shithead.

It's easy to take him around the theater this early, as there's only a handful of classes happening in the rehearsal room and the black box, but nothing on the main stage where all his attention will be in designing the lights. I show him the grid. I show him what we have available on the fly system. I show him the booth and the two spots, though he won't be using either.

I'm about to take him back to the office when my phone trembles.

"One second," I tell him, though he's distracted by a Fresnel he's examining on the lighting rack anyway.

I stare down at my phone in disbelief:

DESSIE

Was it because I didn't put out?

I gawk at her text. Is she fucking serious? I read it seven billion times, growing more pissed with every pass of my eyes over the words. Since Kellen is still occupied, I mash my thumbs to respond:

ME

Why would u say that?

DESSIE

Just wondering why you went cold fish on me.

I've had two whole days to consider what I did.

ME

U didn't do anything. Can we get a bite?
To chat? Breakfast? Lunch, maybe? 10 or 11?

DESSIE

Okay.

Okay? That's it? So is it 10 or 11? Breakfast or lunch? Yes or no? *Fuck, she's being so infuriating!* I gotta remind myself that I'm the damn reason for all this weirdness. It's my fucking fault.

Kellen shows me the screen of his phone, asking me where the office is because he wants to check in with "Ol' Marvin" before he goes. I nod and tell him to follow me, pocketing my phone and swallowing a growl along with all my frustrated thoughts of Dessie.

I lead him to the office doors. After we exchange numbers, Kellen thanks me with a handshake, which I take to be my permission to go before he slips into the office. I check my phone one last time, then shove it away after finding the screen irritatingly blank.

When I look up to push open the glass doors of the lobby, Dessie is making her way in.

We stop, frozen by one another's presence.

"Hi," I greet her first, my eyes wide.

She's beautiful today. Her hair falls in waves and tangles of brown, and she's in a green sundress with yellow flowers along the bottom rim of it, which is about the most colorful thing I've seen her wear yet. I'm already imagining how smooth her legs would be if I ran my hands up them, sliding that dress up with it and discovering the color of her panties. Maybe if I ask nicely enough, she won't wear any at all.

She gives me a little wave of her hand—*Hi.* Her eyes, light brown and shimmering, seem guarded. It cuts me deep that I don't know what she's thinking, if she's already over me, just tolerating me, or still gives half a shit about what went on between us Saturday. I almost devoured her. I was *so close*. She wanted it too. We craved each other's taste all night; I could tell in the magnetic way she drew toward me when I pulled away, or how every nerve in my body vibrated with electricity when her wicked finger traced my tattoo. I'd draw a roadmap of ink all over my body if it meant having her touch all over me.

"How're you?" I ask her dumbly.

She gives me a shrug and a muted smile, then runs a hand through her hair, drawing some of it behind an ear. *God, she looks so beautiful.* She presses her lips together, and for some reason, that makes me think of how she squeezed her legs together when I touched her on my couch.

She still wants me, I decide, a stroke of confidence racing up my back, straightening it. "You wanna grab a bite?" I ask her, crossing my arms and leaning on the glass next to her, which brings me so close to Dessie that I can smell her hair.

"I have class," she says demonstratively, then points at the hallway.

I bite the inside of my cheek, frustrated.

Then her hand finds my arm. I sink into her gorgeous eyes. Just the touch of her soft fingers on my forearm invigorates me to the core. I was a frozen-solid yeti in a realm of ice and endless cold, and she's thawed me in seconds.

"Afterwards, maybe," she adds.

"Afterwards," I agree, my eyes lighting up.

The next second, Kellen has emerged from the hall and his face shimmers with surprise, his eyebrows lifting up high. He says something and Dessie turns around to face him, and the look on her face is, to say the very least, caught off-guard. She seems to sputter and her face turns three shades of pink. No smile finds her, despite her apparent attempt at being polite and shaking his hand, albeit stiffly. The two of them exchange words, none of which I understand.

I feel my pulse throb in my throat.

They know each other. *Of course.*

Kellen says something and Dessie looks uneasy, her beautiful hair dancing as she glances away. Kellen smiles self-assuredly, then puts a big hand on her shoulder and gives it a rub. *The fuck is he touching her for?* She smiles stiffly and seems to shrug away, then gives him a nod and says something else.

All this fucking talking. All this fucking touching.

All this fucking silence.

Kellen says his goodbye, then makes his way around her and gives me a wave, to which I respond with a cold, detached nod. The glass doors close behind him with a gentle thrum I feel through my body.

Dessie's face is visibly darkened by that encounter. She looks up at me and I put on a smile right away, determined not to show the bitterness that's sitting in my chest. I could give two fucks about Kellen, even if he's all nice to me. His presence clearly didn't improve Dessie's day, and it's led me down a path of possibility that I don't want to entertain. Are they old flames? Did he have his hands all over her in New York? Is he some abusive asshole from her past? The possibilities burn across my synapses like wildfire.

I give a sideways nod at the glass, then lift my eyebrows. "So you know him?"

She bites her lip, looks to the left, to the right, and then she double-taps the thumb of a fist to her pretty pink lips—*Secret.*

I nod knowingly. I don't even know what the hell's between them and I already want to pummel Kellen until he's bent in half. "Does *he* know it's a secret?"

She nods, though uncertainly. Her eyes are all over the place, thoughts and worries racing across them.

"Why'd he put his hands on you?" I mumble.

What the fuck am I saying? I can't imagine anything more possessive-sounding to have said than that. Are we in fucking high school or some shit? I want to know what the fuck's gone on between them. Maybe I'm provoking her to spill.

"Maybe 'cause you look so beautiful today," I suggest for her.

Gag me. Someone fucking gag me.

She smiles, her cheeks turning pink. Her eyes averted, she points at her classroom again without a word, then gives me a little wave and walks away. I fight another urge to call after her and say something else dumb. Apparently, I'm just full of dumb words. I'm a dumb word factory.

I want to know what's gone down between them, but maybe that can wait. Dessie's talking to me again. That's fucking everything to me right now.

We're talking.

I take a breath, half the tension inside me released with it, and I push through the glass doors, taking a seat on the bench outside and letting the morning sun bathe over me.

I get to have a bite with her after her class, and that's the best news I've gotten in days.

And if I play my cards right, maybe I'll get a bite of her, too.

DESSIE

We share a table in the UC food court. He's got two giant fried fish fillet sandwiches and I have a grilled cheese.

And the noise here is deafening, even at barely 11 in the morning.

It's amazing, but also maybe a bit sad, how quickly I forgave him. I *think* I forgave him. When I got that text Monday night at the *Throng*, my first reaction was utter, unapologetic thrill. I was so fucking happy to have heard from him, even after suffering nearly two days of radio silence. It was Eric who told me not to answer. "Give him a taste of his own," he insisted, but I think he was channeling bitterness from his own boy troubles and projecting them onto me.

I held my phone that whole night, caressing it like a chocolate addict with the world's last Snickers.

Now here we are, sharing lunch in the dense noise of a hundred people shouting, laughing, and yelling at each other from across booths and tables. As I suffer in the chaos, I peer over the table at Clayton eating his sandwich and realize with a start that this experience is drastically different for him. Where I'm assaulted by the relentless onslaught of noise, Clayton only knows peace.

He smirks at me across the table after taking his first generous bite, chewing with a strained expression on his face.

Well, okay. Maybe there's a form of inner peace that he may

presently be lacking.

After he swallows, he says something to me, his mouth half-blocked by his fish fillet sandwich, hands propped up at the elbows and his meal hanging loose between them.

I can't hear him. Oh, the irony. "What?"

He lowers his sandwich, revealing his sexy, plush lips, then speaks louder. "So you know Kellen?"

I kinda knew that, of all topics to enjoy, Kellen Wright would be the first thing he brought up. "Yes," I say, nodding for emphasis.

"Nice guy?" he prompts me with a lift of his brow, taking another humungous bite of his sandwich.

The way his mouth moves, his jaw tightening and relaxing in his massive, muscular efforts of chewing, is so fucking erotic that I can't stand it. His lips alone are art. Add that to the whole visually-stimulating workout of his teeth and sharp jawline, and I'm about as distracted as a lunch mate can possibly be. I'm already having fond recollections of how his mouth worked mine when my *lips* were his meal.

"Nice," I agree vaguely, nodding again, then help myself to a bite of my grilled cheese.

He asks me a question through his full mouth. I catch exactly zero words of it, lifting my eyebrows in confusion. He swallows hard, then lifts his chin and repeats, "Did you two date?"

I roll my eyes. "My dad ... *mentored* him," I explain, punching the word.

"Your dad? The one who pulled a string?" he goes on, his face wrinkling as he chews.

"Yes. That dad."

His eyes pull away suddenly, and I see a flicker of darkness in them. I've become so adept at reading the little expressions that play war games across Clayton's face. The jolt in his eye bothers me.

"What?" I prompt him, but he doesn't seem to be paying attention, lost in a thought.

Kellen and I met during one of the shows my dad was designing in New York. For the first few days that I knew him, I thought he was a member of the chorus. Then I learned he was a lighting intern of sorts, but thought he was shy. When a Friday night rehearsal came to its end and the last stage light was shut off, Kellen kissed me unexpectedly in the dark behind the fold of a curtain where I was sorting props, proving to me how very *not* shy he was. Then he tried to talk me out of going to the cast party two weeks later where I would then discover how *not* single he was. It was one of my first lessons in how faithless and fickle city men can be, constantly shopping for the next best thing while gripping their girlfriends so tightly.

Maybe I have a soured secret or two of my own that I'm not sure I want to expose Clayton to just yet.

I set my sandwich down, type something into my phone, then give a little wave, drawing his attention back to see the contents of my screen:

I don't know why Kellen's here.
On Monday I found out Victoria knows who I am and now
I'm afraid between the two of them, everyone will find out :(:(

He frowns at the message, then pulls out his own phone and, after cramming the last bite of his first fish fillet, types:

U're cute when u're pissed.

To that, I glare at him.

He chuckles, full-mouthed, then puts a reassuring hand on top of mine and gives it a rub. The very next second, he seems to think that the gesture was too much and quickly retracts his hand, swallowing hard before starting on his second sandwich.

The gesture wasn't too much. It granted a much-needed warmth to the coldness I've felt since leaving the theater.

But it doesn't quite ease my uncertainty about our hot-and-cold weekend. I type, then lift my screen:

Are you going to explain Sunday's silence or what?

His sandwich lowers to the table, a surrender, and his face hardens. He swallows his bite, meets my eyes, then says a couple words too quietly.

"Louder," I urge him.

He leans partway over the table, propped up by his elbows, his arms bulging as he does. "I was a coward," he murmurs. His lips this much closer to me, I could just lean in as much as he is and kiss him right now. "Been a while since I've been with a girl."

"Me too," I mouth.

His face wrinkles. "You've been with a girl?"

I slap his arm, pushing him away with a laugh. He doesn't budge, the stone statue that he is.

"That's kinda hot," he teases me.

"So we've both been alone for a while," I mutter.

He nods resolutely.

"And we're both ... kinda scared ... of each other?" I suggest, speaking slowly.

He shrugs, then nods at that, too.

His shoulders are so big and he looks so delicious in that tight-fitting shirt, the fabric pulling across his chest distractingly. His eyes are alight with interest and his lips ... his lips are *right fucking there.*

Then he says, "You two dated, didn't you."

It isn't quite a question, more of an accusation. I press my lips together, unsure if he's actually asking, or just trying to playfully get a rise out of me again. I smack his arm again, harder than before, and earn a little Clayton-brand smirk of amusement.

Then I decide, of all things, to torture him. I type into my phone, then shove it right in his face. He has to back away a bit to read it:

No. But he did kiss me. I think he wanted to get closer to my dad through me. I felt used. He also had a hot girlfriend in the cast that I didn' t know about. I don' t think very highly of him.

Clayton's chest puffs up after reading that, his jaw tightening. An odd look of validation crosses his face. "Thought something was off about him," he says.

I smirk. "Yeah? Smelled all the lies and deceit he was drenched in?"

Clayton takes a sip of his drink, then says, "Truth is, I resent him being ..." He swallows, rubs his ear, then finishes, "I resent the fucker being here. *I* wanted to design the lights for the main stage show. He took that job from me."

A shiver of worry reenters my mind as I listen to him. It was first born the moment I recognized Kellen at the theater, but I couldn't quite put my finger on what bothered me so much until just now. My father mentored Kellen like a little lighting-god protégé. Did my father have anything to do with Kellen showing up out of nowhere to design lights for the show?

And is that connected with "the string" my father pulled in getting me into this Theatre program?

Am I the reason Clayton's opportunity was stolen?

Just like I'm the reason Victoria's chance at a lead was swiped out from under her ready, able hands?

Is there *anything* my arrival here hasn't ruined?

"Dessie?"

I look up, realizing that I'd gone silent. I don't know if he said anything else, so lost in my own dark hurricane of anxiety that I wasn't paying attention.

"Sorry," I mutter, shaking away my worries. Only time will answer my questions–time and an overdue phone call to my dad. "I resent him, too."

A question seems to glimmer in Clayton's eyes, but he doesn't ask it, drawing his sandwich back up to his lips to take another mouthful as I watch, a mixture of longing and doubt swimming inside me as I wonder if Clayton's pieced it together himself. Does *he* already suspect I have anything to do with Kellen's arrival?

He finishes his sandwich and I finish my drink in silence. He smiles at me twice and I return them with a small one of my own, studying my phone and trying to think about the routine I need to have prepared for my voice class in an hour. Something to do with vowels and combining them with different poses and odd stretches. *Ugh, I'm going to fail.*

When we leave the food court a moment later, he stops me at the door, the blinding sun silhouetting his face in an otherworldly, beautiful way.

Away from the noise of the building and entirely unable to see his face or lips, I only hear him as his voice brushes against my ears. "Do you want to hang out tonight?"

In contrast, he likely sees my face perfectly lit, the sun painting me in the brightest shade of every color it has to offer. "I have rehearsal."

"After rehearsal," the shadow murmurs.

"Well ..." Squinting against the glaring light, I shrug. "I was invited to the *Throng* to sing, but ..."

"Sing? They want you to sing again?"

"I went last night and ... the musicians basically invited me back tonight," I explain. "They want me to sing again, but I don't think I'm going to go," I finish with a frown and a shake of my head.

"Why not? You're amazing."

"You don't know what I sound like! How do you know?" I spit back playfully, peering into the shadow that's Clayton. "I don't think—"

"I'll bring the guys," he says, and I hear a smile in his voice. "We can hang out afterwards if you're up for it. Everyone should hear you."

I smile, despite myself. Clayton at the *Throng* again so I can sing my song to him, my muse who sets my insides aflame? How can I say no to all of that?

"Sounds good," I murmur with a nod.

Clayton leans a bit to my right, eclipsing the sun and giving me the gift of his beautiful face for one fleeting moment.

"See you then, Dessie," he murmurs, the sound of my name through his velvety voice sending a tremor of excitement down my body, before we part ways.

I fly through the vocal performance as if it wasn't ever a vex on my mind. The class even seems to smile back at me, and the whole world spins as if it were the basketball on the end of some guy's finger. *Clayton's finger*. He's got my whole world and he's spinning it.

I don't even dread going into rehearsal as much, despite how horrible my first day was. I sit next to Eric and pay attention the whole time, no "sickly waiting for Clayton to answer my text" distracting me the whole four hours.

And I take Eric's advice and suck. I suck so hard when I recite my lines. I even chuckle at the irony that, despite our requirement of being off-book for act one, we still have to hold our scripts so that we can write down the blocking and directions we're given. Really, each time I look at the script to jot down a note, I take the chance to suck up my next line with my eyes, then suck as I recite it.

Suck Town.

When we break after two hours for a fifteen, Eric puts an arm around me and says, "You're sucking really well today."

"You too," I note, since Eric got to finally do his first Simon scene. "Your 'drunk' is spot-on. I should know; I've seen you at the *Throng*."

"Speaking of, are we still on?"

"Yep. And," I add, giving him my playful eyes, "a special someone and his two roommates are coming."

That stops Eric dead in his green Converse. "No way."

"Way," I state with a grin. "Very, very way."

Eric dances into the men's bathroom with a howl of excitement as I saunter off to the quiet, unoccupied lobby which, at 8:08pm, is somewhat like a very long, dark dorm room, feeling strangely intimate and safe. I stare out of the tall glass windows at the courtyard, watching students pass under streetlamps as the chill of the AC touches my skin, and I pull out my phone.

I need to make a call and I'm not sure I really want to make it. Yes, of course I could wait until tomorrow, but I also need to get some answers to my questions. I'm walking on uneven ground until I do.

I press the phone to my ear, my eyes centering on the back of a bench outside where a pair of lovers are holding each other, the tops of their heads glowing under the pale white streetlamp.

"Dad?"

"Dessie, sweetie," he says, his voice nearly singing with happiness. "How's your life down there, sweetie? Isn't Klangburg just charming?"

"It's really great, Dad. Thanks so much. I'm really having ... I'm really having a time down here," I finish with a doleful sigh.

"Sweetie?"

He hears the doubt, even in my sigh. In complete contrast to my oblivious mother, my dad picks up on every little nuance in my voice; he always has.

"I'm just ... curious ..." I start, wondering whether I really, truly want to broach this subject right now, "how exactly I came to ... enjoy this time here."

My dad doesn't sidestep around any subject. "All I had to do was call up Marv and tell him what a fine, promising young lady you are," he discloses at once.

Marv? "And who's Marv?"

"Marv, sweetheart! The Director of the School of Theatre. Haven't you met him yet? He said he'd see you first thing and make sure you're taken care of."

I feel my head spinning. "*The* Director himself? Doctor Marvin Thwaite?"

"That's the one. Is there a problem?"

I guess I was a bit naïve to not consider who my father's contact was. Of course it'd be someone at the top. "I didn't realize you two knew each other."

"We went to college together, sweetie. He's doing really well for himself, being head of the department and all. Pays to have friends in high places, eh?"

Presuming you don't stoop to an all-time low with said high-placed friends. "Dad, why is Kellen here?"

"Oh, so he's arrived? I wasn't sure if it was this week or next. With all our focus on Winona's show in London, I forget what day of the week it is unless Mia puts the schedule right in front of me."

I don't know who Mia is, whether a secretary or a friend or yet another of my father's countless budding lighting design interns. "He's arrived," I state coolly.

"At least you'll have a familiar face down there with you," he says, meaning well.

No, I didn't tell the story to my dad about Kellen Wright's ill-timed advance on me. Being the selfless (read: spineless) individual I was four years ago, I thought that telling my dad that his twenty-nine-year-old golden boy was making a move on his eighteen-year-old daughter would have put an abrupt and horrible end to the man's career before it even started. For all my dad knows, Kellen is still the angel he pretends to be. And to be fair, even with eleven years on me, Kellen has a youthful face that make him look far more innocent than he is.

"Dad," I say, daring to step on his toes, "did you send Kellen down here ... *for* me?"

My dad seems to find that amusing, breaths of his chuckling dancing through the phone in tiny bursts of static. "Leave the matchmaking to your sister. I'd never deign to commit such an act."

"That's not what I meant," I mumble.

"I sent him there as a favor to Marv," my dad carries on. "You know, to drum up a little media for the school. Ticket sales have been low, interest in the program has decreased, you know how it can be."

"He ... was part of the deal?" I ask, my pulse rising.

"What deal?"

"*Marv* lets me into his program, and you send him one of your lighting designer minions in exchange? Am I ... Am I hearing this right?"

"Sweetheart, you're twisting it around."

"Do you realize that, in doing this, you just took an opportunity from ... from someone else who could have designed lights and actually *learned* something?"

"It's only one show, sweetie, and it's really for the betterment of the whole department. Imagine, when all the shows sell out and Klangburg gets noticed, receiving more funds from benefactors, which can—"

"So it's all about money? Is that it?"

My heart racing, I'm not even listening to him anymore; I just want to pick a fight. I'm furious that I'm—even indirectly—responsible for Clayton having lost his opportunity.

"The 'big picture' is a lot bigger than you realize, Dessie, and you're standing too close. It's better for everyone this way. The school. Its future. Your peers. And you're enjoying your role in *Our Town*, aren't you? Isn't it what you've always wanted?"

I feel like some princess high up in a stony tower and my father's handed me a porcelain doll. Was this handed to me? All of it? I didn't earn my way into this school, fighting hard like Clayton did. For all I know, I didn't even earn the role I'm playing.

Oh, god. Did he even arrange *that?* Does he know Nina too, or did Dr. Thwaite convince her to hand me the lead role, just like I was handed everything else?

I feel sick.

"Sweetheart?"

He's been talking in my ear, but all I feel is rage. I was naïve not to have considered any of this before. It's strange, how a call to my dad can make me aware of the pair of rose-tinted glasses I never noticed were balanced on the tip of my nose.

The lovers on the bench, the ones I'm staring at through the windows, they pull apart and I see the tears in their eyes. In the space of seconds, they're shouting at each other.

How quickly things can change.

"We sent you to Italy," my dad goes on, "but that slipper didn't fit. Claudio & Rigby's was a great opportunity for you, but that ended with an unfortunate exit scene and ... regrettable consequences. Did you ever consider the backlash, Dessie? We sent you on countless auditions and you even got to audit those acting workshops at NYU. We—"

"And so you sent me here," I say, watching the sweet couple tear each other apart through the glass, "but couldn't bear for me to have a normal experience like I wanted, so you made sure to package it all up nice and pretty, dust it with promises of success and a handshake, and let your daughter believe in the lie."

"Dessie ..."

"I have to get back to rehearsal, Dad." My voice is heavy and broken. "You know, to rehearse that role I don't really deserve."

"You deserve the world, sweetheart."

I hang up, clenching the phone as tightly as I am my jaw. The lovers outside walk away, and so do I.

The rest of the rehearsal is considerably less pleasant, and when Eric asks me what's wrong, that's when I engage in my first *true* bit of acting, putting on a light smile and convincing him that I'm totally fine and can't wait to sing my heart out. And for the first time in any rehearsal in my life, a person is actually convinced by my performance; Eric grins, squeezes my shoulder, and advises me to "up the sexy-sexy" in my song tonight. "Get Clay-boy all hot and bothered."

And until I'm up on that stage and singing, I'll sit here and hug my knees to my chest, leaning against the wall and waiting patiently for the storm of my father's words to clear.

Chapter 19

CLAYTON

I wanted to sit in the back where I usually do, but Brant thought it'd be a better idea to sit up close so we can really see her. Surrounded on all sides by other college dudes makes me nervous. I constantly check over my shoulders to make sure nothing weird is happening.

Dmitri's on the other side of the tall table we're all sitting around and he's signing to me what he's saying as he tells Brant about his latest short story, which involves a video game that fulfills any sexual fantasy the player has, and the player in Dmitri's story turns out to have sick, crazy-extreme interests that basically turns the video game into a murderous monster.

Meanwhile, I'm having fun negotiating with a fucking barstool. It's one of those tall seat-like ones where I don't know whether to sit in it or lean on it.

Brant hits my shoulder, then points. I turn to find three people coming in through the doors. Eric, who I met last year but never got to know, leads the trio with Chloe at his side, who looks like the scary byproduct of a raven, Death itself, and an extra from some unreleased Tim Burton flick, if I had to guess.

Behind them is Dessie, the beauty who owns a room the moment she walks in. She changed, wearing a sexy sleeveless red top and tight jeans. *Fuck me ...*

But her face seems pensive. I see the tension in her body before she's reached us. Her foot kicks into a chair and she glares down at it, annoyed. She squints against the smoke in the air, a scowl on her face for a moment as she gazes over the room.

Then her eyes land on me and her expression changes. The tension there drops away. The trace of a smile crosses her face and her stride becomes lighter.

Did I do that to her?

I'm fucking floating right now at the sight of her.

I hope I'm not grinning like a dumb shit, because I'm definitely grinning like a dumb shit in my mind.

"Dessie," I say when she's come to a stop in front of me.

"Clayton," her lips say.

I'm really holding back right now. I want to grab hold of her and claim her as mine in front of everyone in this room. I want every ogling dude in this room to know that she's taken. I want to put my mouth on her pretty pink lips and taste her.

Her gaze shifts, and in the next instant, she's greeting my roommates. Brant gives her half a hug, which is more than I even gave her, the big drooling ogre that I am, and Dmitri offers her a curt nod and a dimply smile after readjusting his glasses. The table only has two more chairs, so Brant offers his to Dessie, opting to just stand squished between Dmitri and her. Eric and Chloe take the two that remain, making our table an unnecessarily crowded one.

Eric reaches his hand over the table, introducing himself to Dmitri, if I had to guess. It belatedly occurs to me that Eric's gay. I snort, amused at the prospect of anything happening between those two. *Good luck cracking Dmitri's bisexual-slash-asexual egg,* I'd tell him.

Dessie touches my arm, getting my attention, then asks what I snorted about. I shake my head, smiling. "Nothing. Want something to drink?" She shakes her head and smiles back. I study the side of her face for a while as she watches the others chat away. I love how her eyes light up, her face turning as she listens to the conversations that break out over the table. I'm not a part of any of them, yet vicariously through her, I feel somehow connected to it all. Chloe says something and Dessie laughs. Eric reaches out and runs a finger down Dmitri's tattoo, seeming to ask about it. Brant leans over the table to shout what I can only assume is something lewd and suggestive to Chloe, who doesn't seem amused by the humor, rolling her eyes. Dessie, however, laughs so hard that she falls into me, her hands clinging to my shoulder as she laughs.

God, I want her to stay right there on my shoulder and make a fucking home. I love when she clings to me. *Before this night is over*, I vow to myself, *I'm gonna get her to claw those sexy fingers of hers down my back.*

Over the next half hour, more people start to pack into the *Throng*, and I feel pretty fortunate that we all got a table when we did. What the fuck with Tuesday nights? It's never this busy unless it's a weekend.

Dessie seems to notice the same thing, because she nudges me and says, *"It got really loud!"*

I smirk and take the opportunity for a joke. "Totally loud," I agree. "Can you ask them to keep it down? Having trouble hearing my friends here."

She laughs too hard at that, then slaps me on the arm and says something.

I focus on her lips. "What?"

She says, *"I'm happy I came."*

Squeezed into the table like she is, her breasts rise and fall with every breath. I don't know if that's due to her bra, or her top, or being squeezed between me and Brant, or fucking magic or what, but I'm enjoying the view as I peer down at her in all her glory.

I lean in and say, "Can't wait 'til you're up there."

She studies my eyes too long, her own glowing in the dim light that hangs above our table. If I'm not mistaking that look, I'm feeling a pull toward her lips. She's inviting me to kiss her, just with that daring, mischievous look in her eyes.

Then she looks up at the stage. I look too, only to discover everyone applauding suddenly.

The very next moment, Dessie's left my side. I watch as the guitarist relinquishes his stool to her, sliding to the side of the pianist as Dessie steps onto the stage. Everyone at my table is clapping, so I do the same, following their lead until I see their hands stop moving. Then the only thing in the room that's got my attention is Dessie.

And she's looking right at me from the stage. Her body glows under the harsh stage light. I have to say, from my experience in technical theatre, it takes a special kind of person to make ugly light look pretty.

And fuck, she does that job without trying.

Dessie's hand runs up the microphone. She brings her lips to it, then introduces herself to the room.

But I can't catch any of the words. Frustrated, I pull out my phone, determined to find that horrible speech-to-text app I'd downloaded. Then, coming to my rescue, Dmitri starts moving his hands for me, and I could kiss him for his keen intuition.

Hey, I'm Dessie, my awesome roommate interprets for me. *Some of you know me from last time. Or last night. Or whatever, I'm not good at these things. Ha! These crazy musicians, Dirk and—what's your name?—Lorenzo, wanted me back here to sing one of my little tunes. Want to hear it? I have something ... but it's a little angsty. I ...* Dmitri stops, looking up at Dessie to gather what's happening, because she's laughing. When she starts speaking again, he resumes: *Alright, then! I'll sing it. I hope you like it. I have no idea what the musicians are going to do, but they're good at improvising. This one's called, "The Liar".*

Dessie closes her eyes to bring herself to that place where all the music and beauty comes from. All that tension I saw the moment she came in, it's like it was never there. Totally relaxed, loose as the breeze, she holds the microphone and kisses it to her pink lips.

And through Dmitri, I watch the words flow:

These nails that I wear,
the curls in my hair,
my talent and my flair,
it's all fake. I'm a liar.

And the makeup on your face,
wearing leather or wearing lace,
or that cologne you embrace,
each just another lie, I say,
just another thing in the way.
You're a liar, too.

That's not how you really look.
Just another billion dollar lie
sold to you by a billion dollar book.
And that's not how you really smell.
Whether from soap, cologne, or shampoo,
I don't think you know yourself as well
as you think you do.

Just like me, an actress who lies all day
reading another line from another play
being some other person, some other name.
We're all liars just the same.

And just when you're ready to let it go,
too exhausted to keep up the show,

you get a glimpse inside another's eyes
and you'll finally see
the only way free
is to be a liar who never lies.

After the last lyrics are signed, the musicians seem to still be filling the space with music, the guitarist's hands strumming as Dessie hums against the mic, her eyes closed and lost in the song.

And I'm lost in her, my arms folded and my jaw tight.

She opens her eyes and they find me.

I wonder if she sees my lies.

My truths.

My way free.

And then the room shakes with applause, and I lift my own hands to join them, watching as Dessie takes in the cheering with a laugh, a pink face, and then a grand, demonstrative bow.

She returns to the table and her friends explode with their reactions, offering compliments and happy faces and laughter. Dmitri tells her how beautiful her voice was, but was worried about what the lyrics meant: *If I've lied to you,* he says to her as he signs at the same time for my benefit, *then I'm totally sorry and, you know, please don't write a song about me.*

After some time, Dessie turns and says something. I look at her, waiting for her to repeat what she said when suddenly there's a screen in my face:

Want to get out of here?

I smirk my consent, then slap Brant's shoulder, telling him that we're gonna head out. Dmitri takes note of my departure, waving goodbye. To him, I sign back: *We're gonna need the apartment for a bit.*

Dmitri's response is a dimply flat-line for lips and a resolute nod.

Good boy.

After leaving the place, my skin feels a noticeable departure of vibrations and noise, drinking in the calm silence of the street like a cool glass of water. Or maybe that's just literally the breeze of the night air on my thirsty skin.

We might as well be holding hands, but we're not. We're not at that point. Honestly, I'm not even sure I'm really the hand-holding type. I don't know why I'm suddenly obsessed with that idea. Maybe it's how close she's walking by my side. Maybe I'm wondering if I should put an arm around her or–

No, fuck that. What am I thinking?

I look over at her. Either it happens to be the moment she looks at me too, or else she's watching me as we walk. I chuckle dryly. Not sure if that laugh came out or not, but I felt it in my chest.

Then I notice her lips move. I might be wrong, but I think she asks if we're heading back to my place.

"If that's okay with you," I say back.

To that, she nods.

I'm fucking floating right now.

When the door's in my face, I can barely get the key in I'm so fucking excited. I've been desperate for another night alone with her for the past three days. I've craved her touch on my skin and longed to put my arms around her body. I want my hands on her skin so fucking bad that I'm practically hopping right now.

"Want anything to drink?" I ask automatically, edging quickly toward the kitchen while peering over a shoulder, keeping her in my gaze.

She bites her lip.

I stop cold at the kitchen counter, watching her. The world grows very, very still. "So ... is that a yes?"

Her lips part. She takes a breath, her eyes lifting to meet mine. There's something very intense about her. I think she's expecting me to make the first move. She wants me to cast everything off the counter with a reckless swipe of my hand before gripping her and slamming her on the counter to fuck her. The fantasy is painted in her eyes. The yearning for it ...

"Yeah?" I prompt her. "A drink?"

Then, the tears touch her eyes.

Uh, fuck. Misread.

"Dessie?"

She shakes her head, the tears sitting up there in her eyes, refusing to fall. Then she lifts her chin and, with a coldness in her eyes, she says something.

I don't catch all her words. "*Liar,*" I think she said. "*Don't deserve,*" I think she also said. My insides turn to stone as I watch her, frustrated by her quick lips.

"Dessie," I repeat, coming up to her and grasping her shoulders with my hands.

She looks away and clenches shut her eyes, her jaw tightened.

She's angry.

"Dessie." I try to get her to look at me, bending my neck and rubbing her shoulders calmingly. *Fuck, her skin feels so smooth.* "Dessie, talk."

"I am talking!" she shouts, her furious, tear-filled eyes meeting mine. I see the shout in her neck pulling taut, her nostrils flaring, her whole body contracting in the effort. *"It's all I ever do!"*

I'm so fucking confused. "I'm sorry," I tell her, all the guilt from this weekend that I thought we had gotten past rushing back into my stomach. "I should not have blown you off. I was scared. I was a fucking idiot. You deserve a guy so much better than me."

"No." Her eyes widen. *"You deserve better than* me," she says, slapping

her own chest. She waves a palm in front of her face once, then throws a thumb past her ear—*Better*. She pokes a finger at her chest—*Me*.

Is she fucking crazy? "I'm the one who doesn't deserve you, Dessie. Don't mistake that for a second. You're too fucking good for me."

She takes a deep breath, shutting her eyes, and then her lips move.

And this time, I catch the words.

Every word.

I knew what she was going to say because it's exactly the conclusion I had come to earlier when we ate lunch together at the UC. Her father got her into this school. Her father is a famous lighting designer. She knew Kellen. She's the reason he's here, designing the lights for the main stage show.

And she's the reason I'm not.

"My being here ... has ruined ... everything," she says.

But all I see is strength in her. Those tears, she won't even allow them the courtesy of falling. She isn't trying to earn my sympathy; she's owning all of this. If she'd ask me, she's owning too much of it.

She didn't ask for Kellen Douchebag Wright.

She didn't ask to get all intimate with me and put herself between me and my dreams. She just fucking met me a couple weeks ago. She owes me nothing.

And here I am, standing in front of this strong, incredible woman who has so much passion in her that she's bursting at every carefully-stitched seam, singing on stages and earning artistic respect from all these beer-guzzling morons. That's respect her father did *not* buy for her, respect she got all on her own.

And here I am with this incessant raging hard-on in my pants that's been distracting me for the past hour, and I don't deserve a single fucking tear of hers.

The truth is, her being here saved me.

"Your dad can give you a school," I tell her, pushing through the vacuum in my ears as my teeth and throat and chest vibrate with my speech, "your dad can give you a whole play," and I see her trying to protest, so I speak even louder, praying my words are reaching her, "but your dad can't give you what you did on that little stage an hour ago. Did you see their eyes? Did you see all those people in that room, the way they listened to you when you ... when you sang?"

Her eyes shift, the tears threatening to spill as she speaks to me through her clenched teeth. *"The one person ... who I want ... to hear that song,"* she mouths, her whole body trembling, *"can't ... hear ... anything."*

"I *hear* you."

Her eyes flash at those words. Her brows flinch as she stares at me uncertainly, the emotion frozen on her pained, broken face.

"I hear you," I repeat to Dessie, every nerve in my body pulling tight. "You aren't the only one who's had parents try to ruin you. You aren't the only one who's fought the destiny that everyone keeps trying to push down onto you. I *hear* you." I even feel my voice cracking. Today might set a new record for how many words I've let myself speak out loud. It's all Dessie; she's pulling me out of myself. "You aren't alone in this battle to find your voice. To find where you belong. To break free."

The emotion hanging between her eyes and mine is practically tangible. I worry there's even tears in my own eyes now, tears I also refuse to spill for that stupid fucking world out there.

"I'm sick of people thinking they know who I am," I whisper, feeling the breath thrust its way out with each word. I take her face, a hand on either cheek, then pour into her eyes. "People trying to tell me what kind of man I am."

"What kind of woman I am," she echoes back.

"Telling me I'm just Texas trash."

"Telling me I'm just a New York snob."

"Dessie, I *hear* you."

The anger has drained from her face, replaced with something else entirely.

"*Clayton ...*" she mouths.

"I hear you."

Our lips collide. Dessie's breath washes over my face in uneven torrents as our hands clasp to each other's bodies.

Her hands grab the base of my shirt. A tremor of anticipation lances up my side as her fingers move.

There goes my shirt.

I pin her to the wall, our mouths still locked as we mutually try to consume the other's face. The warmth between us is a fire I'm helpless to try putting out.

My hands brush up her sexy hips.

She bucks against my body, our lips unlocking so I can free her from that sexy red top she's wearing.

To the floor it goes.

She finds her lips a new meal at my earlobe. Then her teeth are invited to the party.

I moan against her, needles of pleasure racing up my neck and exploding where her teeth dig into me. Doesn't she know how dangerous that is? I could claw the wall until there's nine doorways into my room with the way she's making work of my ear.

I can't hold back any longer. *Goddamn, Dessie ...*

I pick her up under her knees, her arms throwing themselves around me as I push us into my bedroom. The mattress gives as we land on it with a bounce, and she's slammed onto her back. Her eyes flash up at me with alarm.

I hope she can handle me.

I play rough.

Like the beast I am, I crawl over her, then launch at her lips with mine. She reciprocates, just as hungry. We don't let each other utter another pointless word; our fingers and locked lips do all the talking.

I thrust my hands under Dessie, startling her as I aggressively work the back of her bra. I unhook it with blind finesse.

Then her breasts are free and my face is buried in them like an animal. I feel the vibrations in her chest. *"Oh, fuck ... Clayton, fuck!"* I'll imagine she's saying up there, crying the words out for her own benefit.

Then I bite her left nipple for *my* benefit.

I slap a hand over her face, feeding her my fingers as she gasps onto them—I feel her jaw open wide and hot breath push from her gaping mouth. She sucks in a finger of mine while her devilish nails draw down my back, which inspires a deep, beastly growl from my own body.

Her clawing of my back only strengthens the hold of my teeth on her helpless nipple. I bet it's almost too much for her to bear, judging from how her breath against my hand just sped up.

There's something about her surrendering of her body to me, even in pain, that's so fucking erotic.

I release her nipple and reach down, working the buttons of her jeans. Yet again, her eyes gleam as she watches what I do. *These jeans are in my way*, my eyes tell her. *And they're about to not be.*

They slip off her body like butter and find a place to perch on the dresser, or wall, or wherever the fuck I carelessly pitch them.

I yank down her panties and cast them to the side too. She's all mine tonight, and I'll make sure every inch of her knows it.

From the glint in her eyes that looks both excited and scared, I'd say she's learning fast.

With my hardened eyes on her stunned ones, I pull a condom wrapper out of my pocket and bite the end, letting it hang from my teeth as I pull open my pants with force, working the buttons.

She watches, breathing heavy, unblinking.

The corner of my lips curve into a smile as I drop the pants to my ankles, the underwear going with them, and step out of them. I won't be needing those. I watch her zero in on my cock, her eyes widening.

She wants it. I can see the wetness from where I'm looking down at her. I know she's ready for it.

And I'm ready to give it.

I give the wrapper in my teeth a deft tug, freeing the condom, then spitting the wrapper to the side. Watching her with hungry intent, I roll it on.

Her gaze on me is unwavering.

I grip under her thighs and pull her up to my hips, firmly pressed against me.

Her breathing is heavy. She wants this as much as I do. No other words need to be said.

Except perhaps this: "Hold on to something."

Her legs lock behind my back and her fingers claw into the bed, bracing herself. *Smart woman.*

My cock slides right inside.

She gasps sharply, her lips parting and her chest rising, those gorgeous breasts rising with them.

I pump her slow at first, making sure my eyes never leave hers. I want to see every little thing I do to her as the pain and pleasure break across her face in little earthquakes. I want to feel her body as she fuses with mine, her legs locked, her fingers digging into the sheets as she pushes her hips into me, taking my cock deeper.

Entering her didn't sate my hunger.

It strengthened it.

I clasp her shoulders and pull her down hard, forcing her hips to meet my every thrust. I can't get deep enough inside her. It's driving me crazy.

She squirms against my body, bouncing with my fevered, frustrated movements. I don't know what sounds I'm making, but I feel a chorus of grunting in my chest, vibrations working their way up and down my arms as I cling to Dessie and keep her right where I need her. *She is so fucking tight.*

I'm already so close. I've been desperate for this release. No couch-bound fantasy or hallway daydream can possibly match the fire that's ignited between me and her in this stifling room.

I grip her breasts, my thumbs grinding over her nipples, which causes her to throw her head back, our eye contact broken.

And that won't do. "Look at me."

She reels, twisting out of her bliss and focusing her astonished gaze onto me.

"Look at me," I repeat, fucking her into the mattress, my legs flexed taut with every shove, my arms bulging as I brace myself to bear down into her. The impatient look in her eyes emboldens me.

I slide my right hand between our sweat-drenched bodies to skillfully rub her swollen clit. The imminent orgasm becomes evident in her eyes too.

We're both so close.

Her lips part as she spills her breath at me, beads of sweat dressing her forehead and chest, giving the most beautiful sheen to her body. My face reaches for hers, desperate to taste her.

"Look at me," I whisper. "I want you looking at me when you come."

"*Clayton...*" she mouths back.

I feel her contract, and her eyes see heaven as the anguish of release spills across her face. I fuck her through that orgasm, determined to squeeze every last drop of pleasure out of her. I won't let her miss a single breath of it.

"I want to taste you," I breathe at her when her eyes come back. *I'm so close.* "I want—"

And then our mouths connect right on time. I can't hold back. My load empties into her just as a moan erupts from my chest, vibrating through our twisting lips. I shoot over and over again, groaning against her mouth as a cocktail of desire and agony floods every nerve in my body.

Then, all I know is an ocean of calm.

I collapse onto her, gasping for my life. Her breath chases mine, hot against my ear. I feel her tongue there as she kisses the side of my face.

I lift my head. "Dessie," I moan.

She lifts her head for a kiss. I give it to her sweetly, the beast sated for now. Then, she pulls away to say one little word to me.

Amused, I grin and whisper, "You're welcome."

DESSIE

I gently stroke his sleeping face.

He opens an eye.

"Dessie," he mumbles sleepily, grinning.

I bite my lip, a giggle of delirium caught in my chest like a bird in a cage, rattling around and unable to break free. That's basically the only way I can react after a night with a man who made me feel unlike anyone has before. None of the *boys* from my past could've ever done what Clayton did with that strength of his, with that strong mouth, with those massive arms that put me right where he wanted me so he could have his way. I'm pretty sure he's ruined me for all other men, past, present, and future.

I feel the soreness of muscles I didn't know I had. We barely slept. He brought me to orgasm so many more times, I literally lost count.

Clayton's sleepy-eyed face emerges over mine. His lips touch my cheek gently, and then he hovers there, looking down into my eyes.

I feel like I've become a puddle in his bed. Clayton Watts's bed. *I'm a puddle in fucking Clayton Watts's bed.*

"Breakfast?" he murmurs quietly. I nod.

Twenty minutes later, we sit on barstools in front of his kitchen counter eating frozen waffles he tossed into the toaster that taste like makeup sponges glazed with the gooiest syrup I've ever had the displeasure of eating. I'm polite and eat them anyway because, after last night's ample physical exertions, I discover I've worked up quite an appetite and would probably eat the cushion from a couch.

After my last bite, I glance back at the living room to find Brant crashed on the loveseat clutching an orange-and-blue afghan, his mouth hanging open and the remote barely balanced on the edge of his knee, just a nudge away from falling off.

"I guess he didn't make it to his room," I note, thumbing at Brant.

Clayton shrugs as he catches where I'm pointing, then he looks at me and says, "I got class in an hour."

"Me too," I say back.

Then, almost like nothing, he puts a kiss on my cheek and mumbles, "Gotta put something on."

To his sexy back and boxer-brief-sporting ass, I murmur, "Pity."

There's a smile as big as the sky on my face when the morning light touches it. The walk from his place to campus is already familiar to me, as if I'd done it a hundred times. We make a merciful detour to my dorm so I can quickly shower and change and look a bit less ... *wrecked*. Clayton waits for me on a courtyard bench, typing on his phone. When I'm decent again, he walks me back, leaving me in front of the theater to go to his psychology class, and we experience a short moment of not knowing whether to kiss or hug or just wave. I see the uncertainty in his eyes and my hands seem to twitch with the same intentions as his. Finally, he opts to squeeze my arm, which was almost a half-hug, before he goes. His face reddens as he whips around the corner, which makes me laugh.

I push through the glass doors and waltz into the black box for my acting class, zipping right past Ariel, whose blasé stare of condescension at what she likely just witnessed through the window is not missed.

And really, after how close Clayton and I have grown in just one glorious rollercoaster of a weekend followed by a couple of surprise-filled days, how can I let anything—*or anyone*—ruin it?

My good mood is invincible. Nina gives me a harsh yet instructive critique on my performance piece while Ariel watches from the back row, her arms crossed and her eyes narrowed. And how do I come out of that class?

Smiling like a cat with a bird in my pocket.

Fuck you, mermaid. You can't touch me.

I find Sam in our usual spot in the UC food court, and I insist on buying lunch for her. Something tells me she's made a habit of coming here at this precise time because she knows I do. Plus, inevitably, I always give her about half or more of whatever I eat.

"Take off your glasses," I say over my teriyaki sub.

Sam lifts her blunt, horrific eyebrows. "Hmm?" she moans through a mouthful of potato wedges.

"Glasses," I order with a smirk. "Off."

With reluctance, she pulls off her glasses. Well, the bad news is, those thick frames do a good job of concealing how big and bulbous her nose really is. The good news is, beyond those smudgy lenses, she's been hiding a set of soft hazel eyes I've never noticed before. I always mistakenly thought they were brown.

"Interesting," I murmur, studying her.

"I can't see your face," she complains.

"Let's get away from campus," I suggest. "We don't have any classes until tonight. I want to go shopping."

She fumbles to get her glasses back on her face. "Shopping? I don't—"

"You've worn that shirt three times since Friday."

She glances down at her shirt, as if doubting it. When she looks back up at me, she surrenders with an unenthusiastic shrug. "I guess I could use a little shopping. I think there's a thrift shop on Avenue D."

A thrift shop is not what I have in mind for her.

An hour later finds us in a store on the *high-dollar* side of town, much to Sam's dismay. I run my hand through the soft, colorful racks, feeling oddly like I'm back home on some errand in town with my sister when she was a little bit less of a nose-upturned diva. Cece would rush up to a pretty dress, gasping as she spun around and showed it to me held up to her neck and draped down her body. I'd pick a matching dress two sizes bigger and we'd try them on together, then burst out of the dressing rooms at the same time and surprise each other, laughing.

I miss the way she used to be.

Sam moans from within the changing room, complaining about how she looks. "Shush," I tell her. "Get your booty out here and let me see you."

The door opens. I get a good look.

"Alright, not your color. Try this." I toss another one at her. "And please, posture. No one looks good when they're bent into the shape of a coat hanger. Be the coat, Sam, not the hanger."

I guess I'm the new Cece and Sam's my little sister. When she comes out of the dressing room again, her face looks lighter, and I nod with my approval.

What I foretold to be an hour-long overdue outing with my roommate turns into three, and I'm taking her down the street with an armful of bags filled with dresses, shirts, new jeans, and some sexy-ass shoes. I even throw in a few for myself.

"I can't let you pay for all this," Sam complains at the counter of the next store.

"I'm not," I tell her innocently. "My credit card is."

Swipe. *Cha-ching.*

Soon, the front glass window of a beauty salon greets our eyes.

Sam scowls at me. "We're *not* gonna have one of those moments where you push me in there and have them give me some swanky makeover and I come out looking like last year's prom queen."

"No," I assure her. "You'll come out looking like *next* year's prom queen."

Since each stylist's area is hidden by big annoying bamboo walls, I don't get to see Sam until the sun is setting the horizon on fire behind me and the haircut is completely finished. I literally don't recognize her.

"That's ... not the cut we discussed," I murmur, staring at her wide-eyed.

"It's kinda the one I wanted," she says, then rubs her eyes. "I can't see how it looks. They made me take my glasses off."

Her hair is about eighty percent gone. What's left in its place is a short spread of talon-shaped spikes that sweep near the front into some sort of jet-colored tidal wave.

Sam's breathing quickens. "You're worrying me."

I hand the girl at the front counter my card without even looking at her, my eyes glued to Sam's hair.

"It's horrible," Sam groans, deadpan. "It's hideous. I'm gonna scare children. That's what it is, isn't it?"

I get my card back, swipe Sam's glasses off the counter, and put them on her. The next instant, she slumps over to the nearest mirror, then engages in a strange sort of staring contest with herself, many odd, unreadable emotions cutting through her face.

I come up behind her. "Pretty damn hot, huh?" I murmur, breaking a smile.

Sam's eyebrows, completely reshaped, slowly lift, as if she were seeing daylight for the first time. She doesn't say anything, staring at herself in a daze.

Now it's *my* turn to wonder if she hates the cut. "You know, hair grows back," I reason with her, "and if you don't like it—"

"I love it," she says with her brand of deadpan joy. "I love it so much. It's really the best thing. Wow."

Every one of her words, monotonous and flat. She makes "joy" sound miserable. She makes "love" sound like an exhausting climb up a hillside. Yet even with all that indifference that is Samantha Hart, I know better than to rely on the mere sound of her words; she *does* love her haircut. She loves it so much, she can't look away from the mirror.

I smile inside at a job well-done.

By the time we get back to campus, I realize I'm already five minutes late to my lighting crew shift. The glass door nearly meets my nose before it meets my hand, and I stumble going down the short hall to the auditorium.

Clayton waits for me, his legs dangling over the lip of the stage. He's since changed and showered, as is evidenced by the new white shirt and jeans. Also, his hair seems to be fixed up a bit, like he threw a splash of water over his head and gave it a few rubs.

"I'm late," I mouth soundlessly when I reach him.

He seems amused, smirking out of the side of his mouth as he gives me a once-over. "Doesn't look like appropriate attire for crew work."

"I picked up this dress today when I went on a shopping spree with my roommate," I tell Clayton with a coy smile. "I thought that you ... might like it."

"Like it?" he echoes.

From the look on his face, I think he more than likes it.

"By the way," he goes on, "Dick won't be by pretty much for the rest of the semester." I wrinkle my brow questioningly. "It means I'm your boss. It's *my* say on how late or inappropriately dressed you are."

I cross my arms and squint defiantly at him. "So ... am I in trouble?"

Watching my lips so intently, a dark, roguish glint enters his eyes. He nods slowly, then hops off the edge of the stage and saunters up to me, staring down at me over his big chest and intimidating size.

"Big trouble," resonates his deep, silky voice.

I bite my lip.

"I was told to send you to rehearsal after we finish everything on this list." He waves a piece of paper in the air, then slaps it onto the stage. "Just so happens, I finished the list an hour ago."

My heart races. "Oh?"

"But I don't feel like sending you to rehearsal."

"I don't feel like going."

A hand firmly settles on the small of my back. "Let's double-check some of the items on this list."

I stare up into his dark gaze. "Yes, boss."

He grins.

Then, with a superior flick of his chin, he leads me up the steps to the stage. I follow, my heart fluttering excitedly.

"Lighting rack organized?" he inquires, his eyes finding me.

"Check," I say, then press my lips together.

He rounds about the stage, coming to a bunch of hooks that line the back wall. "All the cords wrapped and sorted?"

Feeling playful, I pull at one of the hooks, a set of yellow cords dropping to the ground in a pile.

His eyes zero in on me.

I shrug innocently. "Oops."

The very next instant, he has that cord in his grip. He steps forward, and suddenly I'm against the wall.

"This needs to be wound back up," he says quietly, grabbing me and beginning to loop the yellow cord around my wrists.

"Clayton," I hiss at him, my eyes darting around.

"No one's here," he assures me with a mischievous tone, wrapping the cord around and around itself, then pulling tight. "No one at all." He flips it over the hook, then pulls.

My bound hands fly up with the cable, startling me. *Oh my god.* My heart hammers like a prisoner in my ribcage. My breath is stolen.

Hanging onto that cord, having all the power in his mighty grip, he puts a finger of his free hand into his mouth, sucking it long and hard. I watch his lips work, biting my own.

Then he pulls that finger out of his mouth with a pop and, his evil grin tightening, he thrusts that hand under my dress.

"*Clayton!*" I protest again.

His face intensely boring into mine, his hand negotiates its way under my dress and into my panties with the same slick persuasion as his lips.

His finger glides inside.

A surge of insanity courses through me. *Fuck!* Just one little movement and my body rebels, every muscle in me submitting to the power of Clayton's finger.

Vainly, I pull against the cord, only to remind myself how very trapped I am.

In response, Clayton pulls tighter, stretching me until I'm nearly on my tippy-toes. I'm completely in his control.

His finger pushes in deeper—or maybe he's added a second one, I can't tell.

"Someone's going to catch us," I breathe, fighting my restricted hands—except I don't really want to be free. *Who in their right mind would?*

He leans in, his face inches from mine. "You're so wet," he whispers. "You want me."

"Yes," I say, but the word turns into a desperate moan that pushes out of my throat. *Oh my god.* He's making me so dizzy with his beautiful torment.

"Come on my fingers," he whispers.

"Clayton ..."

"Come for me." His fingers twist.

I squirm against him, pushing my clit up against his palm, rubbing frantically and trying to get more friction. He presses up against my body. I feel his fingers dig deeper, pulsating inside me and working me like a damn puppet.

What the hell is he doing down there that feels so fucking good?

And then I feel myself letting go. I can't stop it. I cry out in his face, my orgasm rocketing through me. Shockwaves of pleasure race up to my fingers, down to my toes, and through my clenching stomach.

I flick open my eyes.

His victorious face hovers in front of mine. Then, his fingers slip out of me and, without breaking his fierce gaze for a second, he brings those fingers to his wicked mouth and slips them in, his tongue dancing up and down each digit as he tastes me.

He lets go of the cord and it slides off the hook, my hands dropping with it. Gently, he unties his thick knot, releasing my wrists and winding the cord back up over his shoulder, like his job's done.

He offers me a wink before tossing the wound-up cord back onto the wall. Then, he faces me to say, "Looks like our little list's complete. You're free to return to rehearsal, Dessie."

Massaging my wrists, I lift my eyes to him, feeling bold, and throw my arms around his neck. I kiss him without warning, tasting myself on his swollen lips. "I think I'd rather work overtime," I whisper.

An amused smirk darkens his face.

I don't suspect I'm leaving anytime soon.

DESSIE

We're only able to get away with our Wednesday Night Lighting Crew Sexcapades for two more weeks before rehearsal would take its due priority, forcing me to attend the earlier and far less desirable Tuesday afternoon lighting crew shift that fits neatly between my movement and voice classes.

Of course, Clayton makes sure to be there during said shifts. Unfortunately, so are five other guys.

We meet up for lunch or dinner on the "good end" of fraternity row a few times a week. It almost feels weird to eat alone now. I always seem to learn a handful of new signs each time we get together. I practice each one to him while he patiently corrects me. I know signing in public isn't something he likes to do, but he's become way more comfortable with it around me.

We both pull each other out of our comfy boxes.

I stay at his place two or three times a week. I'm sure Sam doesn't mind the random nights she gets to have the dorm room all to herself, composing her music at top volume. I told her to install her software on *my* laptop so she can use my computer when I'm not there. Turns out, my computer is approximately nine billion times faster than hers.

She doesn't know it, but I'm totally letting her keep that laptop; I can afford a new one.

It's only a matter of days before Clayton and I become so highly attuned to each other's schedules that we surprise each other after classes. It becomes a routine on Tuesday and Thursday afternoons for him to hang out in the lobby until I get out of my voice class, and then we grab dinner together before I head back to the theater for rehearsal.

"Is this how you do it?" I ask him one Thursday evening after I take a bite of cake, signing that my chocolate cake's tasty. Clayton fights a laugh because apparently I just signed: *Church is tasty!* When I repeat the sign back to him, annoyed, he laughs harder because my second version comes out as: *My computer is a tasty cake!* When I put a piece of that cake into his face, he isn't laughing anymore, and then for a few minutes we become one of "those couples" as I kiss the chocolate off his face. I might say, it's one of the best desserts I've had in a while.

"So, what are we?"

He squints, having missed what I said.

My feet shuffle under the table. *Maybe I shouldn't push the subject.* "Never mind."

He growls, frustrated. He really hates when I don't repeat something I've said.

I lick my lips, still tasting chocolate. I poke my chest—*I.* Then, from the place I just poked, I pull an imaginary pencil out with just my thumb and middle finger—*Like.* I'm drawing a blank for the remaining signs, so I mouth the words, "Whatever we are."

Folding his arms on the table, he leans over and grunts, "Me too."

I smile. I just said I wouldn't push this subject, but I can't help myself. "So ... are we a thing?"

He seems to read my words perfectly this time, as I see a hint of a smirk teasing onto his lips as he studies me pensively. His hesitation almost worries me until he mumbles, "I sure as fuck hope so."

The answer sets a cage of butterflies loose inside me. That sensation never gets old.

Not around Clayton.

Unfortunately, that sensation also happens every time I set foot into rehearsal. Moving to the main stage for rehearsals has pressed the sobering reality onto me that opening night will be on me before I know it and the auditorium will be full of people who've bought tickets to see me in my wonderfully subpar and highly disappointing rendition of Emily Webb in *Our Town*. Nina does nothing to bolster my confidence, constantly barking at me and asking weird questions that seem rhetorical, yet she wants a response each time. And annoying Nina clearly doesn't earn me any love from the rest of the cast.

After an especially grueling Friday rehearsal where I royally flubbed at least five of my lines in act three, destroying any sense of dramatic tension that existed, I meet Eric by the exit door and sigh, asking, "When exactly am I supposed to *stop* sucking at rehearsal?"

To that, he responds, "Yesterday," with an apologetic wince.

But there is one perk to rehearsing on the main stage: Clayton is periodically around, focusing lights in the grid, discussing things with Kellen somewhere in the back of the auditorium, or even backstage as he organizes things and helps the set and props crew. Despite our proximity, we keep everything professional during rehearsal.

Also, I'm rather amazed at how well things seem to be going between him and Kellen. Although, I really wouldn't mind Kellen accidentally slipping on a banana peel in the grid and plummeting to the stage below with a shriek and a bone-crunching splat.

Wow. My bitterness over his presence really knows how to pull the dark and morbid out of me.

It becomes a regular joy of mine to visit the *Throng* every Saturday night for a performance. I meet up with the musicians in my free time, practicing new songs. They help me with melody and song structure, which makes me half-appreciate the attention that Sam gives her own work, with all that knowhow she gains from her classes. I may suck like hell when I'm handed an acting role, but put me in front of a microphone with some keen musicians and I will sing a ship full of men into the rocks at the shore.

Twice, I've caught Victoria at the *Throng*. One time, she seemed to be listening to my song, but with half-opened, unimpressed eyes. The second time, she was carrying on a conversation with the orange-bearded Freddie in the very back during my whole performance.

I don't mind, really. It totally doesn't make my blood boil.

But Clayton Watts sure does, because he's always in that audience, and both of his roommates have taken quite a liking to me. Every Saturday after my gig is over, the musicians compliment me, give me high-fives like I'm just another dude in the band, then throw out their ideas for what they want me to come up with next weekend. "Please write a song about my ex," the guitarist begs me. "She set fire to my bed. She's a fucking lunatic." Then, the moment I step offstage, I meet with Clayton and his roommates, who have taken to sitting with Eric and Chloe. Nothing's official, but I think Chloe might be warming up to Brant, and I may be totally off, but I think there's a spark or two flying between Eric and Dmitri. Clayton did tell me that Dmitri swings both ways, and I can't help but notice how cutely clingy Eric's gotten toward Dmitri, insisting on sitting next to him during my gigs.

"Want to crash at my place?" Clayton always asks, as if he still needs to, even four Saturdays later.

"Good idea," I always tease him back.

And then another night of sweating, wrinkled bed sheets, and slamming his headboard against the wall commences.

I always worry that his roommates get tired of me being around all the time, but they seem to be more amused by it. On my way out one Sunday morning, Brant looks at me over his cup of coffee and says, "You mean you can still *walk* after last night?"

I give him the finger.

He gives me two—placed over his mouth with his tongue wiggling between them.

Good ol' Brant.

It isn't until Monday after my acting class that I run into Victoria and Chloe in the lobby. Chloe's face is a mess of black ink running from her eyes to her chin. Victoria sits next to her with a consoling hand on her back, and the moment she sees me, her eyes turn dark.

I come up to the pair of them, undaunted by Victoria's coldness. "Chloe?"

Chloe gives one short look at me, then sniffles. "That fucker."

"What fucker?" I prompt her.

Victoria sighs, long and dramatically, then says, "Can you give us space, Desdemona? Chloe's having troubles and her *friend* here is trying to console her." She rubs Chloe's back in little circles with one hand, clenching her thigh with the other.

I ignore Victoria's snark. "What happened?" I ask Chloe gently, crouching down by her side.

"That male *slut*," she spits out, sniffling. "Ugh. I'm such a stupid mess. I never get this way over a *boy*. I am such an *idiot*."

"No, you're not," murmurs Victoria, rubbing her back with mounting zest, as if she were trying to scrub the glass off of a window. "You're smart and you're full of love. That *ass* is just a good-for-nothing womanizer."

"Brant?" I say suddenly. "Are we talking about—?"

"Don't fucking say his name," groans Chloe. She practically snarls, her teeth bared. "I could kill him. He doesn't have any feelings. He just uses girls like, like, like, like *rags* and ... and then he just ..."

"We don't have to rehash it all," murmurs Victoria soothingly, and I get the impression that what she *really* means is: *Don't bother letting Dessie into any of this. I'm your real friend. I'm here. Dessie is a bitch.*

I sigh. "I'm so sorry, Chloe."

"None of them are any good," Chloe spits back, her eyes sharp as needles. "Those boys all deserve each other, those woman-using chauvinists."

Is she talking about Clayton now, too? "Wait a minute," I start.

"I warned you," Chloe goes on, looking up at me with those two wet paths of darkness down her face. "I said you should stay away from him. None of them are any good. They're a pack of pricks and always were."

"Chloe," I press on, getting annoyed.

"He's going to fuck you over, too. They're best friends, two peanuts in a shell. When he's bored of you, he'll dump your ass—"

"Chloe!"

"And he and Brant will laugh about you," she goes on, "and share stories about you behind your back. You'll just be another dent on the headboard. Wait for it."

"You don't know a damn thing about Clayton at all," I shout at her, furious.

Something is being rehearsed at the other end of the lobby—six freshmen working on a group project—and they go silent at my outburst. Chloe glares at me from her seat and Victoria, all too ready for another excuse to hate me, just looks up at me with a pained sort of put-on sympathetic expression.

"I think you should go," Victoria quietly suggests.

"I think I will," I respond just as stingingly.

The glass doors shut softly at my back, despite my effort to slam them. I feel everyone's eyes staring at me through the windows as I pass through the courtyard. If I'm honest, Chloe and I weren't really super close to begin with, but I could not just stand by while she poured all her resentment on both Clayton and Brant. I mean, sure, Brant's a total player; I called it the moment I met him at the bowling alley. But if she's mad at him, why did she have to bring up Clayton and pull him into the mix? They might be best friends, but they're nothing alike.

Still, even just thinking that, a seed of doubt has planted itself in my already unrested stomach.

It isn't until I get back to my dorm that I take a glance at the calendar and realize opening night is this Friday.

Of course I knew already, but the days still somehow snuck up on me. I knew it was coming for weeks, but seeing it in black and white makes it a reality.

Too much of a reality.

I throw myself into the bathroom just in time to cling to the rim of the toilet, then proceed to ungently turn myself inside-out.

CLAYTON

Kellen Michael Wright says some scholarly know-it-all bullshit to me in the lighting booth when we're alone. I nod, pretending I heard him.

I didn't hear a fucking word.

People don't realize how much we speak with our bodies. You don't need lips or words to communicate. The flick of an eye says so much more. The tensing of the shoulders. The bend of a back.

Maybe that's why they say eighty percent of sign language is your expression, and not the actual signs you make with your hands.

I get sentences from the way your feet fold when you're seated. Or how your legs are inclined toward—or away—from the person you're talking to. You tell me whether you're comfortable around me by letting your arms hang at your side, or thrusting your hands into your pockets, or crossing your arms protectively over your chest. I note the angle of your head, where your chin points, the wrinkles in your face between which either amusement or resentment is expressed.

It's a fucking book, from one end of your body to the other. And Kellen says it all without speaking.

He looks at me, awaiting an answer to some question I didn't hear.

I nod. "Exactly," I agree, just wanting this stupid shit to be over with so I can get back to Dessie. She should be out of her acting class by now, and it's dress week, which is when life gets tough for both of us. She has dress rehearsal every night while the crews give their full focus to the show, making adjustments to the costumes, set, sound, and lights as we communicate with the director to set up lighting cues, like when the lights come on or fade out or change color, and so on.

It's Monday. Only five days separate her from opening night. I can't imagine what a wreck she must be. It doesn't matter how good I tell her she is; she won't hear a word of it.

Suddenly, the screen of Kellen's tablet slides over the table in front of my eyes. In place of the description of a lighting cue, he's typed:

> Are you here today? Getting anything I'm saying at all?
> Or am I wasting my breath trying to teach you?

I smirk and face him, unable to hide my irritation for some reason. "I must've missed what you just said. Can you repeat it?"

He erases his words on the tablet, then types onto it in front of me:

> Can't rely on you seeing what I'm saying anymore?
> Need me to type everything out for you suddenly???

Looking back at him, I see the exasperation in his eyes. I see the frustration in his hunched shoulders. I also see the curl of dislike in his parted lips, the way it makes his chin dimple.

It's not just my absentmindedness. He's annoyed by something else entirely, and taking into account all of what Dessie's told me about this piece of work—and how public Dessie and I have been over the past several weeks—I can take a guess as to what's tied his pretentious panties into a pretzel: he doesn't like that Dessie and I are together.

"I'm *fine*," I tell his lips, feeling the tension in my jaw work into each word. "Repeat yourself *once* and I will understand."

He mashes his fingers into the tablet, yet again:

> You sure about that??? I' m teaching you
> valuable lessons here. I can easily do this by myself.

I barely read the message. My eyes zero in on his. I give him every ounce of fury behind my gaze as I consider whether to punch him in the face for what he did to Dessie years ago, or punch him in the jaw for the condescending way he's talking to me now, or just let it all go and taking the higher ground.

"I'm here to learn," I say through gritted teeth.

Then, twisting his face away, I see Kellen mouth something to himself.

"What was that?" I prompt him.

He shakes his head, taking his tablet back to resume his work, except this time he ignores me, not saying a word.

I won't let it go. "What did you just say?"

He rolls his eyes, then mouths the word, *"Nothing,"* at me before returning to his little thousand-dollar shiny show-off tablet.

I can't hold back with this motherfucker. "Maybe it escaped your attention, but I'm deaf," I explain to him, drawing his gaze back to me, "and it's fucking rude to say something under your breath when you know damn well I can't hear you."

He studies my face for a moment, pensive and superior. Then, without the assistance of his tablet, he says, *"She told you about us."*

My nostrils flare. I say nothing.

"Yeah," he murmurs, his mouth curling into a triumphant smirk. *"That's what this is, isn't it?"*

I can't be sure of his words, not exactly, but I know the gleam of arrogance in another man's eyes when I see it, even if it's through his pair of designer glasses.

He leans in, his face so close that I smell the onion from the bagel he ate this morning. His lips part and he says, *"You're pissed because I got inside her first."*

My fist meets his face before I draw my next breath.

The force is so strong, he flies back in his rolling chair, knocking against the sound console.

And apparently I'm not done. I'm on my feet and my fist meets his face again because the first time just wasn't satisfying enough.

The second hit cracks his designer glasses in half.

Satisfied.

Kellen's on the floor before I know it, his hands thrown up to block himself against any more surprise fists. He doesn't fight back. He quivers and pushes his back against the foot of the table. I already see his face reddening from my impact. That'll leave a monster of a bruise. It's strange, for as hard as I hit him, for there to be no blood.

I look at my own fist to find a tiny bloody spot where I must've nicked a knuckle on his glasses.

There it is.

I glare at him. "I wonder what Dessie's dad would think about your predatory appetite years ago. His eighteen-year-old daughter back then, with his twenty-nine-year-old ... whatever the fuck you are." I crouch down. He cringes away, terrified. With his hands shielding his face, I can't tell if he's pleading for me not to kill him, begging for his life in a whiny, sniveling voice, or not saying a word at all. "Thanks for teaching me so much about lighting. You really fucking *lit up* my eyes to what a lowlife prick you are, and how much better of a man Dessie deserves."

The way his broken glasses sit askew on his face, his cheek turning redder by the second, I could almost laugh at him.

Until I remember some fifteen-year-old kid from Yellow Mills High on the floor of a locker room, cowering in the exact same way, pushing himself as far away from the dangerous, fist-happy Clayton as he could.

Every trace of bloodlust is gone in an instant.

I leave Kellen whimpering—or trembling in silence, or crying, whatever he's doing—and I shove through the door of the lighting booth and descend the stairs to the lobby.

I haven't been this hot about anything in a long time. I feel my peripheral view vibrating with anger and my teeth are starting to ache.

I just punched Kellen in the face. Twice.

I broke his glasses.

My career is fucking over.

I hardly notice Chloe and Victoria sitting in the lobby when I pass by, but when I do, I'm only met with their glares.

I can't even be bothered with either of them. I need to see Dessie and I need to explain what I've done. *Fuck, it's her opening week*, I remind myself all over again. Why am I so good at fucking things up?

Do I tell Dr. Thwaite, or let the fucker do it first?

I push out of the building, furious. I don't know if I'm more angry at myself, or at Kellen for being a prick, or at Dr. Thwaite for pushing him on me. Who is to blame here? The chemist for not knowing what volatile chemicals he was pouring into the same flask? The flask for containing said chemicals as they mixed and erupted? The chemicals themselves for being so damn volatile, despite it being in their nature to explode upon mixing?

Fuck if I know.

The sky is grey and heavy. Halfway to Dessie's dorm, droplets of rain begin to kiss my hair. I suck the drop of blood off my knuckle, feeling the sting of regret already. *I shouldn't have punched him.* Fuck, fuck, fuck, fuck, double-fuck.

I've ruined everything.

That power-tripping prick is going to go straight to Thwaite and have me removed from the program for my assault. He's going to press charges, hiring his big fancy lawyers with his big-shot money, and rape every last cent out of my bank account, which took me years and years of sweat and tears to earn. It'll all be his, in some sickening turn of irony that began and ended with my fist.

I end up cheek-to-wood when I reach Dessie's, feeling the vibrations of my own knocks as my face presses against the door.

The door opens, nearly spilling me inside, and I find Dessie's alarmed eyes staring back.

I see her stiff shoulders. I see her tensed jaw and lips, the tightness of her fingers squeezing the doorknob, and her taut forehead.

Something's wrong with her, too.

"Are you okay?" I ask her first.

After a moment of indecision, she sighs and falls into my chest, wrapping her arms around me and vibrating with deep breaths that match my own. My clothes are a little damp from the light rain that caught me outside, but she doesn't seem to care. We stand there in the doorway for countless minutes just holding each other, saying nothing.

Whatever's bothering her stays inside her, and what's bothering me stays inside my clenched fists and strained eyes.

After some time, she pulls away and draws me into her room. The door stays open behind me as we lower onto her bed. The windowpane fills with little droplets and streaks of rain. The room is dim and cold, the coldness made worse by the feel of the air conditioning against my rain-speckled clothes.

Dessie faces me and starts to spill her worries in broken signs and words. The gist seems to be that Chloe's heart was broken, apparently, and Victoria and her are saying awful things about me now, for whatever reason. Added to that, she's about to perform this Friday to her first-ever audience since her time in Italy, and she's having a mental breakdown—or something to that effect.

I have my arm around her the whole time, and I can't help but feel comforted by holding her body against mine, no matter the shit that just went down before I took flight from the theater or the turmoil that's making a mess of my stomach.

Despite not being able to keep my hands very steady, I speak back to her while signing at the same time: "You're going to be fine, Dessie. From what I could see in the rehearsals, you look confident up there. No matter how you feel inside, it doesn't show."

"I feel like a failure," she signs and says to me. *"I feel like a cheat. I feel like someone else better than me deserves to be on that stage."*

Half the signs are wrong, but I understand well enough. This isn't a lesson in sign language; it's a lesson in self-confidence, of which Dessie is lacking. How can I convince her of the beauty I see every time she graces the stage? How can I convince her that she commands the attention of the audience even without the assistance of my stupid, inadequate lights?

"See it like one of your songs," I tell her, fighting through the fear of what irreversible damage I've done to my career in the past hour. I'm so angry, I could punch him again until I *do* draw blood—and it'd be blood from his face, not my knuckles. "See it like a song at the *Throng* where you own that microphone and that audience is captivated by you. You have this story you need to tell, so tell it."

Somewhere in that last sentence, my phone shakes in my pocket. When I pull it out, my stomach falls through the floor.

DOC THWAITE

I need to see you as soon as possible.
Can you drop by my office within the hour?

Well, I should've known it was coming. I can't tell if I'm wet from the rain or if there's an instant pool of sweat under my arms. I feel a chill race up my back, but I don't know if it's from fear or anger. *I could fold that fucker in half right now.*

Dessie taps my thigh, then signs: *You okay?*

The last thing I want to do is draw her into my problems. "I need to head back to the theater," I say and sign to her. "Maybe we can meet up at my place after rehearsal? I may ... I may be occupied ... with ..."

"The lighting," she finishes for me, nodding with understanding. *"I need some time alone to rehearse before Sam's back from class,"* she says and signs, using the sign for "restaurant" in place of "rehearse".

And really, I'd much rather be at a restaurant kicking back with her than returning to that theater, where I'm quite sure I'll not be allowed to step foot into another rehearsal ever again.

Needing it suddenly, I push my face forcefully into hers. Our mouths interlock as if they were starved for one another. Her hand grips my arm instinctively, as if bracing herself for my sudden impact, and my hand grips her thigh hungrily.

I could do so much more to her right now. I want to slide that hand up between her legs and make her moan.

Then, I feel her moan.

Oops.

With my hand tucked between her legs with more aggression than I'd planned, my mouth moves down her neck, nibbling as I go. I feel her trembling against me, her fingers clawing into my arm.

When my mouth reaches her breast, suddenly I stop. All the breath falls out of me and I feel myself seize up with anger.

I can't even enjoy this.

I feel the vibration of words in her chest. My face pressed against her, I growl with frustration. I don't know whether to hit someone, break something, or scream out and cry.

Instead, I calmly lift my face to hers. "I gotta go."

She studies my eyes uncertainly, her lips parted.

I take a breath. "Doctor Thwaite. He texted me, called to his office for a ... for a meeting."

Dessie's eyes widen. *"Doctor Thwaite?" she says. "He actually* texts *you? You get text messages from the Director of the School of Theatre himself?"*

I interrupt her with a kiss, causing her to swallow the last word or two. "Being deaf and being the head lighting guy has its perks," I mutter.

Head lighting guy—*not for long.*

I rise off the bed. Before I leave the room, I glance back at her and say, "Tonight? My place, after rehearsal?"

Her eyes small, she simply nods.

Dessie, you know how to break my heart and put it back together with just one simple nod.

I let the door close softly behind me.

The West Hall falls at my back. What was once a light drizzle has grown into a torrential downpour. I feel the thunder at my feet as I plod through puddles in the road. The tunnel under the Art building provides a short reprieve before the courtyard between the Music and Theatre buildings thrusts me back into the unforgiving rain. Edging by the windows under a lip of canopy, I move unhurriedly toward the glass doors.

Twice my wet hand slips on the handle before the damn thing lets me inside. Then, once my feet meet the tiled entrance, I nearly slip, catching myself on the trunk of a fake plant near the door. I don't bother glancing at the lobby to see if anyone witnessed; I just rush ahead, pushing through a crowd of freshmen who look like they're waiting out the storm before heading to their next class.

I make a quick trip to the restroom, using some paper towels to dry off my hair and shirt as best as I can. It doesn't matter how I present myself. I know the outcome of this meeting is going to be the same no matter which way my hair's falling.

I fight an urge to punch the reflection in the mirror. My knuckle's bled enough today.

The office is eerily empty. I see Dr. Thwaite's door is open, so I let myself in. He sits at his desk, an older woman in a chair by his side laughing. When the pair of them look up, the laughter ceases.

I'm ready.

Dr. Thwaite gestures toward a free chair in front of his desk. I take my seat and stare at him. Then, as he begins to speak, the woman at his side moves her hands. Oh, she's the interpreter.

I'm back in high school again, meeting with the principal because of another not-so-innocent kid I beat up, an interpreter seated by the desk, and my sad, irritated parents sitting across from them.

But there are no parents here. Just me, the Doc, and some woman I've never met, an interpreter who is *not* about to get banged in a supply closet after this meeting's over.

The woman signs his words: *Thanks for dropping by on such short notice. We've had a situation arise. Kellen has had an emergency. He let me know through an apologetic email, and he's returning to New York at once.*

I swallow hard, my eyes reeled in on the woman's long, wrinkled hands with the intensity of a hawk.

The woman goes on: *I know the lighting work is mostly finished, but there are still details to iron out before opening night. You are the most intimate with Kellen's design. Is it possible for you to finish it on your own, because of Kellen's untimely and sudden departure?*

I feel sweat all over my forehead. My breath is so heavy, every effort at filling my lungs is exhausting. The room spins around me. Am I the butt of some joke right now? Is Kellen fucking with my head?

The woman prompts me again: *Clayton? Are you able to? If it is too much work, Dick can easily do it on his own. I simply wanted to extend the opportunity to you.*

"Yes," I finally say, out of breath. "Yes. Thank you for the chance," I say to the woman's hands without being able to look Doctor Thwaite in the eyes. I feel like if he saw them, he'd somehow know the truth.

The woman smiles. *Good*, she signs.

I stagger out of the office twenty minutes later after he covers all the details, which basically adds about six to eight more hours this week of work at the theater, which I am more than willing to do, considering I thought, after the incident, that I'd be spending exactly zero more hours at the theater.

I take some time to calm down by the side door where the smokers live in a permanent cloud of smoke around that Arnie dude who always seems to be out here. It's on a bench outside that side door that I stare at my hands and try to make sense out of what happened.

Did Kellen literally just pack up his things and go?

Did I scare him so badly, he opted to hightail it back home instead of confront me again?

Did his guilt over what he did to Dessie outweigh the arrogance he displayed to me?

Maybe that's it. Maybe he couldn't risk me—and maybe also Dessie—exposing what he'd done, ruining his reputation with Dessie's dad and/or Thwaite.

But that doesn't quite add up either. He could simply have played a her-word-against-his sort of thing. I've seen guys like that before, guys who push their weight around, who wear their importance or their family name like armor, invincible to anything that comes their way.

Though, his soft face and those fuck-off designer glasses didn't prove so invincible to my fist.

Rehearsal glues me to Dick and to the lighting instruments more than it does to the stage, which is regrettable since I wanted to watch Dessie and give her some words of encouragement when I see her later. Every action seems surreal now with Kellen gone, likely with the bruise I left on his cheek still smarting, and having had not only no consequence served to me, but being given a reward instead. Dick is far calmer, far more fun, and arguably even more educational to work with. We become a team and end up finishing Monday's work in half the time than we'd expected. Because part of Kellen's work for the funeral in act three wasn't finished, I even get to implement that idea I had, if I were able to design the show myself. Dick goes along with it, happy to just have the work done. *"What the hell was Kellen doing with you that took him so damn long?"* Dick jokes to me, if I got his words right. I tell him it would take anyone longer to hang and focus lights with a stick up their ass, and Dick laughs a bit too hard at that.

When it's nearly eleven and the stars are trying to poke through the pitch-nothing of the sky, Dessie finds me waiting for her on a bench. Her hair is messy and tangled, which gives her this feral sexiness that gets me going the moment I see her. When I bend in for a kiss, though, she seems distracted, her eyes lost in the distance somewhere. "What's wrong?" I ask her, but all she signs back is: *I'm tired.*

When we make it to the apartment, Brant and Dmitri are gone. Normally that means Dessie and I can let loose and have a little fun, but there's tension in her eyes and no smile touches her face. When she sets down her things, she goes straight to my bed and lies down without another word. I watch her through the bedroom door for a moment, confused. Was something said to her at rehearsal? Is Victoria being a bitch again? Victoria attends some of the rehearsals now, sent alternatingly with some of the other costume crew members to tend to meticulous costume adjustments.

For some reason, I'm not too sure that she wants me over there to comfort her. I feel so much distance suddenly, and can't separate my misgivings about Kellen's sudden departure with Dessie's coldness to me. Some dark, piteous part of me feels like I deserve this.

But then why did she agree to come over?

Brant's door opens suddenly and he peeks his head out, his eyes finding mine.

I guess we aren't as alone as I thought we were.

Since Dessie's eyes are closed and she's cuddled up with one of my pillows, I let her rest, closing the door softly, then draw up to the kitchen counter where Brant's perched himself on a stool, snacking straight out of a cereal box. He asks me if things are okay—I assume he means between Dessie and I, according to the nod of his head at my room. I shrug, pushing palms into my eyes and sighing deeply.

Brant taps me on the arm and puts a screen in my face, causing my eyes to squint:

Shes not mad at u bout the Chloe thing, is she??

I read his text several times. Then, I put two-and-two together, and a whole new wave of anger finds its way up my neck, reddening my face. "What the fuck did you do to Chloe?" I ask, turning on him.

"Dude, it wasn't serious to begin with," he tells me, raising his hands in defense, *"and she got all clingy, and then she said she loved me, and—"*

"You have hundreds of girls on this campus to choose from," I throw back at him, my temper set off in an instant, "and you pick one of Dessie's friends?"

"I didn't pick her. She picked me."

"The fuck you did," I retort, shoving a hand into his chest. Brant falls against the wall, and whatever trace of humor was in his face is now gone. "I taught you how to even talk to girls. Remember, bitch? You seem to forget that fact, you scared piece of shit. Back then, you couldn't even approach one without pissing your little pants."

Angry, he tries to throw some signs at me, saying that *I'm* the scared piece of shit—but, for the word "scared", he just wiggles his hands in the air, and how can Brant ever forget his favorite sign "poop"?

"I taught you how to talk to girls to give you confidence," I say over his dumb signing. "Not to turn you into the fuckin' *philanderer* you've become. If the girls you meet were smart, they'd stay the fuck away."

He says something to me, but I'm not in the mood to read lips; it's his turn to read mine.

"And respect?" I push on. "Where the fuck's your respect, Brant? You can pull it out all you want, put your mark on every tree you pass, but you keep that dick away from my girl and away from her friends. It's called fucking *respect*."

He lifts his chin and starts shouting at me. I don't have a clue what he's saying.

"Real smart," I say through all his shouting. "Keep it up, Brant. Keep screaming and yelling at your deaf friend. Scream a little louder, help your buddy out, I can't hear you yet."

He shoves his hands into my chest, still yelling. I hardly budge.

"That all you got, you fuckin' slut?"

He shoves me again. I put a hand on his chest and give him my own version of a shove, and that puts him flat against the wall once again. I see the stunned look in his eye as his hat flips off his head from the impact, dropping to the floor.

I come up to Brant, nose-to-nose, and pin him to the wall with my mere presence. With a growl that's summoned from somewhere dark and deadly, I say, "You're not worth any decent woman's time."

His eyes meet mine. I expected him to knock me really good in the face for that one. Maybe I want him to. Maybe I need to be knocked the fuck out so I can quit feeling all this rage inside me that has nowhere to go. This rage has lived in me for so long, the rage of being submitted to a silent world, of being thrust off the pedestal I didn't realize I was standing on at the smart and tender age of twelve. It makes it so much easier to be alone. It makes it so much easier to hate people. The rage has been my friend since day one, protecting me from the assholes who tried to fuck with me.

All the fury seems to drain from Brant's eyes. This close, I see that anger slowly replaced with hurt.

I swallow hard. I don't know whether to regret the words, apologize, or punch a hole through the wall by his head.

Then his eyes shift. I turn around. Dessie's standing in the hallway.

How much of this did she hear?

She signs: *Is this the "you" that you've been hiding? You have an anger problem?* Her signs are all wrong, but I get the gist, and the gist sucks.

My fists are so balled up, I could draw blood from my own palms.

"I don't have an anger problem," I growl through the stinging silence, then sarcastically add, "I have a *deaf* problem."

He texted me, she returns with her hands, and then she spells out his name: *K-E-L-L-E-N.*

My fist breaking his glasses in half replays ten times in my head. I feel my teeth clattering together.

"*He told me to beware of you,*" she says and signs. Instead of "beware", she signs "scared", which I guess is just as accurate. I watch her lips, each word causing its due damage. "*He didn't tell me why, but I know he left early. Eric told me at rehearsal. What happened? Did he leave because of you?*"

All I can do is stare at her. What would be the easiest thing to say? I punched him because of what he said about her, making me sound like some possessive jerk? Or, had I not stopped, I would've thrown fists into him until there was nothing left of his pompous fucking face?

Why does it feel like I lose no matter what I say?

"He just ... He just had to go." My words ride on the last wisp of breath in my lungs.

Her bag's hanging at her side. I just now notice it. She pulls it over a shoulder, telling me *she* has to go.

"Dessie," I plead.

Then I follow, calling after her. Only once she's outside the door does she finally glance back. It isn't her leaving that hurts me the most.

It's the look of fear in those eyes.

DESSIE

The rain hasn't stopped all week. They're saying if it keeps it up this badly, our turnout for the weekend may suffer.

To that, I say, *let it suffer.*

I couldn't dream of a better outcome than to perform in front of an audience of three.

Or two.

Or none.

I listen to the spattering of rain against my dorm window, not wanting to go to sleep just yet, because that means it'll be Friday, and with Friday comes the dreaded opening night.

I breathe deeply, willing myself to calm down.

I've spent days trying to reconcile how I feel about Clayton, about Chloe and Victoria and their judging eyes, about Kellen and his cryptic warning—or Clayton and his cryptic explanation of said warning. The enraged look in his eyes when he'd finished yelling at Brant keeps resurfacing, scaring me anew.

I know what it's like to get close to someone, only to have them turn into someone else entirely. I know how far a man's willing to go to convince a woman he's the best thing under the sun, while actually being as unreliable as the moon, its phase changing each night.

And I'm so scared to experience that again.

No matter how good his arms feel around me.

Or his tongue.

Or his ...

I run a hand down my body, squeezing shut my eyes and trying to envision his sexy face from the first time he stared at me with that hunger in his eyes. My hand is cool as ice as it makes its way between my legs. I gasp as a finger teases me below. Clayton Watts.

He's bad news, Des.

I huff, annoyed at the invading voices. I try to recapture his face, my finger searching for pleasure. I moan, finding it again. I breathe deeply.

All the new students want him. Stay away.

He's bad, bad news.

No one goes near the Watts boy.

I huff again, pushing away all the stupid warnings from my stupid friends.

Their thorns will prick you just the same. It's in their nature.

I touch myself. I feel my heart picking up pace. I lick my lips and run my fingers up and down my *other* lips. My legs squeeze together instinctively, then open up, desperate for him.

He didn't hear your song. Not one note.

He's deaf.

My eyes flick open. Suddenly, it's not his sexy face that I see; it's his half-turned, oblivious face at the Theatre mixer. The first time I ever saw him. I hear myself trying to get his attention again.

Then, I see him walk away like I wasn't even worth his breath.

I see him after he caught me singing to myself in the auditorium. The menacing twist of his lips into a frown ... the tattoo drawn up his neck ... his heavy-lidded eyes as he stares me down.

I don't have an anger problem.

I have a deaf problem.

For some reason, it strikes me harder now than ever. My fantasy is shattered, and as fast as it'd come, suddenly I'm just a girl on a bed with a hand between my legs.

My eyes pool with tears. I bite on my lip, refusing to let them fall. Then when I turn on my side to sleep, they spill onto my pillow.

I don't know if I get any sleep. I feel like I blink and then the morning's come, and magically Sam and her light snoring are back from wherever she was, and the date on my phone is the one Friday in all of time that I'm most dreading.

It's like I have stage fright and I'm nowhere near the stage.

I want to throw up, but my stomach is so empty and I haven't eaten since breakfast yesterday.

My head spins when I sit up, the morning light touching my face in orange, fiery stripes through the blinds. There isn't a speck of rain spattering on the window; only golden sunshine and birds chirping.

Fucking great.

After I'm dressed for the day and have a bag packed for tonight with my post-show outfit and stage makeup, I catch Sam sitting on the edge of her bed wearing one of her old shirts and staring forlornly out the window.

"You alright?" I ask, joining her by the window.

She smirks and says, "Well. There's this guy Tomas. Spelled without an 'H'. And he wanted to do something with me this weekend."

"That's good news! Oh." I frown. "Do you even like him?"

"That's the problem. I mean, he's cute, I guess." Hearing Sam call a guy "cute" in her monotone voice is probably an experience I'll never be able to compare to anything, ever. "But, like, he plays the bassoon."

I lift my eyebrows. "Yeah?"

"I can't be with someone who plays the bassoon."

I spot the frat boys playing Frisbee in the courtyard, but today they have their shirts on. I wonder if the rain brought a cool front with it.

"There'll be some things about the guys we're into that we think we can't handle," I tell her in a wistful tone, watching as one of the guys races across the grass, nearly colliding into the fountain to catch the Frisbee. "Maybe if we tried to hear the bassoon in a new way, we might find that we can ... *sympathize* with the bassoon. Maybe it doesn't sound as awful as we thought. Maybe it's even ... sort of beautiful."

Who exactly am I talking about right now?

Sam sighs her words: "You've obviously never heard a bassoon."

I face her. "Why don't you bring him to my show tonight? I have a pair of comps. I'll set them aside for you at the box office. It'll be safe, you'll get to see a horrible show in which I showcase my abysmal lack of talent, and afterwards, you'll have the perfect excuse to just come back here if you don't want to spend any more time with him."

"Bassoon boy," she mutters sulkily.

I sit on my bed across from her. My bag lands at my feet with a heavy thud. "I bet you could compose some pretty songs together with your piano and his bassoon."

"Or a flute. Or an oboe. Or literally anything other than a bassoon."

"Give him a chance," I tell her, "but only if you like him. I'm leaving those tickets for you, whether you use them or not."

She meets my eyes with her big, hazel ones. She gives a short sigh, then says, "I never thanked you for all the ... the clothes, and ... for my hair, and ... and ..."

"No thanks needed," I assure her. "I didn't do it because there was anything *wrong* with you, Sam. You should be whatever you want to be, look however you want to look. Wear that old, unspeakable shirt if you want," I add teasingly. "I ... really, I just wanted to show you another world out there. I want you to see other options. I want you to wonder what causes someone to love the bassoon so damn much that he picks it as the instrument to give his music a voice."

"Insanity, probably," she reasons.

"Everyone deserves a piece of the world," I go on, standing on my soapbox in this cramped little half-lit dorm room, "but we aren't all given equal chances in life, are we? Regardless, it's important that we do our best with what we have, despite other people's every effort in keeping us as pressed into the ground as possible. What better way to live than to make those people's efforts a waste?"

I wonder how many times my mother's carefree criticism kept me from pursuing a passion of mine. I feel my beautiful sister's cold eyes as they survey my latest failure, and I wonder how often I've let *their* efforts keep me trapped in this pretty little Lebeau box of expectations of what I ought to be.

To my impassioned speech, Sam lifts her chin and says, "I guess a bassoon can kinda sound like an English horn. Kinda. Not really."

That's a start. "You know what, Sam? I'm starved," I say and realize at the same time. "Want to grab some breakfast with me before class?"

"Yes," she deadpans, eyes widening.

Breakfast never tasted so good. The nerves leave me alone, granting me an oasis of peace as I enjoy a tasty meal. Sam tells me about her midterms, which consist of three separate compositions, a group project involving composers from the Baroque era, and something about music history. She envies my ability to stand on a stage in front of people, and I tell her to hold off on that envy until after tonight.

My acting class is a merciful reprieve, as I'd already performed my pieces last week and simply have to sit back and watch others today as they are systematically humiliated or praised in front of the class by the long-nosed, cool-eyed Nina. I can't be bothered to pay attention to their public torture; I have my own to dread.

After class when I make a quick trip to the box office to secure my roommate's tickets, I'm dismayed to find that the show is nearly sold out already. The best I can get Sam is two tickets on the end of row R, which is not ideal, but it'll have to do.

When the tickets are paid for and left at will call, Ariel floats up to my side. "Picking up tickets for your family?" she asks in a saccharine tone. "I hope you got front row!"

I shake my head without looking at her. "Roommate," I mumble.

"Break a leg tonight," she says almost too quickly, as if she wasn't really interested in who the hell the tickets are for. "I hear the house is nearly sold out."

"Just made that discovery myself," I share. "See you later." I turn to go, sliding out the glass doors.

She follows. "You know, I think it's for the best."

I frown. *What the hell is she talking about?* "Sorry?"

"You and him. Same thing that happened to me, sweetheart. I did try to warn you. Hey," she says brightly, "I have someone you should meet. He's really, *really* sweet. He's a friend of mine. When I first met him, I thought he was gay, but he's actually just super nice and, like, totally not gay. But by the time I found out, I was already engaged to Lance, so ..."

She talks so fast, I have to stop. We barely made it out of the courtyard. "What the hell are you going on about?"

Ariel blinks. "I want to introduce you to him, obviously. I mean, not tonight, of course. It can be whenever you like. I mean—"

"I don't need to meet anyone," I spit back. *Who the fuck does she think she is?* "Why the hell would I need to meet your gay friend?"

"No. He's *not* gay. That's the point, Dessie. I'm trying to introduce you to someone nice, now that you and Clayton are over."

"We're not over," I state. I'm so annoyed, I feel my pulse in my ears.

Ariel sighs and shakes her head. "Oh, Dessie. Everyone has eyes, you know. Eric heard it all from Dmitri, and everyone pretty much knows that you two are caput."

"I think the whole damn department can keep their fucking nose out of my business," I fire back at her, seething. "We're *not* over."

"Oh, Dessie," she breathes once more, shaking her head.

I leave her standing there, unable to hear another breathy sigh or whiny offering from that unbearably annoying ex-girlfriend who acts like she knows what's best for everyone. I never said we were over. And, as far as I know, Clayton hasn't said anything similarly about us. The last time I saw him, he had a big fight with Brant over me and Chloe and using women and ... I had to leave.

Since that day, our relationship has been reduced to worries and wishes that float around in my head. I haven't sent him a text and he hasn't sent me one. Although I think I might've caught sight of him once in the grid, I could be mistaken, and other than that, I haven't seen a trace of him. It's like he's deliberately avoiding me.

If I'm honest, I think he scared himself as much as he scared me.

And really, Kellen's a little shit. Whatever Clayton did or didn't do to him, I'm sure he deserved it. *But still ...*

I stop at a tree just before the tunnel that goes under the School of Art, plopping down in the grass by the side of the pathway and sulking. Nothing lately has been easy. I don't know how I feel about Clayton and I. I don't know what I feel about the show I'm about to premiere tonight. Part of me has been wanting to call my parents all week, but I've refrained because I'm afraid of what they'll say, and whether or not their words will work to completely unravel me before I step foot on that stage. Believe it or not, my mother has a wicked talent of making my confidence crumble to dust before my eyes, even when she's trying to encourage me. And I won't even try to describe my sister's so-called brand of motivation.

I pull out my phone and reread through texts that Clayton and I have shared over the past few weeks. A few back-and-forth messages revive the smile on my face, and before I know it, afternoon's come and all that's left of my day is a light dinner—provided I can keep myself from *un*-eating it—and show time.

After a quick lie-down in my dorm room and a hurried meal in the

Quad cafeteria, I head for the theater to face my destiny. Considering how many footsteps I've likely taken in my life, it's bizarre to me that the relatively short trip from my dorm room to the theater would prove to be such a chore. I'm so nervous that my feet keep wanting to kick into one another. I stumble twice as I pass by the University Center, then nearly walk into the wall as I go through the tunnel under the Art building. I might need new feet before the show tonight.

The sky slowly turns over, the deep dusky blue of evening covering it with the fiery sunset nowhere to be found–its view likely blocked by the scorpion tail of the Theatre building itself–as I make my way in through the side door at the back. The lobby is off-limits to us actors, or so I was told before leaving Thursday night's dress rehearsal.

The stench of stage makeup fills the dressing room. My castmates banter loudly across the room at each other, and there seems to be a hilarious joke every five seconds, for as frequently (and obnoxiously) as they laugh. I take my seat in front of my assigned mirror and, with shaky hands, I pull open my bag and begin laying out all the sponges, foundations, and brushes that I'll need. Then, after quickly changing into a makeup shirt, I begin the process of slowly becoming Emily Webb by smearing designer mud all over my face.

"You ready for this?"

The question comes from the actress who plays Mrs. Myrtle Webb, my mother in the play. "You want me to lie, or say something happy and encouraging?" I mumble back to her.

She chuckles, rubbing highlight on her eyelids. "Truth. I always go for truth."

"I'm scared shitless," I say, hesitating before I apply the tiniest bit of shadow beneath my cheekbones, which I hollow by sucking them in.

"Me too! I always get nervous opening night. Then, once I get the first night out of the way, the rest of the run is a breeze."

Just when I'm about to respond, I hear the squeaking of wheels.

Turning to the noise, I see a costumes rack being wheeled in by two costume crew members, Victoria and some blonde I don't know.

Of course one of them would be Victoria.

The blonde girl tends to a torn gown, taking it to the corner of the room to stitch it up. While she sews, Victoria hangs by the rack, aloof, pulling self-consciously at her turquoise costumes apron, her fingers playing anxiously with a tiny tomato-shaped pincushion that hangs by her waist.

I return my attention to my makeup. I may never fall in love with the musty smell of it. "After opening night, it's a breeze, huh?" I smile at that. "Then once tonight passes, everything's going to be lovely."

"It's really like there's two rehearsal processes," she goes on. "The one you do without an audience, and the one you do *with* one."

"Audiences make everything so weird," I moan, blending highlight on my cheekbones.

"Laughing when you don't expect them to. Not laughing when you do. Applauding too long. Some guy with a horrible cough in the front row. That *fucking baby in the third*."

I laugh a bit too hard at her joke, catching sight of Victoria through the mirror. She's watching me, still picking at that squishy pin-filled tomato and waiting for someone to need something from her.

"Is your family coming this weekend or next?" she asks.

The question makes my hand slip, getting a speck of highlight in my hair. "No," I answer.

"Too busy to come down all the way from New York, huh?"

I have to remind myself that people here know where I'm from, even if they don't know exactly *who* my family is. Well, assuming Victoria hasn't secretly told everyone behind my back.

Then, from the door, two words ring clear through the room.

"DESDEMONA LEBEAU."

I jerk, looking up. Ariel stands at the doorway looking gorgeous in a blue satin gown, her waves of blonde hair cascading down her front. Her lips are a perfect, plush, red rose petal. I'm so distracted with how elegant she looks that I forget she just shouted my name.

A hush has swept through the dressing room.

"Ariel?" I return.

Ariel pushes past Victoria standing by the door, taking three steps into the room, each of her steps in those heels of hers clacking loudly against the floor.

"Desdemona Lebeau," she announces again. "Of course. Every bit of it makes sense now. A person like *you* getting the part that *I* deserved."

I blanch. Now *Ariel* is the one who wanted the lead role? I guess I'd be naïve to think otherwise; *every* woman in the department wanted the part of Emily Webb.

"What do you mean by that?" I shoot back at her, twisting around in my chair.

I couldn't hear my own thoughts a second ago. Now, the dressing room is so silent, I hear the jingle of a hairpin touching the counter at the other end of the room.

"You haven't heard the commotion?" she says, making the question sound like an accusation. "They had to bring in campus security to secure the doors of the lobby."

I have no idea what she's talking about.

"Make way," says Ariel demonstratively, waving her hands around the room like a magician, "for the one and only Desdemona Lebeau. Do you all even realize who you've been acting with? This *princess* here who robbed me of my senior year lead because her famous mommy and daddy bought it for her?"

Oh, fuck.

Fuck this. Fuck that. Fuck mermaids. Fuck everything.

"Ariel," I plead fruitlessly.

"So was this your plan all along?" she blurts, spreading her hands.

"Bring in your parents from New York on your opening night and cause a scene and make this huge deal over your big Texas debut?"

Wait a minute.

Wait one fucking minute.

"They're *here?*" I breathe, horrified.

"And call in the press, of course. Channel 11 News. 13. Whoever the hell's in the area. Weather? Traffic? Who cares. The *Lebeaus* are in town. You are a real piece of work, you know that?"

I can't even produce words. My heart is lodged somewhere up in my brain, and all I can hear is my pulse and my own erratic breathing. The room spins while I try to imagine the horrific sight of my mom and dad in the lobby right now, slowly being escorted like precious pieces of gold into the auditorium to claim whatever seats they must have secured for themselves ahead of time. Did Doctor Thwaite invite them? Did they come on their own, my mom desperate for more attention and my dad curious to see what his darling Kellen has designed? Is my sister with them?

"I'm sorry." My voice is so small and pathetic. I don't know if I'm apologizing to her, or to the whole room. I look around and all I see are confused eyes, contemptuous eyes, blank eyes. I don't have a friend in this whole building suddenly. Even the actress next to me who I was just talking to, she looks at me like I'm a total stranger. "I'm sorry. I was ... I just wanted ... Ariel, I'm sorry. I was—"

"Sorry? Sorry for lying to everyone in this room?" she prompts me, her voice turning all sugary again, the same tone she used to warn me about Clayton. "Sorry for ... what?"

I lick my dry lips. I can't seem to swallow. "I'm sorry for—"

"She's sorry," says Victoria from the costumes rack, "that you're being such a royal bitch, Ariel."

Gasps and whispers wash over the room like a sudden breeze.

Victoria, her arms crossed, saunters away from the rack, facing Ariel in the center of the room. She gives her a pointed once-over.

"Dessie here's sorry that she even *had* to keep her identity a secret," Victoria goes on, "because bitches like you can't handle it."

Girls snicker in the back. The blonde one from costumes gawps at her partner, her stitching work forgotten in her lap.

"You think you're the only one who got robbed of that Emily role? I wanted it, too," says Victoria with a careless sweep of her hand. "Hell, I dreamed about that role all summer. Now, I get to sit backstage and watch Dessie perform it."

Ariel folds her arms, her eyes seething with derision.

"And does that ruffle my pretty feathers? Sure," says Victoria with a shrug. "You know what else does? The sheer lack of roles in the Theatre world for people of color. Am I barging into the dressing rooms of every *all-white cast* to tell them about all *their* precious privilege? Fuck no. I'm a big girl. I'll keep auditioning for whatever the hell I want. I *will* play Emily someday in some other production. But Desdemona Lebeau, she can have *this* production."

"Yeah," agrees Ariel, her tone quickly converted from sugar to acid, "and she can invite her famous parents to have a big showy opening night, and *that's* somehow fair, because—"

"Oh, trust me, I know all about *embarrassing parents,*" Victoria cuts her off, waving her hand in Ariel's indignant face. "You don't want to be moving into the dorms with your dad yelling Cantonese down the halls at twenty words a second, trust me. I can only imagine what kind of hell Dessie has to contend with, and why she had to run all the way down here to Texas to get the fuck away from it." She whips her head around to face me. "Am I right?"

I suck on my own lips.

"And what do I say to that?" Victoria presses on, her eyes on me. "Kudos to Dessie. And what a shame that her damn paparazzi-drawing family had to follow her. I mean, look at her poor face. Does she look thrilled with your news that her parents are here, Ariel?" She turns back to Ariel, needles in her eyes. "Truth, you wanted. Go ahead. Look in her eyes. The truth's been there all along. The only one who's lying to themselves is you."

Ariel looks at me now. I wonder if she's looking for any truth in my face, or if she's just imagining ninety-nine ways to murder me. Her eyes are a completely unreadable mix of confusion and resentment, which is about the farthest from how she'd treated me so far in acting class. For a second, I catch myself wondering if *she*, in fact, was the one dumped by Clayton. I never saw this side of her until now.

Less the mermaid. More the sea hag.

Ariel finally parts her lips, though it takes her a handful of seconds to make any words. "I don't trust liars. I don't like liars. Clayton. You. You're made for each other, a pair of liars."

"We're *all* liars," says Victoria with a roll of her eyes, "or did you not hear Dessie's song? I'm a liar. You're a liar. Yay, let's throw a big ol' liar party and get the fuck over it." She takes two steps toward Ariel. "This is the dressing room. Where the *cast* belongs. Seeing as you're not part of the cast, I suggest you go throw yourself a not-in-the-cast party, and *get ... over ... it.*"

To that, Ariel lifts her chin, too proud to show how deep Victoria's words cut her, and strolls out of the dressing room. The others start to break into murmurs and scandalized whispers, even chuckling.

And I'd risen from my chair and didn't even realize it. My back pressed against the makeup counter, I feel dozens of eyes on me. I have no idea how to feel about what just went down.

Then Marcy, who plays Rebecca Gibbs, tilts her head. In a light and curious voice, she asks, "Who are your parents?"

I swallow, facing her. The others in the room seem to await my answer. Well, out with it. "My mother is Winona Lebeau."

I don't even get my father's name out before three of the girls gasp with their surprise. "You mean the Winona Lebeau who opened *Telltale* off-Broadway?" asks someone across the room.

"Oh my god. She did *Hair* on Broadway. And *Hairspray*, too."

"*Chicago*," throws in another voice.

"She won a Tony two years in a row," hisses someone else.

"Wait, wait. *That* Lebeau??"

"Holy crap. You're Theatre royalty!"

"*She's* Theatre royalty."

"Can I meet her? Oh, *please* let me get her autograph!"

The murmurs of scandal quickly somersault into a wave of joyous laughter and excitement as my castmates start to share stories amongst themselves, bolstered somehow by the news.

And above all that noise and gaiety, my eyes lift to find Victoria's.

I step away from the makeup counter, drawing myself up to her. She smirks knowingly at me while I stand there wondering where the hell her sudden reversal came from.

Well, I do have a mouth I can use. "Why'd you stick up for me?" I ask.

Every lick of bitterness that lived in Victoria's eyes drains away, and suddenly she's the fun person I met in our dorm hallway over a month ago. "I wasn't being fair to you," she murmurs quietly, but I still hear her through the noise. "You wanted to have a life down here that you could call your own. I get it. I totally do. And I'm just *awful* for holding that against you." She sighs. "We make better friends than enemies. Reading scripts until 3 AM with Chloe just isn't as much fun."

I feel my heart swell. I think I needed this, after the fast-spinning carousel my emotions have been on lately. I put on a teasing smile, then say, "You just want my mom's autograph, don't you."

She glances to the left, to the right, then leans in and whispers, "I totally fucking do."

CLAYTON

I'm squinting through the glass of the lighting booth, curious what the hell's happening in the front few rows. I can't quite make anything out, so I pass it off as a bunch of rowdy freshmen, rolling my eyes and kicking my feet up, waiting for the show to start. Really, I don't give a shit about anything until the part when Dessie comes onstage and lights up my fucking world.

I don't care that I can't have her. I don't care that everything's gone to shit, just as long as she's focused, she's happy, and she's living the dream she wants to live.

Regardless of whether that dream includes me or not.

A tap on my shoulder nearly scares the shit out of me. I spin in my chair to find Dick standing there, an excited look on his face. He says some words to me that I miss. I lift my chin and furrow my brow.

"Wi-no-na Le-beau," he mouths, punching each syllable. *"She's ... here. The ... lobby ... is ... a ... fucking ... madhouse."*

I blink. Dessie's parents?

Dick slaps me on the back suddenly, then types something out on his phone and shows me the screen:

You do realize who Dessie's father is, don't you?

I bite the inside of my cheek. Of course I do.

I return his enthusiasm with a slow, cool-tempered nod. Dick says something else to me, then slaps my back once more before excitedly hopping out of the door and down the stairs to the lobby. I lean forward, staring through the glass and focusing on the front rows again. Is all the craziness over Dessie's parents, the celebs who've apparently decided to come and show their support for their daughter?

A sting of resentment touches me. Dessie's no longer mine. Doesn't matter whose daughter she is. Once her father gets word of what a dark and unstable guy I am, he won't want his daughter anywhere near me.

And haven't I said it since day one? She deserves better. I'm no good for her.

I clench my teeth and watch listlessly through the window, waiting for my opportunity to darken one world and light up another.

Twenty minutes later, I get the cue on my phone, texted to me from the stage manager backstage—that is, the *actual* stage manager. I wait for the cue light to glow. The moment it does, I slowly fade out the houselights, casting the audience into darkness, before bringing up the lights for act one.

The *actor* Stage Manager, who acts basically as the narrator of the show, comes out onto the stage, greets the audience, and then presents the scene to them, telling them where the Gibbs house is, where the Webb house is, and so on. Sullenly, I read along with my marked-up script in front of me, guesstimating the lines judging from who's on stage and what's happening.

This whole experience would be so much better if I hadn't lost my fucking temper and punched those glasses off Kellen's face. Sure, it felt good and I gained peace, but I lost something else. And I'm pretty sure knowing that I'd be going home with Dessie tonight would feel a hell of a lot better than that punch did.

This is my own fault. I'm married to my anger. I always will be.

Then the scene finally arrives. Desdemona Lebeau makes her stage debut entering as a young Emily Webb, dressed in a cute sort of early-1900s dress, her hair loose and flowing.

I'm so fucking proud to give her light.

I push a hand against my mouth, sighing into it as I watch Dessie.

It hurts, just to see her.

I saw her every day this week at rehearsal, and every day was a knife to my gut that drew no blood. The wound's always too deep to see, and I went home every night with the pain of it. No amount of squeezing any fucking pillow could quiet the ache.

Against any scream in the world, emotional pain screams louder.

The first intermission almost catches me by surprise, so entranced and pained by watching Dessie onstage that I lose track of time. After a sigh, I suck in my lips and mash fingers into my phone.

ME

Is Brant still being weird?

Not ten seconds later, I get my reply.

DMITRI

It isn't too bad. You know him. I think he's bowling.

Hey, you realize I'm in the audience tonight, right?

I snort. I was so wrapped up in worries and frustrations of Dessie that I completely forgot about him being here to support Eric who, I might add, plays a very convincing drunk choir director Simon.

ME

Yeah, of course. Hope you liked act one.

There's two more. Get ready for some #feels

DMITRI

You should talk to her after the show.

I sigh, pushing my phone away after that text. Doesn't he realize there's really no fucking use? Her parents are here. They pretty much serve as a wall of protection between us. I've already upset her enough.

It's funny, how Kellen lost the fistfight, but won the battle.

I take deep breaths, count the minutes, and prepare for act two.

Houselights down. Stage lights up. We move into act two, taking place three years later—as explained by the helpful Stage Manager. I get to watch George and Emily in a flashback where they fall in love, and then they get married in the present, despite their misgivings.

Dessie kisses someone else's lips onstage, and I feel my cock twitch. I know what power lives in those unassuming lips of hers, power I've had the joy of knowing intimately.

Shit. I'm getting hard. Not the appropriate reaction I was expecting to have.

Act two tumbles into the second intermission, during which I need to take a serious fucking leak. Since the lighting booth so intelligently empties into the lobby instead of backstage, I slip into the main lobby bathroom around the ten-minute mark, just to give enough of the audience members time to handle their own business before I do mine.

After releasing the Nile river into the farthest urinal, I flush it and push my hands under a running faucet, soaping up and scrubbing harder than necessary, letting out my frustration. I splash water over my face, sighing as the droplets race down to my chin.

When I open my eyes, the man at the other sink is staring at me, his eyebrows lifted searchingly.

Shit. Was he talking to me? "Sorry," I tell him. "I'm deaf."

The man seems amused for a moment. He has kind eyes, touched by his smile. Then, to my surprise, he raises his hands: *Are you okay?*

My unintended bathroom buddy signs. Not what I was expecting.

I sign back: *Yeah, fine.*

He doesn't seem convinced. To be fair, I wasn't very convincing. He signs: *How are you liking the show?*

I give a shrug: *I think it's good.* Then, finding myself oddly at ease with this man suddenly, I add, *I'm running the lights up in the booth. I also designed one third of the lighting in the show, though I'm not credited in the program.* With half a smile, I shush him and say, "Don't tell anyone."

He smiles, impressed: *Very nice. Which third?*

The one you're about to see, my hands return. *But really, the only actor onstage who's worth any light is Dessie. She's the one who plays Emily Webb.*

The man's brow furrows: *Why do you say that?*

I don't know what comes over me. This kind-eyed man is suddenly my best friend. He's "speaking" my language. My chest tightens as I sign: *She has so much talent. You don't know this, but she also sings. And her voice ... I can't hear it, but ...* I close my eyes, the feelings I had at the *Throng* surging into my hands, making them move: *But I can "hear" it. I see what her songs do to people. She doesn't get it.* My eyes flip open as I keep signing: *I'm sorry if I seem a bit messed up about her. We ... used to date.*

Now, a real smile fills the man's face. He leans against the sink, studying me as he signs: *Used to date?*

The sting of bitterness makes itself known in my stomach again: *She dumped me. Kinda. Maybe. I'm not sure what we are.*

He lifts a fist with the thumb and pinkie pointed out: *Why?*

I shrug: *Because I ... didn't appreciate how amazing she is.*

He smirks, giving my words some thought, then signs: *Actually, it sounds like you do.*

I tap my wrist, the universal—and actual—sign for "time", then say, "I better get back before someone yells at me. Not that I'll hear them."

The man guffaws so loud, I swear I feel the vibrations through my feet. He nods curtly as I hold the door open, letting him out first.

The lonesomeness of the lighting booth swallows me whole again after that short interaction in the bathroom with Captain Kind-Eyes. I breathe a deep, despondent sigh before I settle back into my chair.

The little red cue light blinks just in time.

I lift the lights into the third and final act—a sobering departure from the first two. Nine years have passed now, and the townsfolk gather for a funeral.

Emily's funeral.

Desdemona appears onstage near a spread of stark-looking chairs, in which are seated other characters from the show who have passed away, including Eric's character, Simon Stimson, who hung himself. I can't even follow her lines in the script, too glued to the sight of her onstage as she watches her own funeral, George crying over her grave.

She isn't ready to join the dead. Dessie, with hope stinging her eyes, begs the Stage Manager to relive one day of her life. When her wish is granted, she quickly comes to regret it as the day speeds by too fast, none of its precious moments able to be held on to. Forlorn, she asks if any of the living really know what a gift each moment of their lives is.

I stare at her on that bleak stage standing in a pool of blue, chilly light, wondering if I know what a gift each moment spent with her was before I lost it all.

I don't appreciate how amazing she is.

Then she surrenders, taking the one empty seat among the dead, the chair that was waiting for her all along. I drain all the saturation from her side of the stage—my brilliant lighting contribution—as the faces of the dead wash over in colorlessness.

I suck in a jagged breath of air, biting on my fist as I watch the third act draw to its sullen end.

How can she not see how beautiful she is?

Cue the lights.

Fade out.

DESSIE

When the curtains close, I feel weightless.

I breathe the deepest sigh of relief.

Eric's hand fumbles for mine as I grip it tight for the curtain call, taking my bow with the rest of the cast. Applause rushes over me in waves, filling my ears as the tears fill my eyes.

Not to sound all conceited or anything, but I'm really proud of myself. I'm, like, *really* damn proud of myself.

The curtains drop again, and Eric reels around and gives me the biggest, bone-crunching squeeze, then he squeals and says, "Oh, what a killer opening night! Dessie, that was just the *best!*"

"You were great," I tell him.

"You know, the key to acting drunk ..." he starts as we head back to the dressing rooms.

"Yes! Is to *not* act drunk! And you know what? I took that advice, so my secret was, I tried to suck really bad," I explain to him, "in hopes that I would fail at sucking and, thus, do a decent job of Emily."

He stops outside the women's dressing room. "I think you did a more-than-decent job. Great leg-breaking, Dessie." He gives me a little peck on the cheek, then giggles. "I can't wait to see Dmitri after! Oh," he says suddenly, his smile breaking. "I didn't mean—"

"No, no, no," I assure him. "Please. They're roommates. It doesn't—"

"I know, but still, y'know." He bites his lip, shuffling his feet.

"Are you two a thing?" I prompt him with a nudge to his side. "You and Dmitri?"

Eric shrugs. "Not really. I think we make better friends. He's sort of an oddball. I guess I kinda am too, but I don't know. If he met a girl or another guy, I think I'd be more happy for him than jealous, if you get what I mean."

I rub his shoulder encouragingly. "I do. You're a good person, Eric. Oh, by the way, Vicki and I are totally talking again."

"I heard! Don't let her catch you calling her that or else it's all over again," he teases me.

"Sure thing, *Other Eric*." I wink at him, then rush back into the dressing room to avoid him smacking me.

After washing all the makeup off my face, I slip out of Emily's skin and jump into my post-show outfit: a sleek, black sleeveless dress cut just above the knee. I pair it with some cute flats (because after doing a whole play, *fuck heels*), then run a brush through my hair to tame it at least a little bit before I confront my family–and whatever insanity is likely to accompany it.

The walk down the halls from the dressing room to the lobby is longer than usual, as if the halls were made of elastic and stretched themselves to twice their usual length. I find a tangle of nerves in my stomach, as if I were still anticipating tonight's performance.

Maybe the *real* show hasn't begun yet.

When the doors to the lobby open, a torrent of noise crashes into me long before any faces do. I gently ease my way through the crowd, hoping to be making my way toward my parents, wherever the hell they are in this madness–if they're even out here. For all I know, they were escorted out a side door or advised to stay in the auditorium until the worst of the crowd dispersed.

Then a sea of heads part and I see my parents.

My mother looks fabulous as usual, her hair perfectly curled and bound up tight to her skull, which shows off her glinting earrings and inhumanly long, slender neck. She wears a deep-plunging blue dress adorned in sparkly gems that gain density near the floor. At her side is my father, who was sensible enough to wear a humble sweater vest with a button shirt gently poking out of the neck. His sandy-blond hair is parted neatly, which is a welcome departure from the usual mess he keeps it in. He notices me first and lets a big grin take his face before he opens his arms.

"Dessie," he sings through the noise of the crowd.

I hug him, squeezing so tight it hurts. "Thanks for coming, Dad."

"Wouldn't have dared miss it, sweetie," his voice empties into my ear, strained from how tightly we're hugging.

My mother's locked into a conversation with Doctor Thwaite, her voice as loud and sparkly as her dress. She has a hand lightly affixed to her chest as the other waves in the air in time to her endless speech.

On the other side of the Doc, I belatedly notice my sister. She's blindingly beautiful in her glittery skintight dress, which looks like it was cut directly from a block of diamond.

"Cece?"

Her smile is tight as a vise when she bends into me for the world's stiffest hug.

"Well done," she moans into my ear in that perfect English dialect. The way she says it, it's like she's commending a toddler for scribbling a circle with orange curlicues around it and calling it a lion.

"Thanks, Cece," I say anyway. "I didn't realize you all were coming."

"Of course. And," she adds with a lift of her eyebrows, her dialect still unbroken, "I do expect you to get your tush on a plane and see me when *my* show opens."

Pleasantries and congratulations and thanks are shared over and over as members of the crowd slowly make their way around, whether by kindly asking my mother for an autograph or by complimenting my performance. With each thanks, my heart swells bigger and bigger.

"It is quite loud here, isn't it?" my mother notes to me before she even offers her own congratulations. "Do you think we could move into one of the back hallways where it's a touch quieter?"

Of course I oblige, because that's what anyone does when Winona Lebeau asks for something. Doctor Thwaite bids them a farewell and a safe flight home before the four of us slip into the hallway that leads back to the dressing rooms, classrooms, and offices.

"Dessie," my mother finally says, bending to give me a little kiss on either of my cheeks. "You sweet thing. Have you conquered your little pond yet? It's such a delight to see you on that stage."

She is so artful at coupling a biting, backhanded compliment with an actual one. "I didn't find this pond to be all that little."

"It's a decent place to grow into the shark you need to be for when you come home and try your hand at more professional endeavors," my mother clarifies helpfully, tapping on her phone. "Oh, Geoffrey, Lucille won't be able to make the appointment tomorrow."

Cece sighs at our mother—even her *sighs* are English. "Quit trying to force poor Desdemona into doing something she doesn't want to do. There's room for all sorts of actors in this world. Some like the bite and the fight of the north. Some like the calm and the palms of the south." She smirks cheekily at me. "I came up with that one on my own."

I bite my lip, unsure whether this is a fight I want to pick or not.

Then my dad says something unexpected. "I think what your mom and sister are trying to tell you, sweetheart, is that you did a very fine job tonight, and you should be damn proud of yourself. And," he adds, throwing an arm around me and yanking me into him for a side-hug, like I'm the son he never had and just won the ballgame, "I appreciate you, Dessie. I'm alive and I want to appreciate every little moment while I'm able to." He kisses the top of my head. "Job well done."

I survey the expressions of my mother and sister. For this brief moment, my mother's still gripping her phone, but her eyes are on me, and my sister's wearing that annoyingly tight and uncomfortable smile, but she also seems to look upon me with a sweetness that's so rare, I thought she outgrew it at age ten.

"Thanks," I tell them. "All of you. It means so much, really, truly. Oh, Mom," I blurt suddenly. "You got a program, right?"

She pops open her purse and fishes it out. "This thing?"

Yes, that folded piece of nothing-paper. My mom's so used to the professionally printed playbills that she likely hasn't seen a folded paper program since 1996. "Can you do me a favor?" I ask her. "Sign your name on it, then write, 'To Victoria,' and put something inspiring. It's for my hall mate."

She smirks knowingly, then takes out a pen from her purse and scribbles dramatically on the paper. When she hands it to me, the front reads: *To Victoria, something inspiring. A friend of Dessie's is a friend of mine. Winona Lebeau.*

I smile, clutching that program close. My mother's sense of humor is still alive after all.

"I really wish we had more time, you sweet thing," murmurs my mother, "but the car and driver are waiting outside for us to catch the red eye back to New York. Your sister and I are heading to London Monday and have so many things to get done this weekend before we set off, but we couldn't *bear* to miss your opening night."

"I know," I mutter miserably. Funny, I was dreading them coming, and now I'm dreading them going.

"We will see you soon for winter break," my father murmurs quietly to me, "and I do promise, I won't meddle. No special treatments. If it's your wish to stay here at Klangburg, you have my support."

"Thanks," I say back, unable to help the feeling that something is missing from this whole pleasant experience.

"Geoffrey, we'll miss our flight."

"Oh, honey," he sighs with mock annoyance. "Can't we waste a few more dear minutes with our daughter?" He brings me in for another tight hug, then says, "And do give my props to the lighting designer."

I smirk into my dad's chest. "He took off back to New York with his tail tucked, I'm afraid."

"The *other* lighting designer," he amends.

My forehead screws up in confusion. *Clayton?* But before I'm able to ask the question, he pulls away and my mother and sister are given room to float forth for their stiff farewell hugs and birdlike kisses. Then, not two moments later, I'm standing outside the glass windows and waving goodbye as they disappear into the night like three peculiar ghosts, my heart heavy and my eyes suddenly deciding they want to spill all that emotion I was supposed to have onstage.

A pretty chime from my pocket startles me, disrupting the calm of the night breeze. I look down at the screen.

SAM

sorry i didn't see you after the show. we waited around for a bit but you were with your family. thank you for the tickets. tomas is cool, i guess. we are at the dorm. please knock if you come back. i think he might kiss me. i dunno.

I giggle, staring at the text. I'm so happy for Sam that I could cry.

I'm a second from putting my phone away when suddenly it starts to ring. I stare at it defiantly. Someone's calling me? Who the hell uses phones anymore to actually *call* someone? I bring it into view and find my dad's headshot staring back at me.

I bring it to my ear. "Did you forget something?"

"Your mother was in such a hurry to leave, I did forget something. It was something I wanted to tell you."

I hear my mother scoff at him in the background. "I wasn't in a hurry, *Geoffrey*, but if you're just so desperate to miss our flight ..."

"What'd you forget to tell me?" I ask, pressing through my mom's fussing.

"I had an experience in the bathroom at intermission," he says.

I wince. "You guys had Tex-Mex for lunch? Am I sure I want to hear about this?"

He guffaws through the phone, deep and heartily. "No, sweetheart. Marv took us out for a nice dinner before the show. My experience involved running into the fellow who ran the lights and, apparently, finished the job that Kellen did not. I got to brush up a bit on my ASL, which I hadn't used since Great Aunt Esther passed away."

I was so young when she died, I forgot that she was deaf.

"Seems we're all skilled in the business of not appreciating what we have when we have it," he remarks. "Fine-looking young man. He had quite a lot to say about what he thought of *your* talent. I didn't know you'd taken to singing again in your spare time, sweetheart."

I clutch at my chest. *Clayton and my dad ...?* "I have," I confess. "I go to a local hangout and ... and there's these musicians ..." I swallow. "He told you about that?"

"He's quite a fan of your music, even without being able to hear it. That's quite a feat, if you ask me!" he adds with a laugh. "You know, the Lebeau talent can come in many forms. I don't think we've had a singer in the family since your late grandmother. Oh, the set of cords on that powerhouse of a woman. Dessie," he murmurs over my mother scrupulously directing the driver in the background, "regardless of its form, you have a voice, and you belong in the Theatre world. Whether you act, or sing, or do it all, you have a spot on that stage, sweetheart."

Tears have a whole new reason to touch my eyes now. "Thank you."

"Anyway, that young man's got it right. I might add that he has a strong artistic voice himself, if that act three was any indication. Marv ought to know the lighting talent that's hiding under his nose." My dad sighs happily into the phone, then says, "Stay safe down here in Texas, sweetie. We'll call you later when we land."

"Love you, Dad."

"Don't ever say I pulled a string. You earned and *owned* that stage tonight, sweetheart, and you'll own the next." Then, after that, silence.

I hug my phone for a moment before finally putting it away for good. I take a deep breath, trying to push away the image of my dad and Clayton sharing a bathroom bonding experience. I could almost laugh, if I weren't feeling so strangely brokenhearted.

When I push back into the theater to get my things, I find the lobby cleared except for two or three stragglers who are laughing loudly and chatting with Eric. He turns around and calls out, "Are you hitting up the *Throng* tonight, D-lady?"

I shake my head no. "Opening night wore me out," I say lamely. "I think I'm just gonna head back to my dorm room and interrupt my roommate trying to make out with a bassoonist."

He winces disappointedly. "Maybe tomorrow night, then."

"Great job tonight," I reiterate before pushing into the hallway.

Only three people are left in the dressing room by the time I return. I pack away my makeup and stow all my things into the cabinet above my station, figuring it to be safe there for tomorrow night's show. With a smirk, I drop by the costumes rack and find Victoria's crew apron hanging there. I roll up the autographed program and stash it into the apron pocket; that'll prove to be a most welcome surprise.

Then, I give my tired face one last, long look in the mirror before dismissing myself from the room with an unsatisfied sigh.

Whipping around the corner, I make my trek down the long hall to the lobby, only to find it completely empty now. Even Eric and his friends have taken off. I stare at the vacant chairs for a while, lost in the memory of how noisy and awful it was just thirty or forty minutes ago.

Why does the silence feel so much louder?

"Dessie."

I turn. Clayton stands there by the auditorium doors dressed in his crew blacks: a black t-shirt that pulls across his chest, black slacks that hang loose at his hips, and a pair of black boots that give his feet such a dominant quality. He wears a leather cuff around one wrist, too, which I notice when his hand goes up to the wall, bracing himself as he leans against it.

And my eyes meet his, dark and focused on me as if he'd been watching me all night. Well, he had been—from the lighting booth.

"Clayton," I return.

"If your parents could hear you sing," he says, shaking his head. "If they could see what you do to a room full of people with that beautiful voice of yours ..."

"You ran into my dad in the restroom."

His eyebrows pull together. "What?"

"You ran," I take a step toward him, "into my *dad*," I take another step, "in the *restroom*."

His eyes flash with realization. Then, he chuckles unexpectedly.

"What's so funny?" I prompt him.

"What the fuck is it," he mumbles, "with me meeting people you know ... in fucking *bathrooms*?"

I shake my head. "What do you mean?"

"Never mind," he finishes with a smirk. "You were saying?"

"Well, about my dad," I continue, trying to sign at the same time. "He said something about us not ... appreciating ... what we have when we have it." Instead of signing the word "appreciating", which I don't know, I spell it out. "Is that something you told him?"

His eyes are so intense right now. He looks fucking famished, like a wolf that's been left in the wild for days with no food.

I see the answer in his eyes. "I may have not given you the chance you deserve," I whisper, drawing close enough so that the spicy scent of his cologne can intoxicate me. I lean against the wall, inches from his face. "Are you afraid of hurting me?"

"I'm always afraid of that," he whispers and signs.

I poke a finger into his chest. "I want to know the real you."

"No, you don't."

"I'm Desdemona Lebeau," I tell him unblinkingly. "I'm a pebble in the shadow of my fabulous, talented sister. I'm a blot on my mother's golden name. I came to this campus and lied about who I was," I keep on, signing as much as I know while pausing to spell out what I don't, "while being afraid of men lying to me about who *they* are, and ... suddenly I wonder if I even have a right to be afraid at all. Am I just as bad as the men who've lied to me in my past?"

He brings a finger to my hair, drawing a strand of it out of my face. Just the sensation of that sends a shiver of anticipation down the whole length of my body.

"So, yes," I conclude, finding my voice again. "That's ... the real me. And I want to know you, Clayton Watts. I want to know it all."

"Maybe I'm just afraid," he says slowly, "that when you get to know the real me, you'll make the unfortunate discovery that I'm ... really boring."

I smile. "I doubt that."

His every breath pours over my forehead. Heat rises to my cheeks as my body instinctively inclines toward him. I don't know how much longer I can contain myself. This week has been an emotional mess without my Clayton.

"I've missed you," he whispers to my ear.

Electricity lances its way down my neck, through my chest, into my stomach, and branching off far below. I crave his touch so bad that I'm worried I might hurt him if I give him every ounce of my hunger right now. I could demolish him.

I sign to him: *I've missed—*

He grabs my hands mid-sign.

I look up at him, startled.

"*Read my lips,*" he mouths without voice. "*I want to take you back to my place right now, and show you how very much, how very, very, very fucking much I appreciate every moment with you.*"

And I read every word.

Ten minutes later, the door to his apartment explodes with the noise of two people who can't catch a breath.

The door slams at my back.

His hand's up my dress and I'm thrust onto the kitchen counter, breathless.

My fingers tangle into his dark, tortured hair. I pull hard, inspiring a deep grunt of pleasure–or pain. His fingers claw at my panties, pulling them down so hard, they tear.

"Clayton!" I cry out as he throws my legs over his shoulder, his face buried in my crotch as he lifts me off the counter.

The next instant, I'm dropped onto his bed.

He straddles me and breathes deep, his eyes feral and black.

He's so fucking hard right now that his cock is about to bust out of those slacks. So I help him out of them. Then he rips me out of my dress. And then his shirt is pitched somewhere and forgotten.

After getting naked in record time, I find myself getting bold, and it's me who's off the bed and throwing him down. Clayton grunts, his eyes shimmering with astonishment as I climb over him like a panther, grinning with my intent.

And he lets me take the lead. I straddle his naked waist, pinning him right where I want him.

There's nothing standing in the way, skin against skin, just sweat and heat and ... us.

"Get on top of me," he says suddenly.

I squint, confused. "I already am," I protest.

Then he makes his meaning clear by grabbing my hips and pulling me forward. Way forward.

On top of his face.

"*Clayton!*" I cry out, gripping the headboard for support as my eyes go wide. *Oh my god, his tongue.* I squeeze my legs around his head, trapping him hungrily in place. If he's going to work his tongue like that, I won't let him stop until I'm finished with him.

His head dives deeper.

Pleasure washes over me as I howl out, clasping the headboard with so much strength, I worry I could break it.

He grips my thighs firmly, encouraging me.

Then he thrusts his tongue in even deeper, breaching me.

My thighs tighten more.

His name's the last word I can manage before his tongue slides so deep inside me that I discover a whole new vocabulary of squirming rapture.

He continues his relentless tongue-lashing, grabbing my ass with his big hands while lifting his head off the bed to push himself as deep into me as he can. He alternates between fucking me with his tongue and sucking on my clit. The tighter I seem to squeeze his head, the stronger he pushes his face into me, consuming me.

I can't stop him if I wanted to. I'm as trapped as his head is. *Holy fuck, I'm at the edge already.*

Unexpectedly, he stops, grabbing my hips and sliding me off of his face as he comes up for air, which causes me to groan in frustration. I was *so fucking close*. He chuckles at my distress. I glare back.

I guess that was the appetizer. Now I'm ready for the main course.

And from the look in his eyes, so's he. Clayton's eager hand slaps the nightstand and, with a quick maneuver of fingers, a condom's freed from its tight wrapper only to be made prisoner to his huge, hard-as-fuck cock.

Then, just when he thinks he's the one calling the shots again, it's me grabbing hold of the reins. I grip his chest and position myself on top of him. *Your meek little Dessie's grown up*, I tell him with my sharp, hungry eyes. My hips dance, smooth as silk as I squirm cruelly, rubbing myself against the tip of his bobbing, furious cock.

This must be really fucking maddening for him. I can drive a man insane in the space of seconds just with my hips.

"Mmm, Dessie ..."

My name vibrates down his chest, ending with a growl.

I lean forward. All my hair comes with me, curtaining our view and providing me a tunnel of deep brown that ends at Clayton's beautiful face. He's looking straight up into my eyes, as if cursing what my evil little movements are doing to him.

"Let me inside you," he begs me, gnashing his teeth.

I bite my lip, then gently lower myself just one, cruel inch.

The tip of his cock slips in.

Agony and heaven in one tiny gesture.

But it seems he thinks two can play, for *he* starts to move his hips slowly. The tip slides in and out, in and out, and soon it's me who's throwing my head back, tortured by his movements.

He slips in some more.

"Fuck," I breathe.

I can't help it. I reach up and grab my own breasts, fingers pinching the nipples.

In one powerful movement, he sits up and catches the small of my back, lifting me. I squirm as Clayton's dick slides another inch into me during the maneuver. *God, I've never wanted to be fucked so badly.* He holds me in his lap, one hand bracing my back and guiding my hips as he works to open me up for him.

Then his mouth replaces my fingers, biting that nipple I was so determined to torture myself.

I shudder in his grasp.

He slips even further inside.

Then he trades his teeth for tongue, bathing my nipple and earning himself an even deeper convulsion of pleasure from within me that I cannot control.

He reaches around and takes a handful of my hair, then pulls my whole body down, slipping completely inside.

An earthquake of flesh, sweat, and heat runs down our bodies as his hot breath dances over my breasts. He moves his hips now, pumping me slowly at first as his mouth hungrily works that nipple he's made his prisoner.

I grab hold of his hair so tightly, I don't know if I mean to keep him on my nipple or pull him away. It hurts so much. It feels so good.

"Fuck, Clayton. *Fuck!*"

Pain and pleasure are such close, fickle neighbors.

He moves on to my other breast, desperate for its taste. Hungry for something else too, he greedily pumps me deeper, harder, faster.

I feel myself tightening around him.

Our fingers grip tightly onto anything they're touching—my ass, his back, my hair, his neck.

Our bodies become a unified machine of rapture pumping in rhythm.

Each breath brings another.

Each thrust inspires the next.

We're both close. I feel his tightness and he must feel mine, because his breaths are coming quicker. He sucks that nipple, giving it his teeth as he dares to bring me even closer to the edge.

I'm spilling over.

I pull his hair hard, craning his neck. He releases my breast and looks up into my face.

"*Clayton.*"

"Dessie."

And then he lets loose inside me, wave after wave after wave of pent-up passion spilling out. My mouth drops as I feel myself climax too, crying out with him.

His eyes never leave mine.

Then our lips lock, sealing the heat between us as we collapse onto the bed, the sweaty sheets embracing us as we gently descend from the unfathomable high we reached together.

His eyes on me. My eyes on him.

Breath after breath.

Epilogue

CLAYTON

– Six Months Later –

The spring musical opens tonight.

I have my first lighting design credit in the program.

I have an opening night good-show gift in my pocket for Dessie.

I'm nervous and I'm excited and I'm debating whether it was a good idea to eat lunch at all, because it might end up all over the lobby floor.

Fuck, fuck, fuck.

I pace in front of the glass windows as the audience slowly gathers, pulling up in their cars, dropped off by taxis, students walking in. I see their smiling faces, couples holding hands, some dressed down, some dressed up.

I wipe a sheen of sweat off my forehead and breathe deep, just like Dessie taught me.

It's hilarious, how shockingly calm Dessie is. She was calm during all the rehearsals, singing her heart out on that stage. Everyone knew she was going to get the lead this time, and it had nothing to do with her dad, or with her name, or with anything other than the fact that she had a voice that could touch every corner of the room and make everyone fall in love with her.

I think back to when she took me home with her for Christmas. Fuck, I could not keep my jaw closed when I saw Times Square for the first time in my life. It was so bright that even after the sun fell, it was like high noon. I had also severely underestimated how cold it'd be. Holy shit. She even warned me. Hell, she learned ten different ways to sign to me how frigid, freezing, chilly, bitter, icy, shivery, and otherwise horribly *cold* it would be that time of year.

I met her parents for the first time. Well, second time for her dad, but really, a chance meeting in a restroom pales in comparison to my getting to meet him officially at Dessie's New York City home. The lights were drawn across the room like a fucking dream, and the tree in the living room spanned to the ceiling. It was *enormous*. I must've stood there for a full minute staring up at its awesome height. Dessie made some joke, asking with her hands if I was figuring out in my head how I'd light the tree differently.

It was in a warm, fire-lit gazebo on Christmas Eve that we had exchanged presents. She gifted me with a hot designer leather jacket that fit so perfectly, I'd swear it was handmade for me. Well, actually it kind of was. Dessie was sneaky about it. Swearing it was to practice for some costumes thing that Victoria was doing, she took all my measurements and, unbeknownst to me, sent them to a contact of her sister's in New York–some up-and-coming fashion designer who spent eleven years in France after graduating from NYU–detailing precisely how she wanted this jacket to fit. And she got the style just right; I look like the perfect mix of up-to-no-good and sophisticated-as-fuck.

My gift to her was a charm bracelet I got for a steal at a pawn shop. It had the exact balance of beauty, fragility, and strength that I felt fit Dessie so perfectly. I'd adorned it with three charms: a musical note to represent her beautiful voice, a little light bulb to represent my visual voice, and a linked "C" and "D" that ... well, they speak for themselves. I left room for more charms to be added on special occasions.

When I kissed her that New Year's Eve, I'd never felt more complete. I was frigid as fuck and couldn't feel my dick, but I watched that ball drop, I had Dessie in my arms, and I was the happiest man alive.

And then she dropped the L word on me.

For some reason, I didn't return it. I felt it. I had it. I still have it, but couldn't get that word past my frozen lips. *What the fuck was wrong with me?* The moment was *perfect* and I let it slip away.

Now, Dessie will be leaving to go back home when this semester's over. And that's just in six weeks. Six weeks I know will fly right the fuck by. Then, she'll have an amazing summer in New York. She told me her sister's latest "gorgeous boyfriend" also happens to be the owner of a chain of popular piano bars, and he was looking for a regular act to rotate through them over the summer. Of course, Dessie was Cece's first—and perhaps only—recommendation.

What do I have to look forward to this summer? Cleaning pools. Landscaping work. Construction too, if I can work something out with Pete like I did last year. Anything to build up the funds for my fourth and final year. Normally, that sounds like bliss to me.

But the thought of staying here without Dessie ... I feel so guilty, to be so fucking happy for her, yet torn apart inside.

I grip my good-show gift so tightly in my pocket, it hurts.

Brant busts through the glass doors, pulling me from my thoughts, and the first thing I notice is a red hand-shaped mark across his cheek. I squint at him, making the universal sign for "what the fuck, dude?" which doesn't take a sign-language-inclined person to understand. He tells me that, just now, his girl from last week ran into his girl from *this* week, a slap or two ensued from one or both girls upon his sputtering face, and now he may or may not have an extra ticket to the show.

I shake my head and laugh, pulling Brant in for a hug and saying, "You're one fucking mess, that's for sure." With a slap to his chest, I add, "I taught you how to talk to girls. Maybe I should have taught you how to keep it in your pants sometimes, too. Moderation and shit."

He smirks at me, points to his red-as-a-tomato cheek, and says, "*With* this *pretty face?*"

Just before the audience is given the five-minute get-your-asses-to-your-seats warning, Dmitri pops in and snatches Brant's extra ticket. Together, they disappear into the theater, chatting away.

Oh, fuck. The five-minute warning.

My good-show gift.

She can't start her show without my fucking gift.

Before I realize what I'm doing, I shove through the double doors leading down the back hallways to the dressing room. My feet carry me faster than I can keep up with them, stumbling twice as I make my way. My heart's thrashing against the bone bars of my ribcage like an angry prisoner determined to break free.

My eyes blink when I reach the dressing room. Where is she?

I spot the backside of Victoria dressed in her costume for the show. I rush up to her and spin her around, her startled eyes meeting mine.

"Where's Dessie?" I ask at once.

She mouths back: "*Onstage already.*"

Fuck. They must've already called places.

"Thanks," I say, then smile tightly. "You look great. Break a leg."

The next instant finds me at the stage door. I pull it open, ignoring the waving hands of someone behind me who may or may not be the stage manager as I fly into the wing, my eyes searching for my woman. I hunt through the darkness, pushing forth. Eyes and faces turn, the actors in the wings who are waiting for the show to start.

I want to cherish every moment I have with her. I ache at the idea that this is our last show together before the semester ends. My insides burn at the mere thought that when summer comes, Dessie goes, and I'll have to spend three fucking months without her.

Every moment matters.

This is the opening of our show together—her as the voice to this show, and me as the bringer of light to her dark stage.

And I need to speak my piece. And I need to speak it now.

And she needs my good-show gift.

To badly misquote Emily-freakin'-Webb from *Our Town*, don't us stupid living people know how precious each moment of our lives is? Even a lazy moment in my apartment, lounging on the couch with Dessie in my arms while we watch some dumb thing on TV? Even another everyday lunch we share in the UC cafeteria? Even a walk to class that we've walked a billion times before? Did I truly appreciate each of those seemingly insignificant moments before they slipped by?

Even now, tripping through the darkness backstage searching for my Desdemona. Even now as the final minutes tick away ...

The final seconds ...

DESSIE

I stand behind the curtain—*breathe in, breathe out*—as I fiddle with my bare wrist. My charm bracelet. I can't fucking find it.

That beautiful bracelet he got me for Christmas.

I wear it for good luck every show—much to my costumers' chagrin. Then yesterday before I left for rehearsal, I couldn't find it.

I am so furious with myself.

But I have to focus right now. There's an audience out there, a show to do, and a cast I can't let down.

When I think about it, Claudio Vergas did a number or two on me. So did the absent Damien Rigby. And the little training-camp-getaway that was Italy, they planted a few seeds that I have come to appreciate. Every mistake I've made has strengthened me. Every crushing defeat and red-faced humiliation has served as a necessary stepping stone to reach this place, right here, in front of the curtain.

I don't regret a single thing. Maybe I'll even write Claudio a letter to thank him. I'll send the letter with a package containing a brand new mug to replace the one he threw at my head.

The audience hums with anticipation. Their excitement feeds me, energy racing up and down my body as I wait for the curtain to rise.

"Dessie!"

I spin, my whole backstage universe knocked to the side. I blink through the semidarkness. "Clayton? What—What are you—?"

His hands grasp mine. "I'm so sorry, Dessie. I didn't give you your good-show gift."

I gawp, freeing my hands from his. "Are you serious?" I sign and say to him frantically, lit only by the indistinct blue wash of light onstage. "Clayton, the show's about to begin!"

"They can't start without me, now can they?" He chuckles, then extends his palm. "Give me your wrist."

After a brief moment of hesitation, I sigh and surrender my bare wrist to him. He pulls something from his pocket, then gently attaches it to my wrist.

My charm bracelet! But there's something added to it. I lift my wrist to inspect the new charm. It's a hand symbol. A fist presented with only the thumb, pinkie, and index fingers extended. It's the sign for—

"I love you, Dessie," he whispers.

I bring my eyes up to his, touched. "Clayton."

"I couldn't stand letting you go back to New York without telling you that I love you. I'm totally fucking in love with you. Maybe you already knew. I want to stop being a coward and just ... fucking *say* it. And I want you to wear it. I want you to wear my love and ... and think of me when ... when you're in those piano bars and you're singing your beautiful fuckin' heart out."

I grab his hands, putting a halt to his frantic signing. He meets my eyes, his own wet with inspiration, with sadness, with several emotions.

Without words, I sign to him: *I wanted to tell you tonight after the show, but if you insist on doing this, well, Clayton, I guess we're doing this right now.*

He stares at me, taken aback. The intensity of his eyes sharpens as he awaits my hands' next movements.

I tell him: *I know we talked about moving in together in the fall, but I don't want to spend the summer without you either. My father wants to offer you an internship at his theater in New York.*

Clayton's eyes shimmer against the dim blue lighting, wide as the eyes of flashlights.

I continue: *You'd work alongside some seriously cool professionals up there. And yes, it's a paid internship. It's an amazing opportunity and it's there for you ... if you want it.*

Clayton's lips have parted as he stares at my hands in disbelief. I watch the warring thoughts race across his face in a matter of seconds. He doesn't know what to think. I wonder if maybe I should've saved this piece of information for later like I'd planned.

He whispers, "I'm ... I'm not a charity case for ... for your—"

"No." I pull his attention to my hands, then sign: *Clayton, this is not a handout. My father saw your work. He thinks you're talented and really likes you. You remind him a lot of himself when he was young and had big ideas.*

The stage manager hisses from the side of the stage that they're ready to start the show. Words squawk at her through her headset, the static carrying to me.

Naturally, I ignore them. I have one more thing to say to my man. *And*—my hands carry on, bringing his bewildered, wide-eyed attention back to me—*for the record ...*

I present my fist to him with the thumb, pinkie, and index finger extended. It's the combination of an "I", an "L", and a "Y"—*I love you.*

The next second, he rushes into me for a kiss. My lips crush into his hungry ones as his hands slip around my waist, pulling me against him with all his strength.

I'm pretty sure I hear some sighs of delight by my fellow castmates, who clearly have been watching and witnessing this whole exchange.

Let's never mind that they have no idea what the fuck I was saying with my hands. That's between me and this gorgeous man that I love.

When Clayton finally lets me go, he whispers to me, "Show time."

"Light me up, love," I return to him with a wink.

He departs through the wing. I face the curtains once again, but with a renewed sense of purpose. I can't wipe the smile off my face as I grip my wrist, my fingers touching the new charm that rests there.

I don't know what waits for us in our future. All I know is, Clayton Watts will be with me every step of the way, and I can't fucking wait to experience every little exciting, precious moment of it. I can certainly tell our summer's going to be a whirlwind of pursuing our passions.

I wonder what new songs will find me in those quaint, New York City piano bars.

I wonder what brilliant strokes of light Clayton will bring to those stages.

I see the crowds. I hear the murmur of an eager audience at the edge of their seats, tittering with anticipation, whispering amongst themselves as they wait excitedly for the curtains to rise.

And I stand here in the darkness backstage, all the music bursting within me and ready to be freed.

The curtains rise. Cue the music.

Lights up.

The end.

Continue for a sneak peek of *Beneath The Skin*,

Book 2 in the College Obsession Romance series.

Thank you so much for joining me for another one of my stories. And if this is your first time reading one of my books, thanks for giving me a try!

If you liked Dessie & Clayton, turn the page for a sexy sneak peek of book 2, *Beneath The Skin,* where we get to learn Brant's story. Our favorite cocky flirt is about to meet his match at the School of Art, where he comes face-to-face (among other things) with a wild and provocative young artist who will claim to be more *woman* than Brant can handle.

Something tells me he's up for the challenge.

Join my Facebook group, Daryl's Doorway, to hang out with other cool readers like yourself and be the first to catch exclusive sneak peeks of my upcoming releases: www.facebook.com/groups/DarylsDoorway

Follow me on all your favorite social media spots!

> Facebook: www.facebook.com/DarylBannerWriter

> Twitter: www.twitter.com/darylbanner

> Instagram: www.instagram.com/darylbanner

Music has been a passion of mine since before I could type words. Check out my original music, remixes, and full soundtracks inspired by my various book series: http://darylbanner.bandcamp.com

Beneath The Skin

(A College Obsession Romance #2)

Sneak Peek

BRANT

I can sweet-talk my way between any pair of legs.

"Yeah, the model can't make it," I explain, working my best charm on the desk lady. "At least, that's what Grace said."

"Grace?" she repeats, her lips parted and her chest rising and falling with anticipation.

I've seen that look a million times. She's already picturing me with my clothes off. If I lick my lips, she'll cream all over her chair. If I give her my best eyes, she'll do anything I want.

"Grace. The head of the Art school," I reply, my voice as light as whipped cream on a nipple. "Now, Irene, I gotta warn you—"

"Irma," she corrects me dreamily, her unblinking eyes glued to me.

"Cute name." I shoot her a wink. "Now, *Irma*, it's very possible that the original model might still show up. So, you know, if he does, he needs to be sent away. Grace's orders."

"Sent right away," she agrees, furrowing her brow.

She bought the whole damn thing. I'd laugh if I didn't think it'd blow my cover. Really, just give me a chance to flash my smile and my baby blues, and I can pretty much get a woman to believe anything.

I lift my brows. "So, doll, wanna tell me which room it is?"

"14 ... um, 1401," she stammers. "Hall A, the first one."

"Thanks, Irma. You saved my life," I tell her. That's what I tell them all—*you saved my life*. Girls eat that shit up.

The professor waits outside the classroom, a woman who looks like she hasn't slept in days. She seems confused when I explain the little predicament, but I have her smiling in no time. She gives me a robe and tells me where to change after giving me a surprised once-over she thinks I didn't notice. Maybe she was expecting an older model.

Maybe I also notice how her breathing changes.

Women is a language I speak fluently.

When I enter the hall in my robe, I'm faced with the backs of the artists at their easels. I lift my chin and lock my jaw. This is going to be so fucking great. I already can't wait to see Clayton's expression when I tell him what the fuck I did today. I'm about to be the envy of every woman *and* man in this room.

I strut through the sea of art students, drawing their attention one at a time as the professor announces my arrival. The lonely stool in the center of the room awaits my tight tush.

"Whenever you're ready," urges the professor, her voice a tad too tight in the throat.

Just when my eyes meet the front row, I see her.

It's the girl I saw earlier in the courtyard.

Boy, she's one fierce-looking woman. Her jet black hair is swept over the side of her slender neck, and her deep black eyeliner gives her a dangerous allure.

Dangerous to *other* men. I face her with my boldest grin, undoing the robe, then let it drop to the floor.

The room sees my cock. I observe their collective gaping.

Yeah, I'm used to that reaction.

The woman in front, however, she doesn't seem to regard it at all, her sharp eyes penetrating me from behind her easel. She crosses her legs, unimpressed, though I'd be lying if I said I didn't see a tinge of amusement in her eyes.

I've got her.

I take my position on the stool, doing that one-foot-on-the-ground-and-one-foot-on-the-second-rung-of-the-stool thing. I rest my hands comfortably near my hips, proudly on display, and throw my gaze to the side, as if that hot woman whose attention I totally have doesn't mean a thing. I know how these mind games work, and she's about to find out how expert-level I am.

The calm room becomes a chorus of pencil scratches, tiny sighs, and creaking from shifting stools.

Unable to help it, I turn my chin slightly, meeting her eyes.

She smirks, bringing the pencil to her lip and biting softly.

Fuck.

Sitting on this stool, totally naked, in front of a class full of women and men who are meticulously drawing my every outline, shadowing my every curve and cut of muscle, right down to my big dick ... I find myself suddenly caught with an entirely different, unplanned concern.

I can't let myself get hard.

Not in front of the whole classroom.

I look away from her. Then, I can't look away, glancing back.

Her tongue teases out, touching the tip of her pencil as she quietly studies me.

Already, I'm imagining what that tongue could do to me.

I'm fucking naked. I have nowhere to hide.

In seconds, I've been converted from the cock on the block to ... the dude with his cock out, exposed to the world, and slowly being worked up and turned on by that dangerous-looking girl.

Is my cock stirring? *Everyone's watching.*

The scraping of pencils on paper. The creaking of easels and chairs. A long breath in the back of the room. The clearing of a throat.

I swallow, bringing my eyes back to her.

She shifts in her seat, crossing her legs the other way.

Fu-u-u-u-ck. Don't get hard. Don't get hard. Don't get hard.

Her eyes draw down my body, landing on my cock. The way she looks at it, I can almost feel her fingers wrapping around it.

The end of that pencil breaches her lips. I catch a flick of her evil tongue, imagining how that evil flick would feel on the tip of my dick.

And her lips, wrapping around the end.

Her warm mouth enveloping it.

I suck in a jagged breath of air. If I control my breath, I can control my cock from getting hard. I hold my breath, blinking and fighting all the blood in my body that's quickly rushing south.

Her lips curve into the tiniest hint of a smile.

Oh, yeah? Does my predicament amuse you?

Suddenly, I find my confidence again. The rush of heat subsides, and I look down at her legs, wrinkling my forehead ever so subtly. I consider what sort of warmth is gathering between them right now.

Haven't I been reading the signs? She's turned on, too.

When I look up from her sexy, squeezed-together legs, her intense eyes are on me, and they've changed. They're defiant. It's like I literally just touched her without her permission.

Now it's my turn to wear the nearly-undetectable smirk of victory.

Her eyes narrow.

I got you.

It isn't much longer before the professor makes her announcement, and then class is finally over. With a careless bend downward, I reclaim the robe, shrugging myself back into it and glancing at my eye-fuck-slash-mind-fuck partner, only to find her packing up her supplies.

In the noise of others chatting and gathering their things, I stroll by her easel, catching sight of her sketch.

"Hmm," I mumble, studying it. "I think your ... *proportions* ... are a little on the small side," I note with a leering nod at my junk.

She regards me with two dark eyes that struggle to hide their amusement. “Actually,” she says, her words seeming to lick my ears with their breathiness, “I think I got it just right.”

She smirks, amused, then zips up her supply bag. *Ouch.*

I chuckle, undaunted. “Maybe you need a new pair of contacts,” I tease her, crossing my arms as I peer into those rich green eyes that glow like pure emeralds in that sea of black eyeliner she wears.

“Nope,” she answers curtly, tucking her supply bag under a slender arm. “Perfect vision.” Her eyes trail down my body like a smooth set of fingers, landing at my crotch. “I just draw it how I see it.”

“I’m Brant,” I tell her. “I could ... give you a closer look sometime. Maybe tonight, if you’re free.”

She lifts her eyes, those gorgeous greens flashing.

She stops my breath.

Her lips curl, amused. “I’ve seen enough.”

Then she turns, her hair flipping, and she saunters away, her ass hugged by those tight, black jeans of hers. I can’t take my eyes off of them.

With a grin, I crack my knuckles. Looks like I have my work cut out for me. Hard-to-get is a game I’m quite used to.

And I’m ready to play.

Want to read the rest of Brant’s story?

Look for

Beneath The Skin (A College Obsession Romance)

coming fall of 2016.

Made in the
USA
Monee, IL